The Art of Failing

The Art of Failing

Notes from the Underdog

Anthony McGowan

A Oneworld Book

First published by Oneworld Publications, 2017

A CIP record for this title is available from the British Library

ISBN 978-1-78607-182-8
eISBN 978-1-78607-183-5

Typeset by Siliconchips Services Ltd, UK
Printed and bound in Great Britain by Clays Ltd, St Ives plc

Oneworld Publications
10 Bloomsbury Street
London WC1B 3SR
England

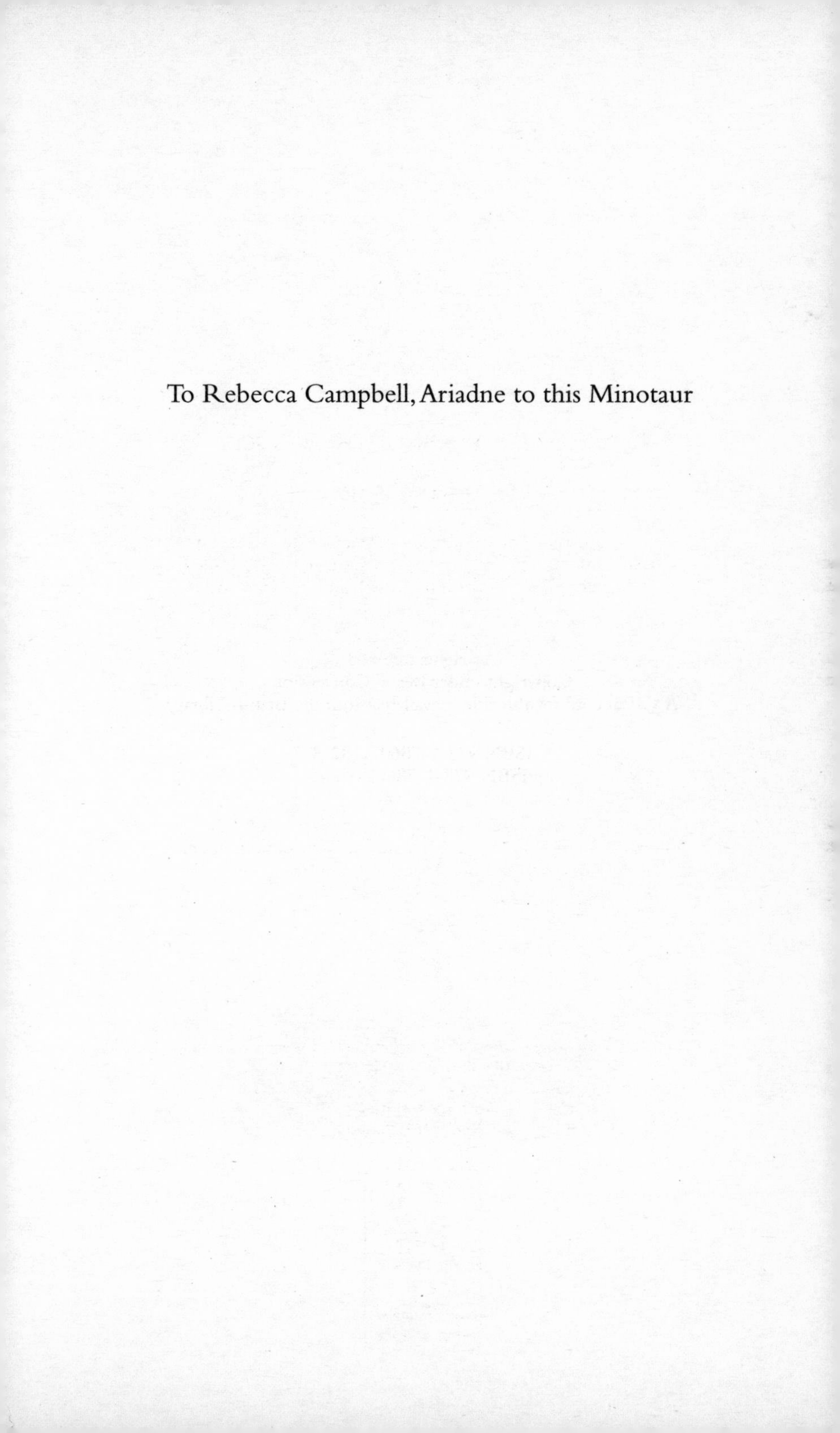

To Rebecca Campbell, Ariadne to this Minotaur

CONTENTS

AUTUMN

I Love You

September 5. I'm back working again at the British Library. It's a forty-minute cycle away through some of the ugliest traffic in London but just getting out of the flat helps goad the slumberous elephant of my creativity back into motion. Or that's the theory. So far all I've managed is to half-fill my Moleskine notebook with a network of scorings and scratchings, like a self-harmer's forearm. And a list of possible book titles. *The Constituents of Glass; The Bad News Bible; Handlebar; The Art of Failing.* And I've almost filled my card with loyalty stamps from the café.

Even if it hasn't yet been a great success in productivity terms, I like sitting in the echoing space of the Humanities 1 reading room, soothed by the gentle susurrus of scholarship – pages turning, the twitch and scritch of tweed, the patter of dandruff falling from scratched grey heads. And there's usually something interesting to catch the eye: a bearded prophet with crammed tissues cascading from his ears like frozen Icelandic waterfalls, or a pretty post-graduate student from, one speculates, Latvia or Montenegro, stretching in a mote-dappled beam of sunlight falling from one of the high windows.

And, until recently, no diplomatic incidents. But then, today, things went awry. I've been taking a banana in for a mid-morning snack. There are, of course, stern injunctions against bringing food into the reading rooms, but I usually conceal the banana about my person, saving a tiresome schlep down to the lockers. Historically, I'd always been broadly banana-neutral, feeling that their function was to fill that otherwise awkward gap in the pleasure spectrum between being hungry and eating something that you actively enjoy. But my library banana had come to be quite important in my life. It was a sign that I'd worked my way through a session, and that I'd be back for more. It was a symbol of hope, rebirth, redemption. And, the thing is, I've discovered that there's a supplementary joy to be had from writing on a banana with a biro. Something about the texture – the momentary resistance, followed by an easeful passage – sets up a mildly pleasurable shimmer across my shoulders. Sometimes I write my name. Sometimes it's just random squiggles.

Anyway, today I was sitting there, daydreaming, when the urge to sneeze came upon me. I plunged my hands into my jacket pockets searching for my hanky. Things were getting critical – I didn't want to be the kind of person who sneezes flamboyantly into the air, like a trumpeting mastodon, or more furtively into his bare hands, which then have to be wiped on the worn furrows of his cord trousers…

So in my panic I emptied my pockets onto the desk – keys, stray length of used floss, a piece of plastic that appeared to have been broken off from some larger piece of plastic the function of which we'll never establish. But also my banana.

And then my hand closed around my hanky, just as the need to sneeze subsided, like desire when you encounter an unexpected wart or a patch of coarse hair on an otherwise lovely woman.

I shrugged, and glanced at the person on my right, expecting a smile of recognition – after all, who has not been disappointed in a sneeze (or in love)?

I'd been vaguely aware that it was one of those prematurely balding young men, whose baldness gives them an air of nervous fragility and helplessness (think Alain de Botton), and so I'd warmed to him. But now I saw the look on his face –

an extreme wariness bordering on hostility – which seemed harsh, given that all I'd done was to nearly sneeze.

And then I remembered the banana, and what I'd doodled on it that morning. Not, on this occasion, a shark's mouth, or a quotation from the *I Ching*. I'd been thinking how central my break banana had become in my life, so I'd written 'I love you'.

And now I'd put this banana love bomb in front of the young man.

I slowly moved my hand to the banana and took back the fruit. I couldn't, of course, stay. As I packed up my things I gave one more fleeting glance at my young man. His expression had softened, into a more neutral 'thanks, but no thanks' look.

So I'll be in the Rare Books reading room for a while, until this all dies down.

Bum Ball

September 6. A limp dappling of autumn sunshine persuaded me that I should walk Mrs McG down to the underground station, efficiently combining this act of conjugal kindness with Monty's urgent need for a morning constitutional. The surging horror of the early commute was over, leaving just the aimless milling of the stragglers and idlers. They reminded me of those defective spermatozoa one reads about, destined never to meet with a comely egg, thrashing in circles, or slumped, broken, at the side of the fallopian tube.

A few people were sitting at tables outside the cafés. Elderly gents with walking sticks and huge, antiquated hearing aids in shades of labial pink. A hipster, his densely-bearded head oddly out of proportion with his puny body, tapping at his tablet. A man in sunglasses stabbed a cigarette out cruelly on the stump of a croissant. It was all perfectly pleasant, and I drifted along, enjoying the wash of images and associations.

The embourgeoisification of my part of North London has taken the paradoxical form of a superabundance of charity shops. My local high street – West End Lane – has six of them, separated by cafés and hairdressers and nail bars and estate agents. We're told that the coils and curlicues of our DNA are made up of meaningful sections of code separated by 'junk'. On West End Lane, all the DNA is junk.

I paused in front of the Oxfam window, and saw in there a deflated gym ball (a piece of exercise equipment that looks like a de-horned space hopper), still in its packaging. The vaguely futuristic, geometric lettering on the box made the word GYM look a lot like the word BUM.

'Bum ball,' I said to Mrs McG in a West Country yokel-type accent.

She didn't laugh, so I tried it again, saying 'bum ball' in a Tennessee redneck sort of way.

Still no effect. Finally, I tried it in Scandawegian.

'Bum ball.'

Nothing.

Aware that there's something cowardly and dishonest in these generic voices, I thought I'd try my only two impressions of actual people. 'Bum ball,' I said in the sneering and sinister tones of 1950s matinee idol James Mason. And then in the extravagantly lisping, spittle-drenched voice of Hegelian provocateur Slavoj Žižek. 'Bum ball.'

I may as well have been talking to myself. So I looked round, expecting to see Mrs McG, her arms crossed, her face bearing the lines of a patience pushed too far, waiting for me to finish so we could get on with the business of the day. But she wasn't there. There were just the other passers-by, trying to ignore the oddly dressed man (I'd pulled a jumper and pair of baggy trousers over my pyjamas, thinking that Mrs McG's polish and fizz would balance my entropic chaos) saying 'bum ball' over and over, in different voices.

For a baffled moment I wondered if Mrs McG had even come on this walk with me. Then, in a brief panic, I doubted her very existence, thought perhaps that I lived on my own in a hostel, or one of those halfway houses for recovering mental patients, and that the wife, the two children (tall, terse, decent Gabe, and operatically exuberant Rosie) and the dog were figments, constructed to console me in my loneliness.

But then I looked back along the street, and saw that they had just stopped for a wee. Monty, being a dog blessed more with irascibility than intelligence, still got confused about which leg to cock, and would go through all the permutations, like a horse performing dressage, before getting it right.

When they finally caught up with me, I said 'Bum ball' again, but just in my normal voice, because my heart wasn't in it any more.

They Whispered Together in the Hallway

September 7. We had a visitation from the dishwasher man. The door is broken: like me, it has lost its firmness of purpose, and just flops open, like a gormless mouth. If it had been a blockage I could have fixed it. I'm good at unblocking things. I have a gift for it, like people with perfect pitch. But broken doors take me out of my comfort zone.

The dishwasher man was delicately boned, and curiously gentle, like an undertaker or an inexplicably ancient altar boy. He quickly diagnosed the problem. It involved springs. I was charmed by this discovery. A spring malfunction was the sort of thing that could go wrong with an 18th-century device, rather than the electronic trash of the modern age. In fact, it transpired that the issue wasn't even the spring itself, but a length of cording attached to the spring. Cording which had, as cording will do, snapped. Who'd have thought that there would be cord in a modern kitchen appliance?

The man searched on his phone for the replacement part. You could only buy the cord with the spring, as a single unit. He showed it to me. It wasn't very expensive. But it still seemed needlessly extravagant to buy a new spring, when all that was required was the cord.

'I have cord!' I said, brightly.

The family was all there, in the kitchen. Rosie, Gabe and Mrs McG, all watching intently. They emitted a short but intense collective groan. A sigh, perhaps, more than a groan. The man looked perplexed.

'Wait,' I said.

I went to my toolbox. Within it was my collection of cords, amassed over the years. I offered them to the man, like a stall-holder in a Middle-Eastern bazaar. There were odd shoe laces, random lengths of generic string, sections of electrical cable.

'Please, dad...' said Gabe.

But I wasn't listening. 'There's something here,' I said, rummaging. 'Something right. Something good.'

I found it.

'It's Kevlar coated,' I said, admiring it like Gollum with the One Ring. It was the cord from an old set of headphones, long disintegrated.

'Strong!'

I showed the man how strong my Kevlar cord was by pulling it taut between my hands. It sang there, like a bowstring.

And it did resemble, vaguely, the cord in the photo on his phone. The man looked at Mrs McG, and at the children. His eyes were kind. Rosie was close to tears.

'Darling...' said Mrs McG – to me, I think, not the dishwasher repair man. 'It's OK. Put the string away, now. You can save it for another time. Something else might break. Or your shoes, your shoes...'

I knew I was defeated. I put the string – I mean, the cording – back in my toolbox, with all the other broken and useless things.

He's coming back another time, with the spare part.

They whispered together in the hallway, before he left, making plans.

The Commode

September 9. I was ambling along West End Lane with Monty, when a van pulled up outside Oxfam. A solidly built man got out, and started to unload various things onto the pavement, intended, I assumed, for the charity shop. Among the bric-a-brac – a broken lampshade, a jigsaw puzzle of Ely cathedral, an ancient stuffed donkey with the bemused expression of someone confronted with a new, but not necessarily unwelcome, perversion – was something that perplexed me for a few moments. It was a sort of chair arrangement, made from white-painted tubular steel and padded vinyl, with an oddly complicated seat.

After a moment I realized it was a commode chair, i.e. a chair with a built-in chamber pot, for the use of the elderly and infirm. I was just thinking this was a slightly eccentric thing to offload to a charity shop when the man propped a small balalaika against it. And then I was lost, imagining the owner – an elderly gentleman, with wisps of white hair – sitting on the commode, his long nightgown pulled up over his bony knees, and plucking the balalaika. 'Lara's Theme', perhaps, or a jaunty Russian folk song. I did speculate, in passing, if perhaps it had been a carer who had played the balalaika to entertain the old man while he was on the commode, but then I realized why the two were being given away together – it could only mean that the old fellow had died. Possibly – indeed I rather hoped – while playing a gentle melody on his instrument.

'Can I help you?' said the van driver, a touch more aggressively than I thought was necessary.

And then I wondered if perhaps I'd been partially re-enacting the last moments of the commode-user's life – the final strums, each one more feeble, the slumping head… It's something I'm prone to do, I mean helping the imaginative act with a few physical movements, but on a smaller scale, in the way that ontogeny (the development of the foetus in the womb) was once said to recapitulate phylogeny (the successive evolution of the vertebrate families).

And so perhaps I'd looked a bit strange standing there, with Monty on his lead.

'No, sorry, I was just…'

Of course there was no way to finish the sentence, so I let Monty drag me away.

Heimlich

September 10. It had been a difficult day, full of those stuttering moments of inelegance and awkwardness in the choreography of life – you attempt to hold the door open for an old person but it slips from your fingers and traps them half in and half out of the charity shop; you fumble for the right change, those same fingers suddenly huge and blunt, insensate as skittles, and, in the end, simply thrust your open hand towards the frightened girl behind the till, leaving her to pick through the coins; you try to pay your wife a compliment, but add a Baroque flourish at the end, which makes her think that you're taking the piss, signalling not your love, but your contempt.

So I took Monty out for his late walk along the grim and blaring Finchley Road, reliving each embarrassment, probing them, the way you stick your spit-moistened finger into the corner of a crisp packet to extract the last savoury morsel, the powdery crumbs and crystals of your woe. Vast trucks and frantic emergency vehicles thundered by, each one making Monty – who isn't a courageous dog – cringe and whimper into my leg. The streetlights somehow had the effect of intensifying the darkness, casting complex shadows that hid the big puddles of black water.

But I wasn't really noticing the world, lost as I was in the corresponding darkness and damp of my own thoughts.

And then I sensed more than heard a disturbance behind me, and looked back.

It took me a second or two to process what was coming. It was a very small man – one might almost say a dwarf – propelling himself with the aid of crutches along the pavement, at high speed. He used the crutches like an extra pair of legs, making his motion resemble a gallop, or the scuttling of a giant spider.

I saw, as he came closer, that his diminutive stature was almost entirely down to his legs, which were tiny and somewhat twisted, hence his reliance on the crutches for locomotion. He was moving so quickly and recklessly that it looked as though he were fleeing something in terror. Or, possibly, pursuing me in a hot rage. His face was contorted in a way that supported either hypothesis.

Monty growled, and then flattened himself against me, like a wet newspaper in a gale. I tried not to gawp, but it was impossible, as the dwarf was heading straight for me.

And then, a couple of yards in front of me, he stopped, dead. He looked – no – stared – right at my face, his own carrying an expression now of amazement.

And in that moment I knew why.

We looked identical.

It was me.

We were one.

I mean he had my face. I saw it, he saw it. He was a tiny version of me, and I was a giant version of him.

His lips parted, and I thought he was going to say something, utter some curse, or deliver a cryptic message. But nothing emerged, beyond his breathless panting. It was clear that he felt the same dumbfounding shock as I did.

And what could one say?

And then, without a word or parting gesture, he raced off again, as if he had remembered what it was he fled or pursued, sweeping past me with that reckless, galloping, four-limbed gait.

Safe, now, Monty re-emerged into the world, and offered a gruff rebuke to the back of the retreating dwarf.

My thoughts after this strange meeting were confused and murky. Of course I was struck by the fact we looked identical. And I wondered from whom (or to whom) he was fleeing. And I thought about how much harder his life must have been than mine, and how trivial my general mithering concerns and complaints were in comparison.

I have rather a common face, and have had doppelgänger-ish encounters before, but none as uncanny as this. I don't know what it means. But I gave the dwarf a name, which fitted him like a gimp mask. Heimlich.

Heimlich, my dwarf doppelgänger.

Let's Have a Quiet Night In

September 11. My Garrett Ace 250 metal detector has arrived.

I don't know quite how this happened. Have I always, at some deep level, wanted a metal detector? Does it symbolize a yearning to find a spiritual meaning in the wastelands of my life? Or is it simply the delusion that I will find treasure, *real treasure*, doubloons and pieces-of-eight, and be able to sleep on a bed of gold, like Smaug?

Mrs McG, obviously, hates it. She says it's my mid-life crisis. But, frankly, I don't see why my mid-life crisis couldn't have taken the form of a sports car, or affair with a sexually uninhibited circus acrobat.

Anyway, it's the single uncoolest thing I've ever bought. Except maybe 'Let's Have a Quiet Night In' by David Soul, although at least then I had the excuse of being eleven.

The Iron Lung

September 12. I was trying to explain to Mrs McG why I need to work at the British Library, rather than my small, windowless study, with its faint smell of disappointment and burnt electrical wiring. I fished around for a metaphor.

'Writing used to be like breathing.' I demonstrated some excellent, state of the art breathing techniques. 'But now asthma... emphysema...' Again, I wheezed and coughed my way through an illustration, as though I were a 1940s Public Information Film, warning against the dangers of inhaling petrol and, probably, masturbation. 'I need... I need...' There was something I was reaching for, a memory of a thing, the right thing. And then it came back to me: the iron lung.

I hadn't thought about the iron lung in a long time. I used to be obsessed with it, as a small boy. It goes back to the polio epidemics of the 1940s and '50s, an active folk memory when I was growing up in the early 1970s. There were still a few kids around then with callipers clamped to their legs, watching with hate in their eyes as you played football in the streets. If the disease affected the muscles of the chest, the patient – usually a child – wouldn't be able to breathe, and they'd be encased from the neck down in an air-tight metal drum, which used negative air pressure to force air in and out of the lungs. You might spend weeks or months in there, lying immobile in that steel coffin…

It terrified me, and yet there was something weirdly attractive about the idea. Isn't the greatest of all freedoms the freedom from responsibility? How nice to be able to offload all decisions, even the decision of whether or not to breathe, to the experts, to the machines. And there was something else, something sexy, something space-age, in the idea of a gadget breathing for you. The machine in you, and you in the machine.

And then later, at university, I invented a small perversion, which I called the Iron Lung. I developed it with a girl called Roxanna, who looked like a balloon-animal version of Botticelli's Venus. It's essentially a kiss. You form a tight seal with your lips, and then, as one person breathes in, the other breathes out, passing the air directly from lung to lung until a mild narcosis sets in. It's more fun than it sounds.

So that's what I needed, and I thought the library could be my iron lung. To breathe for me. To put its lips to my lips.

And so I said, 'Iron lung,' and Mrs McG looked puzzled, and then annoyed, perhaps thinking it was some insult I was hurling at her.

The Sex Act

September 13. Having nothing else made from precious metals, I decided to test out my metal detector's 'gold and jewellery' setting on my fillings. I got on my knees, opened my mouth, and raised the contraption. The machine beeped crazily, like an orgasming R2-D2.

Then Mrs McG came into my study without knocking. Her eyes widened and she accused me of trying to perform a sex act on the thing.

Now I'm convinced I've given myself some rare form of head cancer, caused by whatever rays and beams the detector transmits. Taken together, the embarrassment of being caught fellating the Garrett Ace, and the anxiety over the pulsing tumour, have robbed my new toy of its sheen and glamour. I've put it at the back of the coat cupboard, where I expect it will lurk for the rest of its natural life, to be stumbled across with surprise and regret every decade or so.

The Compound Eye

September 15. People don't really get me and Mrs McG. I mean as a couple. Her friends all used to think she was too good for me. My friends tended to agree. I don't think anyone expected us to last this long. Obviously, we're different, but I always thought that that's what you needed in a relationship. No point having two useless ditherers, or two coolly efficient robots.

She's beautiful, of course. In another guise, I wrote this about her.

Ugliness comes to us in a million different forms, limping, hunched, ill-knit, diseased, mutilated, poor. Ugliness is democratic: most of us partake in it in some aspect of our being, and this chiming with something in ourselves makes for the most human of responses – our hatred and our pity. Of course Homer made his squabbling, anarchic rebel Thersites, for me the true hero of the Iliad, *as ugly as death; and death soon found him, cloven, for his egalitarian fervour, by the beauty of Achilles.*

Beauty comes in fewer guises: as yielding feminine comeliness, in fatal, dark-eyed elegance, in stretched and sinewy Giacometti forms.

Celeste's beauty is of another kind. It has a cold, flawless crystalline perfection about it, like an electron micrograph of a mosquito's compound eye. It is the beauty of a stiletto, of a panther, of an impossible equation, of the silence at the end of everything.

It isn't, perhaps, the beauty I would have chosen, but it was the beauty I got.

But it's not really my attraction to her that baffles people.

I suppose there's a five per cent chance that she'll kill me one day.

Low Stakes

September 17. I've invented a new pastime. I call it Hedgerow Russian Roulette. It involves randomly eating fruits and berries I find in bushes along the side streets of West Hampstead. My reasoning is that I'd be bloody unlucky to find any single berry deadly enough to kill me. It's not, really, the sort of game I'd want to play with the kids, but it makes my solitary perambulations so much more entertaining. And the beauty of wondering if that small purple berry will dissolve your liver is that it takes your mind off those deeper issues – deeper even than your liver. The imponderables. But now it suddenly strikes me as odd that we call them the imponderables, when these are precisely the things you spend your life pondering.

The Borges Balalaika

September 18. The balalaika-and-the-commode incident last week has reminded me of a record my parents used to own, stored in the mahogany radiogram that took up one whole wall of our house. It was called something like *The Magic of the Balalaika*, or perhaps just *Balalaika!*, and it featured on the front cover a balalaika orchestra, with a comical range of balalaikas, the smallest about the size of a yogurt pot, the largest with the bulk and heft of a Soviet-era Lada.

And I always wondered, why stop there, with a balalaika the size of a car, I mean? And perhaps some insane Tsar – Ivan the Ridiculous or Dmitri the Shit – would do that, go on, I mean, and order the construction of increasingly colossal balalaikas – the size of a barn, the size of a palace, finally one that would cover the entire country, crushing the serfs beneath its huge triangular mass.

But empires fall, and giant balalaikas decay, and so almost nothing of the wooden colossus remains – a jagged splinter here, a monolithic peg there, in remote parts of the country, for those with an interest in such things.

Rude Man

September 19. I was walking back from Hampstead after dropping Rosie at school, when I saw two ladies with big dogs approaching on the pavement. They had the look of successful career women who have married stockbrokers and given up work and vaguely resent it, but not so much that they want to go back to work and lose their lives of leisure and boredom. And that was just the dogs.

I tried to work out which way to go round them – inside or out – watching their hips to see which way they were inclining. But I'd left it too late and I was stranded in the middle of the pavement, as they parted, tutting, on either side. I smiled apologetically, acknowledging the mild awkwardness of the situation, but they had already bustled on.

Then one said in a piercing voice, 'Rude man!'

I wanted to explain what had happened, but realized the moment had gone.

This has probably ruined my day. But it's also made me consider how we think about other people. They clearly thought I was the kind of arse who believes he owns the pavement, even though in reality I'm a pathetic shrinking violet, and the last thing I want to own is some pavement. I don't really know any unpleasant people. Often acquaintances will say of someone, 'he's a monster' or 'she's horrible', and then I'll meet them and think they're perfectly fine. So, are all judgements of this kind based purely on the fact that occasionally we have conflicting interests, and those with whom our interests conflict are inevitably 'horrible' in our eyes? Because I assume that no one looks at themselves in the mirror and thinks, actually, yes, I'm the evil sod, here. Or are there really some objectively nasty people? I don't really know. I didn't get much sleep last night so I'm not sure what I think about anything.

Brown Stars

September 20. I was going through an old notebook the other day, when I came across the words 'brown stars'. Just that, on a line by itself. Nothing to indicate the context. I wasn't sure what I'd meant. Was I simply pondering matters astronomical? Perhaps I'd been referring to brown dwarves, the rump left when a star loses the will to go on…

But that didn't seem right. There was something else nagging at the periphery of my vision.

And then today it came back to me. I'm in the infant class at junior school. So it must be Hull, in 1969. And it's coming up to Christmas, because we're drawing nativity scenes. I'm not a gifted artist, but I'm trying really hard, my tongue sticking out of the corner of my mouth, my brow wrinkled in concentration. Some of the kids have their own stash of vibrant felt tips or precise and delicate coloured pencils, the kind that came in a flat tin, with a compartment for each pencil, and more colours than a boy like me could imagine, so many shades of blue and green. But I don't have coloured pencils or felt tips. I have to use the stubby wax crayons provided by the school. I draw a stable. I draw some shepherds. I imagine I attempted a donkey and an ox. And then I colour in the black of the sky. So far, so not terrible. Then I try to fill the black night with stars, culminating in the great star above the stable and the manger and the baby Jesus. But the yellow crayon will not show against the black. No matter how hard I press, my star emits no light. I try some other potential star colours. Orange. Red. Even a green. But the black night is too strong. A girl near me has done something clever. Perhaps guided by the teacher, she has first coloured the sky in yellow, and then covered the yellow in a layer of black. Then she has scraped the black away in a star shape to reveal the gold beneath. Her stars shine with an extraordinary, nuclear vibrancy. I hate and envy the girl. I keep on trying to find a colour that will stand out against the black. Eventually I reach for a brown crayon. And it works. There is a brown star in the black sky. Relieved, I add more brown constellations.

At last, satisfied, I bring it to the teacher. She has big hair and moles, which frighten me. And when I show her my nativity scene she shouts at me, her voice crackling with scorn, 'Brown stars! Stars aren't brown. Why have you done the stars brown?'

I try to explain, but I don't have the words. But the unfairness of it makes my eyes sting with tears. Even now I can feel myself twitching at the injustice.

Anyway, brown stars. And I wondered if that was the key. That ever since that day in Hull in 1969, I've been drawing brown stars. That I'll be drawing brown stars forever.

Popcorn, Poppadoms, Miso and Milk

September 21. I went shopping this morning for, among other things, popcorn, miso and milk. I forgot my shopping list, so, as I wandered aimlessly around Sainsbury's, I recited 'Popcorn, miso and milk'. For some reason, I found it slightly easier (or perhaps just more pleasurable) to say 'Popcorn, poppadoms, miso and milk', although I didn't need or want any poppadoms.

So I was doing that, wandering up and down the aisles, muttering the mantra. Then, without consciously willing it, I found that – still muttering – I was standing in front of the section where they have miso and other Eastern oddities. I noticed that a smart young man with a South Asian background was next to me. A customer, I mean, not a Sainsbury's person. He had the look of someone who, though from a disadvantaged background, was making the most of things, working his way up diligently on the retail side of the electronics business. He looked over as I was saying 'poppadoms'. His face became confused, then angry. I think he was about to confront me, but then thought better of it, and span away. I realized that he probably thought I was saying 'poppadoms' etc. 'at' him, as some sort of mildly surreal racist attack, which I found utterly dismaying.

I didn't know what to do, so I hit on the idea of wandering around, muttering 'Popcorn, poppadoms, miso and milk' in a slightly louder voice, hoping that our paths would re-intersect, and he'd take me for a madman, not a racist.

Alas, I never saw him again. The shopping trip was ruined. But then I asked a sales assistant where the popcorn was (it's quite elusive – the uncooked type, I mean), and he took me to the spot. Going by his accent, he was African. I lingered to chat with him, again half hoping the Asian guy might see me, and realize that I'm not racist. But he never showed up. After a while I realized that the Sainsbury's man was anxious to get away. But I felt a little cheered by our interaction. 'Enjoy your movie,' he said, pointing at the popcorn.

I trudged home with my heavy bags, still muttering 'Popcorn, poppadoms, miso and milk' in a desultory, self-mocking fashion.

'What did you say?' asked Mrs McG, accusingly, when I came in.

'Nothing,' I said.

When I unpacked, I saw that I had, entirely unconsciously, bought some Sharwood's poppadoms.

The Secret Way of the Drunk

September 22. As a writer of books for young people, I am compelled at times to visit schools, whereupon I caper and cavort in an attempt to make the kids like me, and therefore buy my books. It's shameless and depressing even when it goes well. But at least it forces me out into the world, reorienting and recalibrating my sensory and social apparatus. Writers live solitary lives, and without that tethering we can become strange. A little, I suppose, like those who become (as opposed to being born) deaf, and whose voices float further and further away from what they had been, acquiring that unearthly haunting quality, like the sound of a harmonium drifting from a distant church.

Yesterday's school visit was a moderate success. The school was private, and all the kids very well behaved, eerily mature and polite. I'm always dismayed when a teenager looks me in the eye, shakes my hand and says, 'How do you do.' I'm more comfortable among the uncomfortable, the shufflers, with hands in their pockets, wary of eye contact, or indeed of any form of unnecessary touching.

And besides, I was just another service offered to them, like the enormous grounds, and well-appointed music room, and fanciable French teachers. But they were allowed to buy books on account, which would later be charged to their parents, so we did some good trade.

I got drunk on the way back, and then I forgot how to get from Liverpool Street to West Hampstead. It was one of those times when you're convinced there's a secret, rather cunning way to do something, but you just can't quite remember it. A new monorail, or a secret tunnel…

Human Resources

September 23. Got a new job starting at the end of the month, teaching creative writing at Royal Holloway University. In theory, it's part of the University of London, but it's in some far-flung region known to geographers as Egham. It's only a few hours a week, but it's my first salaried employment in ages, and the admin is proving rather stressful. They want all kinds of obscure documents (a P45, for heaven's sake), as well as proof that I'm not a former Somalian pirate or Peruvian llama shagger trying to work here illegally.

And I keep reading and re-reading a letter from Human Resources, and I can't for the life of me work out what it's trying to say, or what they want me to do. Seriously, I'm thinking about going off the grid and living on roadkill badger carcasses in the New Forest. I could satisfy my creative urges by dancing naked in the moonlight, or by sneaking into villages and daubing limericks on pavements using my own faeces.

Yes, all that is preferable to reading the second paragraph of the Health and Safety document.

Mrs McG Never Lies

September 24. Mrs McG never lies. She has a very uncomplicated relationship with words. There is a cup on the table. Objects are arranged in the world. The objects turn into ideas in her head. Words cleave to the ideas. That's her template for everything, no matter how complex or nuanced or intangible.

But, for me, the serpent of doubt slithers in. Every stage – the arrangement of matter, the perception of those arrangements in the mind, the expressing of the thoughts as words – is knotty and difficult. The truth becomes a thing not that you might reveal or conceal, but something that you can never find in the first place.

I tell a couple of stories when I visit schools. One is about the sly bullying and betrayal of a vulnerable kid by a version of me. The other is about the accidental slaying of a dog with a crossbow. I ask the audience to try to guess which is true, which made up. I ask them if it matters, does it make any difference to them as stories. In other words, is truth an aesthetic quality, something that makes art and stories better? Of course, all they care about is whether or not I killed the dog. I give different answers depending on my mood. And now I can't remember which is true. Though it's strange how the young are much more moved by cruelty to animals than cruelty to people.

But this difficult relationship between the world, the mind and language is what Mrs McG describes as lying. And I suppose she's right. I'm guilty of telling people what they want to hear, of trying to avoid the difficult truths, substituting kindness (or weakness) for honesty. But where I would lie, Mrs McG remains silent.

Because, as I began, Mrs McG never lies.

Arlo

September 25. I went for a drink with my writer friend, Arlo, last night. As usual we spent most of the evening discussing his complicated love life. Being single, he has one. He hooks up using Tinder. His latest adventure featured a huge performance artiste called 'Slobzilla'. She'd created a video installation, in which she emerged naked from the sea and proceeded to squash a reasonably accurate model of London made from cardboard boxes, bearing down on St Paul's Cathedral and Big Ben with her titanic breasts and Hindenbergian buttocks. It was all on YouTube – Arlo showed me on his phone.

He told me that when they met up, Slobzilla produced a clipboard, and asked him a series of questions both intimate and slightly surreal (13. Have you ever had sex in a paddling pool? 22. What are your views on fisting?).

After that their evening took on a densely sordid texture, marbled with a doomed poignancy, like blood in a stool sample from a cancerous bowel. The story left me feeling sad and somewhat astonished at the things that people do to each other in the pursuit of pleasure. Or in the flight from loneliness.

The Wrong Transsexual

September 26. I was sent out by Mrs McG to get some paint. She gave me a little tester pot with the details on, and strongly suggested that I try to find the same sales assistant she'd had on an earlier visit.

'You'll know her,' she added, helpfully, 'she's the transsexual. She's really good. She really knows colour.'

It was all a lot to keep in my head – the tester pot, the amount needed (2.5 litres), the transgender issue, etc., so I was a bit worried. I got to Homebase, and was immediately struck by how depressed and useless everyone seemed. I don't suppose it's a great place to work – it had the feeling of a decayed spaceport in a far-flung colony, long neglected, indeed forgotten, by Earth.

I'd assumed that I could just go by the code on the tester pot, and find the right sort of paint on the shelf, but it proved more challenging than that. A man – not transgender – told me it had to be specially mixed up, as you waited, which was a new one on me. Then he pressed a button and said someone would come along and help me – the transsexual, I hoped.

A minute or two later a lady appeared. She had very strong glasses in a distressingly organic shade of pink. I wasn't sure if they were the sort of glasses a transsexual would wear, and there were no other obvious giveaways, so I just hoped for the best. We had quite an enjoyable chat about the whole paint mixing process – slightly flirtatious, you'd have to say. She seemed touched that a customer wanted to engage her in discourse, and we had a bit of a giggle, especially during the stage where the paint was vibrated in a special chamber in a way that was undoubtedly slightly kinky.

It turned out to be a pleasurable shopping experience – she even came and opened up a new till for me, which didn't seem to be part of her normal, paint-mixing duties.

But then, as I cycled away, the doubts began to grow.

Those glasses.

It wasn't that you wouldn't expect a transgender person to wear them, because they can have the same terrible taste as everyone else – more that they didn't seem to be the sorts of things that someone who cared (and knew) about colour would pick.

So I decided that I'd probably got the wrong person. She could still have been a transsexual, of course, just not the right transsexual.

So now, back home, I'm worrying over my tactics, should the paint turn out to be the incorrect shade (summer codsperm, rather than winter seahorse phlegm).

If I admit that I had the wrong person (who may or may not have been a transsexual) then I'd have to shoulder the blame, and take whatever sanctions follow.

However, if I insist, to protect myself, that I had the correct transsexual, the one who knows about colour, then that might cause more damage. You see, Mrs McG has had a difficult time, with her mum being poorly, and me being a knob-head, and her faith in the colour-matching abilities of the transsexual in Homebase has been the one still point in her turning world. And if I take that away from her…

Well, anyway, you see the problem. I might just hide the paint and tell her someone stole it from my panniers while I was buying some stamps, and then she can go and locate the right transsexual tomorrow.

Gender Troubles

September 27. Some time ago I bought two cans of Right Guard Total Defence antiperspirant. One had writing on it in a sort of, well, mauve, I suppose – somewhere in between pink and purple. The other came in a nice, firm, masculine blue. The idea was that Mrs McG and I would have one each, of the appropriate, er, sex. Now I've just discovered that they are both labelled 'For Women'. It seems that I have been using lady antiperspirant.

I can't say I feel actively violated, or even outraged, by this, but I am a touch thrown. I'm all in favour of a little gender slippage, but I like to know exactly what I'm getting into, and to discover only after several weeks that I've got lady armpits is… unsettling. Plus, well, a lady antiperspirant really isn't up to the heavy workload presented by my intimate areas, certainly not when I'm in the throes of a high-octane event. So, anyway, I may have to write a stern letter about this to the appropriate regulatory body.

Paint is Shit

September 28. Trouble. Remember the incident with the paint and the transsexual?

Well, it was the wrong transsexual, and it is the wrong paint.

Our Polish decorator just led me by the arm and showed me the first swipe. Rather than the pale grey, like a kittiwake's back, that I was expecting, it's a sort of yellowy, skidmark brown.

'Paint is shit,' said the Pole, morosely, but accurately.

This is going to be fantastically inconvenient. The lesson is: don't trust what it says on the outside of the tin, especially where the label is merely a long string of numbers and letters. Always open the tin and have a good peer. There may be a metaphor about gender in there, somewhere, but I'm not going to poke about in it.

(Later, Mrs McG and the painter decide that in fact the paint has 'gone off', which is not something I knew paint could do. So it may have been the right paint, and the right transsexual, but the paint then transformed into something else. Don't suppose I'll ever get to the bottom of it.)

Whither the Fog?

September 29. It was quite misty this morning, a few wisps of opacity hanging in the grey streets. Oddly, the patches of mist seemed somehow lighter than the adjacent air, in that paradoxical way that the moon can sometimes make a cloud appear blacker as it passes.

Anyway, it struck me that you hardly ever seem to get decent fog these days – I don't mean pea-souper style smogs, I just mean ordinary, honest, healthy fog. I remember as a kid there'd be many mornings when you couldn't see the bus until it was almost on you, and the fog plastered your hair wetly across your face. So what's happened to all the fog? Is it a global warming phenomenon? Or perhaps it's to do with wind farms, those ominous, beautiful turning blades dispersing it, like a flapping duvet removing the stale residue of an ill-timed emission. Also, how come it never rains and, er, fogs at the same time? Can birds fly through thick fog without crashing into trees? If you went out into a thick fog with a naked candle, would the fog put it out? Can you capture fog in a jar, and take it home? Could you sell flavoured fog as a low-calorie snack?

The Angry Prostate

September 30. Just walked past a new shop in West Hampstead called Health City. There was a big sign in the window suggesting strongly that my prostate needs attention, in the hectoring manner of a First World War recruitment poster. Next to it was an enormous model of an engorged prostate, looking like something concocted by the *Dr Who* special effects team, c. 1975: a shambling, glaucous monster, with one baleful, red eye.

'You're mine,' it seemed to say. 'You're mine.'

It was almost impossible to tear myself away. The red eye of the prostate, like the red eye of Sauron, saw me, held me…

I'd still be there now, a chained worshipper of Cthulhu, if a group of young women hadn't come by, already tipsy, laughing loudly, shaking me from my reverie. No one likes to be caught staring at a large model of an inflamed prostate by a group of giddy girls.

A New Phase Begins

October 1. A new phase in my life began today – schlepped along to Royal Holloway to perform various acts of administrative necessity, prior to starting my stint as visiting lecturer on Wednesday. So far in my life every new phase has been slightly worse than the preceding one, and I've no reason to believe that the pattern is about to change.

However, it really is quite an impressive campus – especially the main building. It looks like one of Louis XIV's spare palaces. Egham, though, is almost impossible to get to from West Hampstead, requiring a bicycle ride, two trains and a bus. On the days when there's work to be done on the track, they offer a replacement hot air balloon service.

Oh, and I had a drink in the student union bar before my meeting with Human Resources, and was dismayed to find that mine was the only alcohol being consumed in the whole place. All around me young people were slurping at paper buckets of coffee, or sipping at energy drinks. Students today are a sensible lot. Doubt they'll be erecting barricades or manning picket lines or rioting, like in my days at Manchester in the 1980s. The most one might hope for from them is a Twitter campaign on the need for transgender-friendly bicycle racks. When I was being interviewed for a PhD scholarship, one of my fellow shortlisted candidates told me that his thesis was on how modern UK policing was transformed by the tactics devised by the Greater Manchester Police Force for dealing with the student demos of the mid-80s.

'I was there!' I said. 'I threw a paper aeroplane at Michael Heseltine!'

This other candidate was a pleasant and a worthy young man, wearing a blazer and a tie and a pair of grey slacks, his hair combed and neatly parted. I can't remember what improvised costume I had on. Possibly the 'country-doctor' suit I'd bought from a charity shop in Manchester. The interview was at the Open University – it funded a single arts postgraduate studentship each year, although there were a couple of hundred similar science scholarships. It was worth quite a lot of money, but it meant you were supposed to live in Milton Keynes and wander round the campus, trying to make it look like a real university. That put a lot of arty responsibility on your shoulders.

The police guy should have got the scholarship. The world would have been a slightly better place. But I had one of my good days, and I managed to make my ludicrous thesis idea – 'Conceptions of Male Beauty, 1750–1850' – sound cutting edge, relevant, cool. At the time I was drowning in quicksand, and the scholarship was the jungle vine that I grasped, and used to pull myself just clear.

But what I'd really like to know is, does that kind of quicksand really exist, or was it just invented for the Johnny Weissmuller *Tarzan* films? Has anyone ever truly been lost beneath the lumpy black tarry mud, sinking slowly, waist, chest, neck, head? A last bubble. Finally, the arm reaching up, the fingers stretching, then curling in death. Perhaps at the seaside, but in jungles?

It loomed large in my imagination as a kid. On building sites and waste ground, we'd check carefully for quicksand, or its close relation, sinking mud. But sinking mud only ever took a welly, and never a young life…

My Chlamydia Levels are Low

October 2. There was one mildly diverting incident while I was at Royal Holloway yesterday afternoon. As I was leaving the student union bar, I saw a basket full of small boxes, in a blue-and-white livery resembling the old Tesco Value range, with a sign saying 'Free!' I paused and picked one up, thinking it might be some pink wafer biscuits, or cup-a-soup, or something else useful.

Then I saw that it was a 'Chlamydia testing kit'.

For a moment I wondered if perhaps my chlamydia levels were actually a bit low, and if I should take the test in case I needed supplements, or just some more, I don't know, bananas, or walnuts, or however you get your chlamydia naturally.

Then I recalled that it was one of those troublesome STDs. The sort of thing that might begin as a minor itch, but, if left untreated, would lead to bunged-up piping, sterility, a generalized shrinking of the genitals, madness and, ultimately, death. Again, I briefly wondered what the test might entail. Swabs, I thought. I may have briefly mimed the various options for swabbing and smearing, orifice-wise.

And then I looked up and saw that a small group of female students were watching this performance. I couldn't think of a witty thing to say, so I bustled into the loo near the display, the testing kit still in my hand. Safely inside, I marvelled at the new trend for having men's lavatories without urinals, before quickly realizing my mistake and rushing out of the Ladies'.

The girls were still there. They were rather sympathetic, actually, to the confused elderly transsexual with his unfortunate ailment. I put the box back. Half wish I'd brought it home, just to see what was in it. But it might have been a hard one to explain to Mrs McG.

Mouth Feel

October 3. One of the surprising things about Mrs McG is her habit of inserting a sliver of tongue during a perfectly ordinary hello/goodbye type of kiss. Even after all these years it still manages to discommode me. I suppose it's her equivalent of one of my greatest inventions, the Deafening Kiss. It's exquisite in its way (the Deafening Kiss, I mean). What you do is sidle up to someone, in full view of the dinner guests, or the party crowd or whatever, put an arm around the victim's shoulders and kiss them on the ear. The key is to deftly draw out the air from the ear canal, creating a total vacuum. Then you complete the kiss with a loud smacking noise. To the outside world it looks like the sweetest gesture, but to your quarry it provides a sharp shock, forcing them to reel away cursing you loudly. You then appear innocent, and terribly wronged. Or, if the other party is a stranger, like a desperate pervert.

But this isn't about my kiss, but hers. For a naturally unaffectionate creature, she's a wonderful kisser. It's all to do with what confectioners call 'mouth feel'. According to market research, what we consumers crave is an initial resistance from a firm outer coating, followed by a melting interior. What we don't like is a sticky outside leading on to a tough core. Or sticky giving way to more sticky. Or hard followed by more hard. No, it has to be firm then soft.

This all reminds me of my first ever job. I was eight years old. Graham Doran's dad worked at the huge Trebor sweet factory outside York. Graham was in my gang, the Low Garth Rangers (we lived in Low Garth Road). It was *my* gang, in that I was the guiding spirit, although not, in fact, its leader. My formal position was Gang Doctor. And my not-particularly-arduous duties were to carry around dock leaves in case of nettle rash; to urinate on grass cuts; and to 'operate' on Simon Morley's compliant sister, Mary. Graham's house was a kind of sucrose heaven. His mum used to mix up something from a tin called Creamola foam, a kind of fruit-flavoured liver salts. It exploded in your mouth like a pineapple hand grenade. She brought it down from Scotland, the spiritual homeland of rotten teeth, where it was favoured by serial wife killers as the best way to dissolve the body. Graham's dad used us as guinea pigs for new sweets. We'd be strapped into an apparatus, like smoking beagles, and a probe would inject confectionery matter directly into our gullets. Not really. Trebor specialized in chews, and we tested out the new flavours: rhubarb and custard, liquorice and apple, whale and bacon, lemur... We had to fill out forms rating our response to flavour, texture (i.e. mouth feel, but *avant la lettre*), and it was fantastic, in a dental-caries-nirvana kind of way, but nobody at school believed me, and it earned me the reputation, slow to shake off, of a confabulist.

But I was talking about kissing. Kissing Her. I've had girlfriends who got things the wrong way round, sloppy, drooly lips first then all clashing teeth, as well as one or two all drool or all teeth. But she got her mouth feel exactly right. Hard and then soft, hard and then soft...

After the first kiss I knew that I didn't want to kiss anyone else ever again, and that I still wanted to be kissing this mouth in forty years' time.

She was twenty-four years old, and I was twenty-eight.

Anyway, the tongue thing still startles me, like a fly taken by a chameleon. Zip, done.

My Medical Training...

October 4. Earlier on this evening I was walking Monty along the Finchley Road, when I saw a group of three drunk men engaged in a clumsy pavement ballet. One staggered and fell, half on the pavement, half in the busy road. The other two could barely stay on their feet, and their attempts to drag their friend back towards safety looked like killing all three of them. It didn't help that they'd all reached the stage of drunkenness in which your trousers tend to fall down, requiring constant holding up with one hand.

So I helped them drag the now unconscious and bloodied first faller back on the pavement. A few other people began to gather. The three men were Polish, and the two still standing had no English at all, which is unusual. I helped to get the prone man into what I vaguely recalled was the recovery position.

'Do you know first aid?' someone asked. 'Yes, I do,' I replied confidently.

I've often claimed to be medically trained, based on the fact I did two weeks of a medical degree, and then a couple of years later a half-day first aid course. But then when I tried to recall my medical knowledge, it seemed that all I could remember was a simpleton called Russell, who tried to give mouth-to-mouth to the resuscitation dummy by applying his lips to the (female) dummy's pert breast.

And now people – a smartly dressed woman, a couple of shopkeepers and a delivery man from the pizza place – were looking at me, as if I would take charge. I felt panic rise.

'I'd better go and get help,' I said, and picked up Monty and ran down the street, and round a corner, to where I knew there was a dense patch of rhododendron bushes, perfect for lurking and skulking.

I crouched in the bushes, in a state of near terror. Much to my relief, about five minutes later, I heard a siren – obviously someone had called for an ambulance. I waited another few minutes, not wanting to be seen by any of the other bystanders. But just as I emerged, the smart lady walked by, observing me suspiciously as I brushed the leaves and twigs and detritus from my clothes. I held Monty out towards her.

'I found him,' I said, by way of explanation.

'You were gone a long time,' said Mrs McG when I got in, in her usual sharply accusing manner.

'I had to help a drunk Polish man,' I said. 'He fell down. My medical training...'

Infinite Regress 1

October 5. Just had an email telling me that the London Book Fair will have a stand at the Frankfurt Book Fair. Don't know why, but this tickles me. Perhaps it's an infinite regress thing. On that London Book Fair stand at the Frankfurt Book Fair, there'll be a leaflet advertising the next Frankfurt Book Fair. There'll be a photo on the front of the leaflet showing, among others, the London Book Fair stand at the Frankfurt Book Fair. If you zoom in on that photo, you'll see there's a leaflet...

A deeper question is why the mind both delights in and dreads the infinite regress. I think, from the storyteller's perspective, the delight comes from the fact that the picture within the picture within the picture means that the story will never end, but carry on moving forever. Which is where the dread comes in: we never reach the referent, the thing in itself, the point. Which is where the delight returns: the point is the story. Don't ask for the meaning in the pattern in the carpet: the meaning *is the pattern.* I remember once seeing some film of an aquatic worm, or perhaps a species of sea cucumber, swimming in the open water. Its mode of propulsion was bizarre and glorious. Essentially a living tube, the creature moved by turning itself inside out in a constant peristaltic wave, its insides becoming its outsides in an endless cycle. Although, now I think about it, perhaps that's a metaphor for something else entirely. The constant exposing of one's inner working. My friend Arlo always said I was like the Pompidou Centre, with all my pipes on the outside.

The Dream of the Street Surveyor

October 6. I don't really believe those street surveyor people you see with their gizmos on tripods are actually doing anything useful. I think they're like trainspotters and it's just a hobby. I mean, if you were ever actually to ask them, 'Excuse me, what are you doing that for, I mean the thing you're doing, with those gizmos on the tripods?' they'd just look embarrassed or hostile. It's not as if, having surveyed a street, anything can be done about it, if it's found to be faulty in some way, out of alignment or in the wrong town or whatever. And, just like trainspotters, you never get a lady street surveyor, and it's not as if it's heavy work or anything. Which proves it's just an Asperger's spectrum thing.

Although now I think about it, I'm rather drawn to it, either as a career or hobby. It's the very ineffectuality that appeals. If it does no good, then equally it does no harm. And so you are freed from any sense of responsibility or guilt. You can go home at the end of each day, rejoicing in the fact that the world is exactly the same, and no worse, because of your actions.

On the Sadness that Affects You When You Come Home Late and Find Your Family Asleep

October 7. You come home late from teaching and find everyone's asleep. You creep silently into three bedrooms and kiss each forehead, aching with lovesadness. The dog looks at you in the murk, flicks his tail twice and goes back to sleep.

Then you realize how hungry you are, and you eat seven Weetabix.

Songlines

October 8. I had a dismaying experience last night. I was feeling tired and vaguely ill, but dragged myself along to a social function, where I self-medicated with free champagne and Kettle crisps. It wasn't really my sort of crowd. The venue was the hospitality lounge at a cricket ground and it was full of narrow-lipped sportswriters, fantastically monomaniacal on whatever their subject happened to be (Argentinian midfield playmakers of the 1950s; Latvian pole-vaulters; transgender golf), interspersed with red-faced men in expensive suits, equally enraged by the England Test team selection criteria and the uncontrolled immigration of blacks, Turks and transgender golfers.

As anyone who's ever met me knows, I have a relatively limited range of conversational subjects – I term them my Big Seven – and I always look to them for salvation when I'm in socially awkward situations. I was holding forth on one of these (no. 4: The demonstration, with idiosyncratic proofs and amusing digressions, that deaf people are not, in fact, deaf, but just pretending: anyone can say 'Pardon?') when an acquaintance who happened to be there told me to stop saying the things I was saying, and say some other stuff instead, on the grounds that my current subject was inappropriate and uninteresting.

On reflection, I was forced to concede that he was being nothing less than factually accurate. This was a disaster. Like the Aborigines in Bruce Chatwin's *Songlines*, I rely on these topics to orient myself both spatially and temporally, not to say intellectually. If I have to cut one of my Big Seven, I literally won't know where or when I am. And they're also all linked, so, if one falls, they'll all fall. The options are stark: think of some new things to say, or don't go out any more. I'm drawn to the latter.

Tiny Jumpers for Your Feet

October 9. For most of my adult life I've been a wearer of the cotton sock, with a single, disastrous and short-lived flirtation with a silk-linen blend. However, I've just bought a load of M&S woollen socks. They look like tiny jumpers for your feet. They make me happy in the way that few other things do.

And now I've got a horrible feeling that this may come under the modish Danish concept of 'hygge'. Finding joy in small domestic delights, in cosiness and comfort. Excitement provided, perhaps, by popping out to chop some wood, before you come back inside to enjoy a warming cup of blandness, sprinkled with, I expect, cinnamon. Your partner, her legs pulled up under her on the clean lines of the sofa, flicks through an architectural magazine. She has lovely eyes, although her honey-coloured hair has fallen over them as she reads. But now she looks up and smiles. Her eyes also seem to be honey-coloured. As is her skin. If she had some honey, doubtless it would be honey-coloured. 'Yergy-flergy blinky-blonk,' she says.

It's probably an invitation to the bedroom. I run my hand through my beard. 'Blinka yergy-flerg,' I reply, having learned the language by studying wood-burning stove catalogues.

Helga goes on ahead of me while I finish up the intricate carvings on the small, honey-coloured wooden box we plan to use as a cinnamon caddy...

And now it's been Danished, I see what is fatal in this discovery of pleasure and solace in small things. Fatal for our souls, in that we stop striving for greatness (or even goodness); fatal for society, in that it makes us content with the state of the world. If Clement Attlee's socks had been softer would there have been an NHS?

Apart from the Money

October 10. Double teaching today. First the absurdly young students at Royal Holloway, then, in the evening, my first

Faber Academy class of the season. The Royal Holloway kids were bright, but didn't really know anything that wasn't on their syllabus. There just isn't the time for them to read widely and weirdly, which is the main requirement for being a writer. But they're sweet kids, and I think they appreciate the fact I'm going to try to help them write something that other people might actually want to read.

The Faber class consisted of fifteen eager women writers. No men. Luckily, my usual tsunami of testosterone helped balance the room. Distressingly, none of them wanted to go to the pub after the class, which is the main reason I teach, apart from the money.

The Lines of the Sad Drunk and the Happy Drunk Are Not Parallel, But Eventually Meet at the Point at Which You're Just Drunk

October 11. Back from a moderate debauch in Cambridge, I had to take to my bed with some sort of malaise – headache, feverish shivering, vague mental disorientation. The heart says Dengue fever, the head suggests hangover.

The debauch followed a rare success. My talk went well. The audience were shocked in the right places, laughed at the jokes, nodded at the profound bits. But what I've found is that the lines of the sad drunk and the happy drunk are not parallel, but eventually meet at the point at which you're just drunk.

Mrs McG being quite kind, by her standards... She brought me a sandwich. At least I think it was a sandwich. I suppose it might have been the ironing. So I lie here listening to the *Sword of Honour* trilogy on the radio. What appalling, witless trash it is. Waugh really is overrated. Or perhaps I'm just Waugh weary. And now I'm slightly ashamed of that joke, as of an unattractive girl I've just snogged behind the pub, and now won't talk to.

While Vermin Swarm Over His Soiled Loins

October 12. Well, what a terrible day. Began with a bitter argument with Mrs McG. On the whole she tolerates my inability to drive, earn enough money, talk intelligently to her friends, buy her flowers and undertake housework. But occasionally some casual misdemeanour will cause the effluent to overflow the septic tank. This offence will often take the form of me insisting on some small point of domestic efficiency – turning off lights, screwing on toothpaste tube caps, stacking the dishwasher correctly, etc. This morning I rashly suggested a reform of our Tupperware storage regime. I suppose she regards these quirks of mine as being like a tramp fussing over his bow tie, while vermin swarm over his soiled loins.

The end of the day matched the beginning. I taught a class in the evening, and managed to get a puncture in town and had to make a desultory trudge home, wheeling the maimed bike. Everything in between was rubbish, too.

The only thing that cheered me up even slightly was the film of some really useless Native American dancing I saw on the internet. I'm a notoriously bad dancer ('the dying buffalo!' as my poor dead cousin, Liam, once declaimed), but even I could have made a better showing. It's a myth that only the developed world can produce shit art.

Okapi

October 15. Rosie wanted to go to the zoo. I told her that I'd take her to the even better 'free' zoo. It's the bit of Regent's

Park where you can see over and through the railings to some of the animal enclosures. We stood in the drizzle for a while. You could see the giraffes and then, gloriously, a flash of okapi. But soon Rosie grew restive, so I told her an edited version of my okapi story.

Some years ago, when I was still in the habit of drinking all day in public spaces, I found myself in this same section of the park, just outside the zoo. It was late at night, and I deduced that my best chance of getting some kip was to hop over the fence into one of the pens, where I could bed down in some straw, safe from interference by the vagrants in the park. I knew the lions and tigers and leopards and wolverines and whatnot were fully enclosed, so I was unlikely to be molested by a large predator, although if truth be told I wasn't thinking all that clearly.

I can't remember quite how I scaled the high perimeter fence, although drink has a way of helping you overcome obstacles of that nature. So, there I was, in some paddock, with a farmyard sort of ambience, and a pervasive stench of vegetative animal excrement.

I found a loose pile of straw, and formed it into a rough bed. I had a big coat in those days, Yugoslavian Army surplus, designed to withstand the rigours of the Balkan winters, and without that I'd probably have frozen to death, and been found the next morning by the keepers. As it was, I was merely very cold, and my knackers were clacking like an executive toy.

But I was just beginning to drift off, soothed by the distant lowing of the llamas, and the gentle whoops of the gibbons, and the digestive rumbles and gut-blasts of the Indian elephants, when suddenly I heard the thunder of hooves approaching, and a frantic whinnying. I looked up to see a strange vision before me, and it took a moment or two before I realized it was an okapi, that gentle and elusive forest cousin of the giraffe. Gentle, in normal circumstances, that is. This one was clearly enraged. It was rearing like a stallion, and emitting that unearthly cry, like a soul in torment.

One of its sharply hooved feet thudded down inches from my skull, and I took that as a sign that I should make my exit. So I did, pursued by the okapi. I'd never before heard of this extreme territoriality in the okapi, and I thought, briefly, that there might be a scientific monograph to be written on the subject. But then I was back over the fence, and decided to make my uncertain way back to my official lodgings.

As I staggered down the street, I realized that there was movement from within the folds of my greatcoat. Somewhat dismayed and surprised, as there had been nothing of that nature going on for quite some time, I pulled open the coat, and something fell out. I picked it up, and found that it was a baby okapi. I considered going back and throwing it over the fence, but the alarm had been raised. A siren was blowing, and searchlights were playing across the pens. I couldn't afford another zoo-related offence on my record, so I scurried away, the okapi tucked back inside my coat, and under my jumper, a Fair Isle sweater I'd won in a game of chance.

It was strangely comforting having the little chap there inside my jumper, and it soon settled down and went to sleep.

However, by the time I'd reached my lodgings, it was dead. Having no money for a kebab, I roasted it in the communal kitchen, and ate it with some stale bread I found in someone's cupboard.

It was the finest thing I've ever eaten, as tender as spring lamb. But hunger, of course, is the best sauce, and I'd had nothing inside but for the drink all day.

I'm not saying I felt good about it, and early the next morning I went back to the park, to pay my respects. I stood at the railings and looked through them, at the mother okapi.

She was standing over the pile of straw, making a sound that was so close to human weeping that I was unmanned. She looked at me with those huge brown okapi eyes, and I stared back, and I think she knew the truth, as she went rigid, and then bared her long, ungulate teeth. I felt shame, and regret, and a sort of disgust at humankind for always destroying what is most gentle and most beautiful in the world.

But also, beneath it, hunger, because once you've tasted okapi, no other meat will suffice.

'Is it true, Dad?' asked Rosie, when I'd finished.

'What?'

'The story, is it true?'

'Ah, truth. Truth is like looking into the murky waters of a pond, and you think you see a fish down there, turning in the depths, but it might just be the play of light and shade, or a bubble of methane emerging from the sludge at the bottom.'

'I hate you, Dad,' said Rosie.

The Return of Heimlich

October 17. I saw him again. Heimlich, I mean, of course. I'd begun to think that perhaps I'd imagined the dwarf, or at least distorted reality to create a diverting illusion. But no. It was just after nine in the evening, and the roads were quiet. Monty and I were picking our way along the backstreets, sniffing at the bloated rubbish sacks, which slumped and lolled like casualties on a medieval battlefield, bowels spilling from their slit torsos.

It was Monty who sensed him first, and gave a low growl, with more fear than fight in it. This time he was coming towards me, on the opposite side of the street. There was an incline and I sensed that his progress was laboured, his breathing ragged. In the effort to keep up his pace against the slope, he flung his crutches forwards, and dragged his poor blunt lower half along with an effort as much mental as physical. His hood bobbled behind the dense black curls of his hair. Every few yards he glanced back over his shoulder, surely confirming the hypothesis that he was fleeing some terrifying pursuer. The dim orange streetlights added to the ghastliness of the scene, etching deep grooves of blackness into his tortured face.

This time Heimlich did not see me. I wanted to call out to him, to find out his story, but short of rugby tackling him I couldn't see how I could stop him. And soon he was lost again in the gloom. I crossed the road, and thought that I could at least wait for whoever hunted him. I imagined hounds straining at the leash; men in leather jerkins, some savage, some blankly implacable. But they were just obeying orders. There would be a lord there too, astride a frothing charger.

I waited two, three minutes, listening for the baying of the hounds, the crack of the whip. But no one came. The mystery of Heimlich would not be solved tonight. Monty looked at me, trying to understand what I wanted, why we weren't already on our way. He had already forgotten Heimlich. Would that I could.

Graveyard Fruits

October 18. My latest round of Hedgerow Russian Roulette. This morning I was walking through the lovely graveyard of St John's in Hampstead, when I saw what I thought was either a vine, heavy with grapes, or deadly nightshade. Imagine my satisfaction on tasting one and finding it a perfect, sweet grape. I was moved by the whole thing – wild grapes in England in October, amid the fallen graves and dark-hearted cedars. And I'd walked right past this spot at least a thousand times before without seeing the vines, which added to the mystery and magic.

But then the Garden of Eden/forbidden fruit thing kicked in, and I realized that I was naked, and I hurried away from the approaching sirens.

How Attempting to Fix a Problem Can Often Make Matters Worse

October 20. You put some milk on to heat. You keep a reasonable eye on it, but then find yourself distracted by something on the radio – a *Woman's Hour* feature on the first all-female attempt to conquer the South Pole without sanitary protection, say, or the revelation of a politician's addiction to auto-erotic asphyxiation – and then you hear the characteristic soft fizzing music of milk boiling over. You rush to the pan, and attempt to transfer it to the sink, thinking this is the best way of containing the disaster. As you carry it, the pan continues to froth and boil, covering the space in between the hob and the sink in spilt milk. The nanosecond you reach the sink, the pan ceases to boil over. You then think, well, if I'd just turned off the gas, and left the pan there, there would have been far less mess, and you resolve to do just that next time. And then the next time comes, and the special kind of panic you feel about boiling milk kicks in, and you do it all over again.

The Probability of Leaves

October 21. I walked down to get myself a soothing mid-morning cheese and onion pasty when a gust of wind shook the plane trees that line my street. Thousands of leaves blew down around me. One landed at my feet – it was huge – unnecessarily so – the size and shape of a T-rex's footprint. And then I thought, as I've thought before at this time of year, about the infinitesimally small chance of me seeing this particular leaf – one of literally billions in my part of London – fall. And if that can happen, then anything is possible, no matter how unlikely, horrific or terrible.

Blow Gently into Its Face, as You Would to a Baby

October 22. I've been told that the way to stop milk from boiling over is to blow gently into its face, as you would to a baby.

A Feather, a Child's Finger Bone, a Teabag

October 25. I was sent out last night to the Tesco Metro for emergency supplies. The charity shops (I had to pass six on the way) had left out their unsellable stock for the bin men – broken-backed pushchairs, spoutless teapots, baby mattresses, stained with troubling areas of burnt umber, and dull amber, unstrung balalaikas, copies of my second novel, etc. etc. As I shambled along, I saw through the murk a figure hunched beside one of these trash piles. It was a man going through the rubbish. From the look of him he was just a notch or so up from utter dereliction, and his face, curiously boneless, wore a haunted, Dostoyevskian expression.

Then my eye was caught by an object on top of the pile of garbage. It took me a second to work out that it was a lady's hat. The sort of thing a divorced woman would wear to her second wedding in, say, 1963. A veil made of nylon netting. Some other sad decorative elements – a feather, a child's finger bone, a teabag.

And, as I watched, I saw the man stretch out his arm and take hold of the hat. And then, as I knew he must, he placed the hat on his head, and tamped it down. At the same moment he looked up at me – I was only a couple of yards away by this time. Our eyes met, and I saw the spasm of shame pass across his face. And then his expression changed: it became a look of recognition and understanding. He knew that if our places were reversed – if I'd been the person to see it first – then I too would have taken the hat, and put it on my head. And then I looked down and saw that my arm had, of its own volition, reached out towards the hat. I filled the gap in time with a throat-clearing noise, and then we exchanged almost imperceptible nods, and I hurried on to buy the oven chips, a three-pack of Mars Bars and a tin of Andrews Liver Salts.

On the way back I saw that the man had gone, and so, of course, had the hat. That was probably a good thing. Not sure how I would have explained it to Mrs McG.

I Don't Know How Long It Can Last

October 27. I heard a sound like a sigh this morning. No, more complicated, a sigh with bones in it. Almost the sound of a medium-sized bird, a wood pigeon or a crow, say, making a messy landing in the top of a tree. I investigated and saw that our drying rack had collapsed under the weight of the clothes. It's one of those foldable ones, that look like the fossilised skeleton of a prehistoric accordion. I felt oddly privileged to have actually witnessed (aurally) the collapse. Usually that sort of domestic disaster happens when you're out or otherwise unaware, and you just discover the horror later. Somehow this felt special…

I was looking at the pile of bones and ragged flesh (OK, mainly my underpants, T-shirts and some towels), when I realized Mrs McG was at my shoulder.

'I'll have to get a new one,' she said.

I had the feeling that she might have been looking at me, rather than the broken rack.

'I can fix things,' I said, and my voice may have cracked, a little.

'It can't be fixed.'

Then she left for work.

I spent the day binding and splinting the broken leg. And I found myself uttering soothing words. 'There, there. It's OK, shush, now, shush.'

It's standing again now, but I don't know how long it can last.

The Importance of Silence

October 28. For reasons beyond my capacity to explain, or even fully comprehend, at the school gates this morning I was handed an enormous aluminium fish-slice. I found this immensely burdensome on the way home: it was the combination of the absurd domesticity of the object, combined with a distinct whiff of perversity – it was the sort of implement you'd ask a fat man to spank you with at a suburban orgy. I tried various concealment strategies, before wedging the spatulate end into my back pocket, with the long handle then passing up inside my coat (the handsome one bequeathed to me by my uncle Jock, who worked at the Golden Wonder crisp factory in Edinburgh).

I then stuck on my ear phones, and was in the middle of developing my theory about the importance of the three seconds of silence after a song stops, which are filled with more musical meaning than everything that goes before, when I felt a sharp rapping at my shoulder. I turned to see an angry-looking middle-aged lady, waving the fish-slice at me. Evidently it had dropped out of my pocket, and the lady had been shouting at me, as I was lost in my soundworld. She really did look quite cross, although I suspect it was a lifetime of romantic disappointment more than the fish-slice incident that was responsible. I imagined an unsatisfactory first husband, perhaps a door-to-door surgical appliance salesman, with gum disease and a big shoe.

But then as she passed the fish-slice to me, something made her face soften. Perhaps our fingers brushed together on the long handle. Perhaps she just understood my embarrassment, and its causes. Anyway, she then unfurled a smile so dazzling I briefly thought that I too would have sold trusses and support bandages door-to-door for her, if I'd known her in 1973. I don't think it was a romantic moment, but as I thanked her and walked away I felt flooded with love for the world.

The Frog and the Bluebottle

October 30. I recall reading, many years ago, that frogs are able to chew with their eyeballs. This is possible because they have no solid palate, and can compress their eyes down to crush and manipulate whatever grub they've taken into their mouths.

Two days and two school visits have done for my ego what the eyeballs of the frog do to its dinner, the crushing coming from an unexpected direction.

Yesterday at a tough but in many ways excellent school in Newham, I was booked in to talk to the whole of Year 7 in two tranches. 'And each child will be getting a free book,' the enthusiastic librarian had told me on the phone. 'I'm sure they'll love it if you sign them for them.'

Ah, that's nice, I thought – 180 new adherents to the Cult of McGowan. And then it transpired that the kids really were getting a free book each.

Just not one by me.

It was funded by a charity, which was donating books by various other authors. The kids were clearly baffled by the whole affair, the disjunct between the books they were being given and the shambolic character before them. Was I a real author? Why weren't any of my books among the freebies? Was I famous? Did I know J.K. Rowling? If I was a real author how come they'd seen me chain my bike up in the shed? But they wanted me to sign the books anyway. So I did, trying to give an abstract quality to my scrawl, so it could easily have been that of J.K. Rowling, or Jacqueline Wilson, or Andy Stanton.

And then today at an equally excellent (but rather less deprived) school in Essex, the delightful deputy head showed me into the office where, 'The ladies are dying to meet you!'

I knew what was coming, and my heart sank.

They'd seen my 'handsome' publicity photo.

Over the years I'd got used to the disappointment on the faces of those who thought I was going to look like *that* in reality. But this time it was different. I got rank hilarity. They laughed. Guffawed, even. I joined in the fun with some Quasimodo-style capering and bell-ringing. I then had to go and talk to two hundred kids in the school hall. Unsurprisingly, when I put my foot down on the accelerator, there was nothing there. Performing like that needs an inflated ego, not one punctured by reality. You need to believe in the myth of yourself. Need to be both the God and the High Priestess, offering sacrifices at your altar, naked under her long robe, her hungry hands roaming all over her lovely body, cupping each full... What? Sorry. Drifted off.

Anyway, I tried, I really tried, but I felt like a bluebottle battering itself against the window, unable either to understand its captivity, or cease its futile buzzing.

On the way home, glowering skies and dead fields, and then the steel fury and futility of the Olympic park, and then the obscene machismo of the City. Tomorrow should be better: I'm not doing anything or going anywhere.

We've Kissed and Made Up

November 1. Well, today has begun with a piece of startling good fortune. I cycled in to the British Library for my first full day of actual writing in weeks, only to discover that I'd forgotten my library card, without which the brutal security personnel forbid entrance, and if you try to sneak past them they beat you up with truncheons, grind your spectacles under their hobnailed boots, steal your dinner money, etc. etc. So I had the option of cycling home, my morning entirely wasted, or stumping up the £5 for a day pass. These are the sorts of problems that I find most irksome. Dealing with them requires no moral or actual courage. No praise accrues to those who overcome such minor inconveniences. There's no heroism or renunciation, or transfiguration. No Richard Strauss tone poem to celebrate your victory over the monsters inside and out. They just fuck up your day.

But then, as I decided to pay for the day pass, the sweet-natured, round-faced person on the desk informed me that the forgotten pass had run out yesterday, so I was entitled to a *free* renewal! I could have kissed him on his plump, bureaucratic lips. So, I'd lost a penny and found a pound. Except I hadn't actually lost the penny, and it wasn't a pound, but five of them.

Even the photo was less awful than usual – my previous three passes have all made me look like a debauched post office worker, caught in the midst of an act of self-pollution at his counter. The new one made me look like a former bank robber who has decided it's safer to make money through internet fraud. Which is an advance.

Anyway, me and the world have kissed and made up. For now.

The Swedish Edition

November 2. My publisher has sent me a Swedish version of one of my books. Foreign editions always cheer me up, and induce general high spirits and a feeling (however fleeting) of wellbeing and self-satisfaction. Perhaps it's the slight distancing or pleasurably alienating effect, akin to the adolescent technique of lying on your arm to numb it prior to masturbating, so it feels like someone else is doing it.

So, I was performing, for my own amusement, a comedy version of scenes from the book, in my best Scandawegian accent, when I heard a snorting sound from the hallway. I went to investigate, and saw that our front door was wide open. Outside there were two decorators painting the communal stairway and varnishing the doors (which was why Mrs McG had left it open, without warning me). They tried to sober up, but the sight of me was too much, and they were soon gripped again by painful guffaws.

Being a man of the people, I didn't want to appear snooty or unapproachable, so I threw myself into explanation about the Swedish edition. I showed them the book. They'd stopped laughing by now. I think they understood. I went back to the kitchen and considered carrying on with the Swedish performance, to show that I wasn't intimidated. But the moment had passed. So I made some toast.

The Lavatory Habits of Famous Authors

November 3. Trying to sort out the mess in my study I found the notes I'd made on an old acoustic typewriter for an interview with Anthony Burgess, in 1989. It was to be my second piece of paid journalism, for a shoddy and pointless magazine called *Writers' Monthly*. I'd shamefully given Burgess – whom I've always revered – the impression that I was working for a more prestigious journal – the *New Statesman*, I think. Anyway, I turned up at his suite at a once grand, now somewhat faded hotel in Mayfair – heavy doors, but worn carpets, that sort of thing. His wife, Liana, met me at the door, and fluttered gracefully before retiring. I was a few minutes early. I waited for Burgess, who appeared shortly, arranging his dress. He smiled and shook my hand, and we both sat down.

Then his face went rapidly through a range of emotions, from confusion to what looked like rage. I wondered what I'd done. Had he seen through my ruse about working for the *Statesman*? Then he thrust his veiny and liver-spotted hand down inside his baggy tweed trousers. Again, I had no idea what was about to happen. After a moment he withdrew his hand. It was holding a pair of reading glasses.

There was a beat or two of silence, and then Burgess moved his head towards the door from which he'd entered.

'Lavatory,' he said, enunciating each syllable with phlegmy precision.

I imagined the scene: he'd been reading in there… the bell… a rapid, perhaps premature completion… the spectacles deposited in the helpful well formed by his trousers and undergarments, and then forgotten as he hurriedly pulled them up.

From that point on the interview went like a dream – Burgess was incredibly entertaining, but also interested in me and my 'career' (I was only twenty-four, and didn't have one). We drank whisky, although it was 10 a.m. And then at the end I realized that in all the excitement of the discovered spectacles, I'd forgotten to turn on my tape recorder. I didn't have the courage to tell him. So I went home and tried to recreate the interview. The shitty magazine didn't take the piece, and all that remains of it are those typed notes on yellowing paper I'd stolen from my day job at HM Customs & Excise. My career as a literary journalist died, and it was six years before anyone paid me for anything of a literary nature again – a poem – £6 from the *London Magazine*, then edited by the great Alan Ross.

Nipples

November 4. A couple of days ago I was pottering about in the kitchen when Mrs McG said, 'You can't wear that.' She pointed at my nipple. I looked down, startled. There was a horizontal tear in my pyjama top, roughly in the nipple area.

'It's only a flesh wound,' I said. 'Nothing fatal.'

'No, I'm sorry, it has to go.'

'But I only wear it in bed. It's not like I'm going out, er, dancing in it or anything.'

She smirked at the idea of me dancing.

'I don't want to have to look at it.'

'But it could be useful,' I said, playing for time.

'How?'

'You could, er, tweak me. On the nipple.'

I performed a tweaking gesture. Not on my own nipple, which would be obscene, but just vaguely, in the air, as if forming a shadow puppet.

'Why would I do that?'

'It might be fun.'

'I mean, why would I tweak your nipple through a hole in your pyjamas, rather than in the general course of things?'

I didn't really have an answer to that. I did, in fact, think it would be more amusing to be tweaked through a hole in your pyjamas than in most other circumstances. But that's not the sort of thing you can confess to. I made another tweaking gesture, more feeble than the first, and she knew she had her victory. But I hoped that she might forget about it.

Then last night, when I went to my, er, pyjama place, I found the bottoms but not the top. I knew what had happened. And this morning when I was putting the bins out, on impulse I opened the sack. I had to dig down a bit, but I found it there. I looked at the top for a while, maybe three or four minutes, thinking about taking it out, shaking off the coffee grounds and eggshells. But I didn't.

Bury My Heart

November 6. It suddenly struck me this afternoon that no child would ever again play Cowboys and Indians. As a small boy I had a big shoebox full of cowboys and Indians, some on foot, some mounted, and would enact major battles between them. Often my US Cavalry, aided by civilian cowboys, would launch retaliatory raids against a tepee village full of painted braves. No women and children were slaughtered, of course. This was before *Bury My Heart at Wounded Knee*. And I know it's still possible to buy toys like those, indeed my own boy once had a full Playmobil set of cowboys and Indians, though I'm not sure how much play they got before they were sent to the desolate reservation of the cousins.

I'm thinking more about the live-action version. It's just impossible to imagine kids today stalking through the undergrowth, preparing an ambush against the Cavalry. The laughable idea of a child from the iPad generation pretending to fire a bow and arrow, or miming a scalping.

And what this must mean is that somewhere out there is the last little boy (or girl, I suppose) who ever played or ever will play Cowboys and Indians. And of course they wouldn't know. They'll just continue living their life, having their own children, growing old, dying. Perhaps at the end they'll drift in an opiate dream back through the years, and ride the range again, and sleep by the fire on the open prairie, with the coyotes howling. Or is that the Indians…?

I wonder if it's me?

Manly Glue

November 7. Like most (I guess) artists and writers there are times when I feel like a spent force, that there's literally nothing left in the bag, that the drink, the ketamine, the incipient mad cow disease have taken their toll. And then, suddenly, it comes back – just one idea, perhaps, but enough to make you think that you've still got it, that the Nobel is still within reach. And so, this morning, I realized that rather than prying open my wardrobe door with my cracked and broken nails, I could just glue the handle back on. After two years…

And for the gluing on of the handle I used my special *manly* glue. Ordinary, *non-manly* glue is merely squeezed from a tube and daubed onto the items that need attaching. But *manly* glue begins life as two different pastes that must be mixed together with a matchstick before they acquire *manly*, adhesive qualities. Even better, it comes in a double-barrelled apparatus, like a cyberpunk syringe. The whole performance has made me feel at least seventeen per cent more masculine.

Strike a Chord

November 9. Going into town to meet a friend for lunch wearing a cord jacket and cord trousers in vaguely similar, but different, hues. The jacket is a sort of browny-green, like fresh cowshit, whereas the trousers are more greeny-brown like, well, I suppose that's one of the possibilities for cowshit, too. I know this is wrong, but it's too late now to do anything about it, even if I could, which I can't.

The friend is an aspiring writer who, I think, has one eye on my potential to help her career, while the other (eye) moves with chameleon ocular independence, and rank erotic covetousness, over my lovely body. I'm looking forward to striking heroic, self-sacrificing poses as I gently reject her, while leaving a tiny crack of light, just in case I'm in need of an ego boost sometime in the future.

She's very attractive, but I've told Mrs McG that she has a weight problem, and an unsightly skin condition.

'She gets through drums of, ah, emollients,' I said, not sure if that was the right word. 'It's psoriasis,' I added, authoritatively, like a highly-paid consultant skin man, 'with some, ah, nodular formations.'

Mrs McG wasn't really listening, which was a good thing.

'We're at the amelioration stage. Palliative, that is to say. All we can hope is to make the patient more comfortable.'

But as usual the final syllables flopped dead into the empty air.

Anticipation Is Always the Best Part

She cancelled.

The Armenian Despot

November 10. You trundle down in the old apartment lift, staring at yourself in the mirror, and running through a few of your old facial expressions, partly to relieve and expel some of the night's anxieties, partly just to get the faces out of the way before you have to confront the world. So out, in quick succession, come: the Armenian Despot Contemplating the Annihilation of His Foes; Me, I'm Afraid of Virginia Woolf; the Elderly Welshman Trying on His First Sports Bra; Confucius on the Lavatory; the Masturbating Macaque, etc. etc. And just as you're mid-transition back to your normal face (Depressed Author, Surveying the Wreck of His Hopes) the lift opens and the attractive downstairs neighbour begins to get in, then stops, reverses, and says, 'I'll take the stairs.' That'd be awful, if it happened, wouldn't it?

The Elephant with White Ears

November 11. For the writer, whose days are spent in solitary contemplation of his failures, publishers' parties have a very special place. Their professional value – the networking with editors and publicists, the sucking-up to senior management, the establishment of your place in the Byzantine hierarchies of publishing (what's below a eunuch, but above a galley slave?) – is less important than the opportunity they present to restock the wells of despair and humiliation.

The Random House party has long been a special one for me. It was my first (at least the first I attended in my own right, rather than as a plus one) and the only one I've ever really loved. I've got genuine friends among both the staff and the writers, and the booze flows, and there's always an after-party that, traditionally, ends with me as the last person in an empty pub, weeping into a pint glass half filled with the dregs of other glasses. The day after, my publicists will email me a list of the people I have to apologize to, along with a dry-cleaning bill and, not uncommonly, a comment too cryptic for me to decipher – 'The elephant with white ears – it's a no-no'; 'she isn't a lesbian'; 'you realize he was in the SAS and could have cracked your skull like a walnut?' and so on.

Anyway, it's party season again, so I tried on my blue velvet suit, sixteen years old now, and veteran of almost every publishing party I've ever attended, to make sure the previous season's letting-out of the trousers was still adequate.

And in the pockets I recovered enough detritus to reconstruct the whole of last year's party. A cloakroom ticket; napkins scrawled with barely legible messages ('*Something something* by ten thirty or I'll *something* kill you'); the small bicycle light I'd thought lost forever; a tightly folded A4 sheet, revealing a photocopy of someone's buttocks – Philip Pullman? Michael Morpurgo? I'll probably never know; broken cocktail sticks.

And then, triumphantly, what I at first take to be the mummified finger of a child but which, on closer inspection, turns out to be a cocktail sausage, blackened, shrunken, desiccated. But still surprisingly tasty. We're ready to rock.

It'll Mask the Taste

November 12. Baked some cookies to make up for the fact I gave the kids a dully utilitarian dinner. I've never made biscuits before (I'm a perfectly adequate cook, but I don't really bake, apart from bread), but all seemed well – they looked like nice big flat cookies. Then came the eating stage.

'Dad, they taste funny…'

'What do you mean, funny? They can't be funny. It's your imagination.'

Then I tasted of the cookie, and found it to be funny. Too much bicarb – soapy aftertaste.

Really quite depressed about this. I feel that I've let everyone down, including the ingredients. All that butter and sugar… for nothing, nothing. The kids were actually quite supportive about it. My son patted me on the back.

'I'll try it with Nutella later,' he said. 'It'll mask the taste.'

But it's no good. We all know that I made some soapy cookies, and now everything is lost.

Set Dressing

November 14. As if things weren't already bad enough, I've just found out that one of my early adult crime books – *Mortal Coil* – was used as 'set dressing' on the *Alien* prequel *Prometheus* – without doubt the worst film I've seen in the past five years. I was proud of the book at the time... seems a sad fate to become decor for a shit SF movie.

Stopping by Woods

November 15. Walking this morning with Monty through the woods near Golders Hill Park, while Mrs McG jogged ahead. Monty loves her much more than he loves me, and wanted to stay with her, but his tiny legs just weren't up to the job. He ran along with her for a while, but then gave up, and waited, panting, bewildered, depressed, for me to trudge up. In general he likes us to stay together. It's probably a pack thing. Unless he senses some undercurrent...

This part of Hampstead Heath is one of the gay pick-up areas. Occasionally, a head pops out of a bush, and gives me a quick peruse. If they see Monty first, the hopeful face perks up. He's a very gay dog. But then he'll see me, stumping along behind him in my cords, and his face falls. They can always tell that I'm not up for fun.

But that wasn't my point. The woods are varied and interesting, with oak and birch and other scrubby trees, alder, blackthorn, lime, elder. Though, to be frank, most tree names are just floating signifiers to me, unconnected to any actual thing in the world. A few I remember from childhood – the helicopter tree (sycamore); the baby mouse tree (pussy willow). The rest are just tree trees.

Anyway, I was walking through the trees, with only the mounds of used condoms, soiled baby wipes and rubber gloves to connect me to the modern world, when I came across a patch of more open woodland. These were immensely tall, grey-trunked beech, and the ground beneath them was curiously clear, other than for the spongy brown duvet of ancient beech mast, delightful to the foot. I remembered reading somewhere that beech trees secrete toxins that inhibit the growth of other vegetation near to them, which both accounts for the openness and gives it a faintly sinister turn.

But the fact remained that this uncluttered spot was charming, even on a dull November day. And then I wondered if there might be something about the relative proportions of the trees, and the spaces between them, that accounted for the aesthetic pleasure to be found in their contemplation. I did a rough calculation. All the beech trees were approximately the same height, and they were equally spaced with a precision just a little less than geometric. But that wasn't it. I mean it wasn't simply that they were regularly spaced. And then I realized that the spaces between the trees were about half the height of the trees. Could there be a universal principle at play here – that the human eye, and, perhaps, the wondrous mind of Nature itself, might derive satisfaction from arranging objects half as far apart as they are tall? Was this also, perhaps, the ideal distance for humans to be apart? – coincidentally the distance that would separate you if you held hands with your arms comfortably extended.

I eventually found Mrs McG, and excitedly told her about my discovery. I planned to call it the McGowan Organic Ratio, or maybe just McGowan's Law. But she was unimpressed and immediately found flaws with the hypothesis.

Back home I tried to organize my desk in accordance with the McGowan Organic Ratio. Unfortunately, I didn't have enough things the same size to properly put it into operation. Except for beer cans.

Mrs McG came in halfway through the experiment.

'What are you doing?'

'I'm just, er, arranging things.'

I think she knew I was testing my hypothesis, but she didn't say anything about it. Later on she came back and put the empties in the recycling.

Any Trousers Shortened

November 18. For reasons I don't want to go into, I was loitering on West End Lane with Monty. For want of anything better, I found myself looking into a dry-cleaner's window. There was a big sign, saying, ANY TROUSERS SHORTENED, £7.50.

The longer I stared at it, the stranger it seemed. It was that 'ANY'. Were there other dry cleaners who would refuse to shorten *some* trousers? If so, what sort of trousers? Loon pants? Jake the Peg's (with that extra leg)? Or perhaps a pair made for a performing octopus…

And then I imagined pushing things to the limit. You know those enormous trousers made for circus stilt walkers, with legs thirty feet long? Asking to have them taken up to fit a normal leg. Let's see their smug 'ANY TROUSERS' faces then! But then I realized that these were ungenerous thoughts, and I moved on.

Next, I paused in front of one of the charity shops (the street goes shit café–charity shop–shit café–charity shop all the way down). There was a pair of red braces in the window. Two things occurred to me as I was looking at them. The first was that it was about time that I acquired some braces, as the solution to the trousers-falling-down issue. Not, I hasten to add, in the spirit of 1980s Wall Street excess, but more like a 1950s lower middle class father-in-law, doing that thing where you hook your thumbs in the braces and simultaneously extend the arms and bend at the knees.

The second was that if you spend any time gawping at a charity shop window, especially if you're fairly obviously wearing your pyjamas underneath your clothes, the attractive but snooty American lady from the flat downstairs will walk past, and you'll be compelled to make one of those pointless hand gestures that don't mean anything beyond 'I have no explanation for this'.

I Know Him Better Than He Knows Hisself

November 19. On my way to Egham this morning I sat opposite a woman who was speaking at terrific volume into her mobile phone, despite the fact that we were in the quiet carriage. It was impossible not to listen. I suppose I should have blocked it out somehow, or moved away, or told her to keep it down, but I have to admit that the content was rather compelling.

The woman had a certain faded grandeur – still quite attractive and I'd guess she was something of a stunner ten years ago. She was wearing a fur coat, and heavy gold jewellery that tinkled – no, more clanged – as she moved.

Her story, despite the screeching tone, had a poignancy.

'But you don't understand him the way I do. He told me he loved me. I'd have him back in a second. The thing about Shaun is that he changes his mind all the time. He'll say one thing, then twenty minutes later he'll say something else.'

I imagined Shaun leaving twenty minutes of silence in between each utterance, but I don't suppose that's what she meant.

Tears kept welling up in her eyes, but somehow they never fell, as if she were reabsorbing them.

I had some marking to do, so I reached into my bag. When I brought the papers out, a vegetarian sausage roll I'd brought with me for my lunch, propelled by the latent energy of its compressed plastic packaging, went skittering across the table, coming to rest, quite naked, against the lady's handbag.

She looked down at the sausage roll, still speaking – 'I've known him fifteen years. I know him better than he knows hisself.' Her expression changed slowly from anguish to puzzlement. You could see her trying to work out what this could mean. Was it a message? A gift? She looked at me for the first time – a literal up and down. Not bad, ten years ago, she might have thought.

And then she half poked, half flicked the sausage roll with a long, heavily knuckled finger (she was wearing glossy brown nail varnish, which seems to be a thing at the moment), sending it sliding back across the table to me.

By then it was Egham, and time to get off.

'Don't forget your sausage roll,' she said in a flirty way. And then, into the phone, 'No, not you, him, a man on the train.'

I've just eaten it, cold and dense as osmium.

It's Quite Possible He Died

November 20. Finally applied for a replacement provisional driving licence, some fifteen years after losing the old one. I suppose that this means that I'll have to actually learn how to drive.

My inability to drive was for a long time the biggest source of conflict between me and Mrs McG. It wasn't so much having to stay sober at parties that annoyed her – unlike me she doesn't need to be three quarters drunk before she can have a normal conversation. It was more the long drives on holiday, or to see family.

I don't know why I've never learned. Or, rather, the reasons are so many that it would be tedious to list them. But one might begin with idleness, a fear of mowing down pensioners on zebra crossings, a reluctance to enter the adult world, the rival pleasures of cycling and the desire to get three quarters drunk at parties so I can have a normal conversation.

And my two feeble attempts to learn ended in fiasco. The first was with someone called Tony, whom I flagged down as he drove by in his driving instructor car around West Hampstead. He was a cool guy, and I quite enjoyed our first lesson. He kept asking me to pull over, while he popped out to chat with friends. After the third stop, I realized that he was a drug dealer, and so I reluctantly ended our relationship. My second and final instructor, Stevo, had been recommended by a friend of Mrs McG. Stevo had taught the friend to drive a decade earlier. He turned up in a 1980s Yugo 45, a design based on an early 1970s Fiat 127. (I can't drive but, being a boy, I know something about cars; and being me, I have an interest in shit things, and failures of all kinds.) The instructor almost entirely filled the interior. He must have weighed twenty-seven stone. His right thigh and buttock overflowed his seat, and I had to feel around under the marshmallowy flesh to find the handbrake. I could have been wrong, but I thought he enjoyed this, though it might have been in the way a buffalo likes to have his ears and nostrils cleaned by an oxpecker, rather than a sex thing.

When we ground into motion, Stevo directed me towards the northern suburbs. I'd never managed more than fifteen miles per hour on my trip with Tony, but soon I was on a dual carriageway, and had hit fifty.

I looked over at Stevo.

He seemed to be fast asleep.

'Er, *hello*,' I said, a little panicked.

He jerked awake. 'Just resting my eyes,' he said. 'Can you pull in here…'

It was a drive-in McDonald's. He extruded himself from the Yugo, ordered two Big Macs, and talked me through my errors, before we moved on to his failed marriage and successful diabetes.

I can't remember who pulled the plug before Lesson 2. It's quite possible he died.

Anyway, that was all years ago, and I really need to do something to help restore my depleted testosterone reserves. It's learn to drive or get into cage fighting.

It Was Biblical

November 22. I spent most of today trying to unblock our kitchen sink. I usually quite like unblocking things. There's a problem in the world; you apply yourself to fixing it; the problem goes away, leaving you satisfied and feeling a little more manly. The trouble was that my unblocking activities (two different unblocking solutions, one long length of wire, repeated plunging) initially proved utterly futile, leading to a mental condition generally described as 'rage'.

Two things exacerbated this condition. The first was the UTTER DROSS put out by Radio 4 today – the most embarrassingly humourless comedies; turgid, badly written, hopelessly acted dramas; that appalling *Woman's Hour* interview with Cher (part of their Worst of the Year compilation); musical sketches that make you wish the human race had never discovered music, or started trying to be funny. And the second thing (those others were merely subsections of the first thing) was that Mrs McG was in bed all day with a 'cold'. And of course she's entitled to do that, but it means I had nobody to complain to about the shit radio and the blocked sink.

So, having failed, I tried the ultimate solution (literally) – a special super-concentrated hydrochloric acid that only professional plumbers and those licensed to engage in chemical warfare are supposed to use. I was meant to dress in a full Noddy suit, but I just held my breath ('CAN DESTROY LUNG TISSUE IF INHALED').

The result was far worse than the earlier failures. The blockage was unmoved, and a belch of acid reflux dyed the sink black. This added an extra element of desolation and danger to the affair. Having her shiny sink dyed black is one of those things likely to induce the Wrath of Mrs McG.

But I couldn't let the sink beat me. In the end it was epic, it was biblical. I tracked down a bloke from the estate who knows a bit about plumbing. He came round and shook his head. There was nothing to be done. We were going to have to move out. Possibly leave the country. West Hampstead was going to be like the area around Chernobyl. The wolves would come back. There would be beavers as big as bears. I suggested having a final go with the plunger. Three of us (Mrs McG rose briefly from her sickbed to help) blocked up the various orifices, and plunging commenced. There was movement. A rumble from the innards. And we were free! Another application of the lethal acid helped things further. I now have a sink that works. The acid stains will remain as a permanent reminder of the bad times. But I don't care. This year may still suck, but with the power of a leech rather than Nosferatu.

You Can't Turn Down Free Rubber Gloves, Can You?

November 23. After a few days of vaguely heart-attack type pains, I make it to the Doctors, and immediately start to feel better. So I engage the attractive middle-aged receptionist in some flirtatious banter. She has a delightful, tittering laugh.

And then the doctor is gratifyingly energized by my symptoms, which I under- rather than overplay.

'Right, we'll get a full set of bloods, plus an ultrasound, and the gastroenterologist will have to have a look down there.'

Of course this all delights me further. But then comes the killer blow. 'And we'll need a stool sample.' That deflates me somewhat. 'You can pick up the stool pots at the reception.'

A few minutes later I'm back with the attractive receptionist.

'I need some, er, the doctor said to collect some, ah, stool thingies.'

She seems more amused than repelled by this, and efficiently goes about her business. 'There's a spoon in the pack. You can use that. You don't have to, you know, do it in the pot.' She taps the lid of the pot with a long, densely lacquered nail.

I feel the need to recover some sense of agency here. 'Yes, I know,' I say, 'I've, er, had experience.'

She looks quizzical. I don't want her to think I'm the kind of person who regularly needs his stool samples tested.

'I have, er, children,' I say, rather gnomically. And then go on, 'And…' I mean to say 'a dog', but temporarily can't remember the word. 'A Monty.'

'A Monty?' She's going to think Monty is my elderly boyfriend. Probably a theatrical type, a big name at the Old Vic in the 1960s.

'Yes, he's not a person. He's a…' Still the word 'dog' escapes me. I grope for an alternative. 'Animal,' I say, finally, rather too loudly. It's almost a shout. Then I repeat 'Animal' in a normal voice.

'Animal?'

Obviously, the flirting days are over for us. She's wondering what kind of animal. Or I would be, if I were her. Octopus? Gibbon? Sloth? Could be anything.

'He's just a dog,' I say, remembering the word at last. I try to get some resignation into it, as if she'd tried to insist that I kept a wolverine in the back bedroom. 'Just a dog.'

'Do you want gloves?' she says, before I go. She holds out some blue rubber gloves. I take them without looking in her eyes. You can't turn down free rubber gloves, can you?

Stoning the Dragon

November 24. Talking to my students today about stories from the Bible that could be (or have been) updated/retold, I asked for some ideas.

'Cain and Abel,' suggests one, vaguely.

Another looks at her, puzzled. 'Which one's that?'

'Er, not sure. I think it's the one where he throws a stone at a dragon.'

Now I'm intrigued.

Dragon?

In the Bible?

Behemoth…? Leviathan…?

No, wait, there is a dragon in Revelations, isn't there?

'Oh, no, not dragon,' continues the student. 'Giant.'

Slowly it dawns on me.

'You mean David and Goliath?' I suggest.

'Yeah, them.'

I was teaching over my lunch hour, and so had a blood-sugar crash on my way back to the station at Egham, requiring the taking on of some heavy fuel. A fish and chip shop had a sign saying CHEESY CHIPS. Now, if you go to a posh burger place, this means chips drenched in a thick, orange cheesy sauce, the texture of warm snot.

And that was exactly what I wanted.

A few seconds after ordering, a sealed polystyrene box was handed back to me. I opened it as I walked away down the street. What it contained was chips with some grated cheese on them. Just sprinkled over the top.

The jolt was almost physical. I was angry. I was upset. But I couldn't go and complain, because, after all, they could plausibly argue that what they meant by cheesy chips was chips with some grated cheese sprinkled on them. I wouldn't have a legal leg to stand on.

So I ate. Mainly I brushed the cheese off and consumed the chips in their natural state. But sometimes I ate a chip with some cheese adhering to it. I've had worse things in my mouth. You hardly noticed the cheese. Still, though, it was a dispiriting journey back to West Hampstead.

Sober Thoughts

November 25. After a week (which is to say three days) being dry, I've concluded that it's much better to be slightly drunk than sober, but also a little better to be sober than totally arse-holed. So it makes me wonder why evolution didn't make us slightly drunk all the time. You'd get all the advantages – a heightened mood, increased conviviality, greater creativity, optimism, etc. – without the disadvantages of being either really drunk or stone cold sober. And no one would ever think of getting hammered if you were always slightly pissed, for free. Except, now I think about it, perhaps evolution has made us slightly drunk, just that we don't realize it, because it's our base state, and that below this is a level of supernatural sobriety. And you do sometimes see people like that, don't you? I think I might need to go and work this out properly with equations and stuff.

Toothpaste Caps and Babies' Heads

November 26. Well, that's rather thrown me. For reasons I can't go into, because of the emotional distress it would cause, I wanted to move the cap from one of those tiny tubes of toothpaste you sometimes get, on to a full-sized tube. I had a theory that this would be possible, as it would be more efficient to have one cap size for the different sized tubes, rather than having to retool a whole production line... Anyway, guess what? The cap for the smaller tube was *too big* for the bigger tube. It was as if you had a theory (which I do, sort of) that babies had exactly the same sized heads as adults, but then when you measured them, you found the babies' heads were *bigger*.

The aesthetic and ontological consequences of all this are still to be discerned. But I'm unsettled, truly I am.

But, just to clarify, I don't believe that babies' heads are bigger than adult human heads. I just don't have sufficient data on the subject to make an authoritative ruling.

What Does Monty Think About the Lift?

November 27. Two or three times a day I get in the lift with Monty. A door opens, he gets in. The door closes. Then it opens again, and we are in a new place. Do you think he has any idea what's going on? I don't mean, does he understand the precise mechanics of the lift – who does? – just the idea that he's in a box that moves vertically through space.

It reminds me for some reason of Arthur C. Clarke's Third Law – Any sufficiently advanced technology is indistinguishable from magic.

I Desire Windy Nights

November 28. Just now I was composing an email, and thought I'd written (as part of a sentence): 'despite endless rewrites...' When I looked up from the keyboard to the screen I saw that what I'd actually typed was: 'I desire windy nights'.

I'm a hunt and peck typist, so occasionally odd things appear on the screen, but still...

And I wonder, has my subconscious spoken, and do I truly desire windy nights? Trees tossed in a gale, slates torn from the roof, a heavy-haunched lass from Huddersfield, flapping the duvet...

The Bonjela Junkie

November 29. There's a special type of vanity that concerns itself with working out just how vain you are. My own vanity takes that particularly negative, English form of generally hating everything about my appearance, with particular hot-spots of loathing centred around my hair, my unnaturally short legs (and the compensatory lengthened torso, without which I wouldn't be able to reach the ground), my manky big toenail and my massive, Jamie Oliver-style fat tongue.

Of these by far the most inconvenient is my fat tongue. Its bulbous proportions make it difficult for me to pronounce certain words, e.g. Saskatchewan and syzygy. And it's distressingly prone to being bitten (by me, usually). Which is exactly what I did last night on an epic scale, first filling my mouth with blood, and then rendering me agonizingly mute. (I wonder if animals bite their tongues, dolphins and lemurs and so on, or if it's a peculiarly human problem?) I slice into mine every couple of months, always in the same place, near the back, where now my poor tongue is scarred and knotted – thereby, of course, increasing the likelihood that I'll bite it again. If the trend continues, my hugely engorged and goitrous tongue will one day make it impossible for me to close my mouth, and it'll look like I'm halfway through eating the Elephant Man, forever.

Anyway, this latest tongue mishap has come at a most inconvenient time, as I have to be professionally loquacious later on this evening.

The gig is an odd one. A group of children's writers decided to hold an auction for the benefit of the tsunami-hit Philippines. Arlo and I thought that rather than donate a signed book, or a stained undergarment, we'd offer up a night out on the razzle with the two of us. Half a dozen women bid for the privilege, lured, perhaps, by the out-of-date photos... And it all might well have been fun, if it weren't for my forced muteness. I can't even apply Bonjela, lest it spark the old addiction back to life – and I don't want to go through the terrible Bonjela withdrawal symptoms again (neuralgia, wind, etc.).

Just hoping a day of tonguerest might do the trick. We'll see.

A Charitable Twitch in Roderick's Perineum

November 30. My tongue was OK, once the numbing effect of the alcohol kicked in, and the evening was a riot. Five of the 'winners' were aspiring authors, and Arlo and I handed out wisdom like drunken Solomons ('Kill your darlings'; 'Never begin a book with the sentence: *A twitch in Roderick's perineum could mean only one thing: it was time to change the awkward-to-reach light bulb in the oven.*' Etc. etc.). The sixth was an old friend, a well-known writer of lesbian mermaid stories. She's one of my favourite people in the world to flirt with, as it's a bit kinky (she's a lesbian!) but also quite safe (she's a lesbian!).

The only slight downside was that I think Arlo only agreed to take part as he thought there was a chance of some action, which might assuage the loneliness in his heart. But there wasn't, although he shared a cigarette on the step of an O2 phone shop with someone who'd come down from Hull. At least we raised a few hundred for a good cause. Whatever it was.

WINTER

The Helmet

December 1. Well, that was awkward. Delivery man at the door. I buzzed him in. The cranky old lift had to go down and up, so I thought I'd use the couple of minutes it would take to arrive to try on my new cricket helmet, which was on the bench by the door. But it got sort of jammed, with my glasses stuck up inside it. So I had to sign for the parcel wearing the helmet. Must have looked peculiar. I thought about trying to explain it, but realized that could only make matters worse.

The delivery was of a Japanese edition of one of my books. I was still wearing the helmet, so I took the opportunity to pick up my cricket bat and practise some Kendo swipes, emitting a guttural and vaguely oriental 'Yah!' and stamping my foot, as you're supposed to do, with each killing vertical slash.

There was a knock and a throat clearing from the door, which I'd left ajar. Turned out there was a second parcel.

'Just a bit of the old Jenga. I mean Ken Dodd. No, Kendo, Kendo,' I said.

Probably time to have an early lunch.

Attack-Dog Hair

December 2. Popped out for a haircut. Alas, the eccentric Egyptian ('You, me, we are falcons; together we fly!') was absent, as was the entertainingly grumpy French lady (Me:

'Please don't take any off the top.' Her: 'Why? You look stupid.'). So my hair was cut by a dour Tunisian, who didn't engage much in conversation, except to say that he planned to set up a business training 'attack dogs'. And he gave me a dour, attack-dog sort of haircut. I've been trying to read the troubled recent history of his country in the haircut – the years of drab, inefficient, randomly brutal dictatorship; the hope of the revolution; the slow death of those hopes. And perhaps it is all there, in my short back and sides.

A Kindred Spirit

December 3. On my way back from some slightly confusing book events in Hounslow (confusing for everyone – it was the awards ceremony for the Hounslow Children's Book of the Year, or something like that, but I didn't have a book in the running, and was there as a sort of generic author, and made a generic author speech, except it had, I suppose, more excrement references in it than most author speeches), I walked around Waitrose for a while, in a listless sort of way, not sure what I wanted. I picked up various things, studying them for differing amounts of time, not obviously related to their intrinsic interest or my current needs. Mustard. Cornflour. Saffron. Dog food. There was a longer queue at the automated tills than for the humans, so I went the latter route.

I vaguely put my basket – which I'd thought was quite full – in front of the check-out person. He didn't look like the usual Waitrose assistant – who around here tend to be middle-aged women, or relatively posh kids. This was a salt-of-the-earth working man, with the look of someone who learned about socialism at night school. His face was lined in a way that suggested both good humour and moral seriousness. If I were being critical I'd say his hair – thick and black – looked a decade younger than the rest of him. He scanned the items in my basket, as I daydreamed.

It – the scanning process, I mean – seemed to be over too quickly. When I looked down, I saw that I appeared to have only bought a couple of items – a pizza (spicy Calabrian) and some scones (reduced).

'Is that it? I thought I'd got more, er, items...' I said, straining to see round his till, in case anything had got lodged back there.

The man smiled ruefully. 'It's the ozone, I reckon,' he said. 'Messes you up.'

I nodded, unsure where he was going with this.

'Only this morning,' he continued, 'I got in the lift, and I honestly didn't know if I'd just come in, or was just going out. I stood there for ten minutes, thinking it through.'

I smiled more openly, now. Yes, we were kindred spirits. I paid using contactless, even though it only came to four quid.

'You take care, sir,' he said.

I replied in similar style, and would have shaken his hand, if I'd had one free.

Chilli Soap

December 4. Was on a train yesterday, when I felt a hay-fever nose-run coming on, so I got my hanky out to have a good blow (I'm an impressive nose-blower – the guitar-tuner on my phone tells me that I produce either an E flat, as in Beethoven's 'Eroica', or a C minor, as in the Symphony No. 5. At times I also emit something very close to the plangency and yearning of Wagner's *Tristan* chord...). Anyway, I was startled to sense something odd in the hanky. It was like the glaucous carapace of some huge beetle. No, not one, several of them. I imagined a foul nest of some kind, full of moist corruption.

At that point I made a noise somewhere in between a screech and a squeal, which I tried to conceal behind a cough. Then the contents of the hanky spilt out on my lap. It took a few moments to comprehend what was there. And then the confused images resolved themselves, and I saw that it was four or five thumb-sized pieces of soap.

A few baffled moments of contemplation followed, until I remembered how I'd come by them. I was at my in-laws' house some weeks before. I went to the bathroom and, while washing my hands, saw the pieces of soap in the bin. It seemed a waste to discard them thus, when there were multiple washings to be had from them. So I wrapped them in my hanky, and then forgot about them.

But I was still now left with the dilemma of what to do next. I couldn't, I felt, just leave them on the crowded train. That seemed to have health and safety implications. But I didn't really want to put them back in my pocket. I was worried what any observer might think. A man making a violent cry, then staring at some pieces of soap, then putting them away again in his pocket, as if the oracles had spoken. I'd just eaten a packet of Kettle crisps, and I still had the bag. I decided that the only acceptable course of action was to put the soap shards in the bag. I'd completed this whole process without looking up, so I had no idea if the rest of the carriage were engrossed in this performance, or lost in their texts and phone-games. I stared at the floor, holding my crisp bag, until my stop. Now our soap dishes are loaded with sweet chilli-flavoured soap fragments.

The Blank Card

December 5. Just got a Christmas card from one of my publishers – utterly blank on the inside. Not so much as a scrawled x, or smudged thumbprint. Nice to feel such a cherished part of the team. Bit of a throwback to the good old days of rejection letters:

'Dear Sir/Madam,

Your novel/poetry collection/play (delete as required) is…' etc. etc.

I suppose the next stage is silence.

Mrs McG picked up the card in the hall on her way out. She looked at it from various angles, trying to read the signs. I mean read the sign that there were no signs. She's smart. She knows. She looked at me and shrugged.

'What time are you home?' I asked.

'There's a Faculty thing…'

'So, late, then…?'

'Ish. Hard to say.'

She opened the door, and, rather than going back to my study, I waited with her for the lift to come clanking up. Monty appeared, hopefully, his lead in his mouth.

'Sorry, Mont,' I said. 'Not now. Walky later.'

But he wasn't looking at me, but at her.

The Continuation of November by Other Means

December 6. In December 2004, I went to my first Random House Children's Books Christmas party. It was held in a lovely room full of people variously clever, famous, glamorous, odd, interesting, weird, wise. It seemed like a kind of heaven, even for someone like me, who knew no one, and who had but the most tenuous of toe-holds on the literary world.

And every year since, over the course of the eleven books I've published with them, and always wearing the same blue velvet jacket, I've returned. Each time I've known a few more people, and sucked ever more juice from the pomegranate. Perhaps, at times, a little too much juice, for the truth is I can be a bit of an arse (though a good-natured one, I trust), and have been prone, historically, to the occasional faux pas. But one had the sense that whichever way one turned, there'd be a friendly face, a Steve here, a Bali there, a Chris or two, a Paul, a Shannon, a Natalie, a Kelly, a Louise, a Matt. The bearded illustrators. Other illustrators in unnecessarily complex hats. One or two others I always talked to without ever quite realizing who they were (sure it was mutual).

But this time I haven't made the cut. I don't have a book out with them this year, which is the usual baseline requirement. Unless you happen to be a name. No one will have a quiet word, beforehand, to advise me to behave myself. No one at the end, when the pubs are finally throwing out, to say that I wasn't too bad this year.

It's made my December feel rather drab and melancholy, like the continuation of November by other means.

When the Last Word is Spoken...

December 7. I know instantly when I've used (written or spoken) a word for the first time because of the physical sensation, a shiver of pleasure that runs across my shoulders. Just wrote 'tantamount', and got that thrill. It's not at all an unusual word, just one I've never had the occasion to use before. And now my linguistic universe is a tiny bit bigger, and better.

This joy in the new reminds me of the very first time I tasted a curry, in Rusholme in Manchester, in my first week of university. Up until then my culinary universe had been Irish peasant food, requiring heavy sprinklings of salt and ground white pepper to get it up to the level of the merely bland. And now here was something extraordinary in my mouth, flavours that I hadn't even imagined might exist. It was as though my mouth had lost its virginity.

I suppose if one lived long enough, one might use up all the words. I wonder if you'd know, if some internal bell would tinkle. And then you'd lie down, and quietly die. They should set up a computer program, like the one that searches for the next prime number, and it would speak every word in every language, and when the final word had been uttered then... Well, I was going to say the world would end, but of course it wouldn't. That's just whimsy.

I Didn't. Wee in It

December 8. I found a tiny bottle of wine Mrs McG had bought to make some risotto. I tried to drown my sorrows in it.

It proved insufficiently deep.

But luckily I then found a normal sized bottle of wine, overlooked in the fridge. I filled up the little bottle from the normal sized bottle, so Mrs McG could still make her risotto.

But then I drank that up, too.

I thought about doing a wee in the tiny bottle, just to create the illusion that it was still full of wine, thinking: Mrs McG isn't going to be making the risotto any time soon, so I'll be able to replace the wee bottle with a wine bottle.

But the neck was quite small – the neck of the tiny bottle, I mean – and I feared my aim might be insufficiently accurate.

So I didn't. Wee in it.

I've hidden the tiny empty bottle behind the cornflakes.

I think deciding not to try to wee in the tiny bottle shows a new maturity.

Bakewell Sadness

December 10. Just wandered out of the British Library to get a revivifying mid-afternoon Bakewell tart, only to discover that Pret a Manger has replaced them with a 'seasonal' mince pie. From my point of view, this is like going up to someone expecting a nice kiss (light and quick, but with the ghost of a tongue) and receiving, in its place, a sharp seasonal kick in the nasticles. I had to get a 'Pret Bar' instead, which had dried fruit embedded in some sort of matter made from sweetened wood pulp and bat guano. And I thought the stroll would solve my plotting issue. But it hasn't. I'm losing today.

The Sinner Saved, and All That

December 11. Putting up Christmas cards on the mantelpiece. The usual robins. Some Breughel peasants trudging through the snow. The new craze for putting yourself and your children on the front, done, I suppose, to assuage the father's guilt about his affair, and the mother's shame at her drinking. The children looking stunned or bored or on the verge of tears. It strikes me that we get fewer cards than we used to. Too early for Death to play a role. The price of stamps, perhaps. Or the winnowing of friendships. The awfulness of e-cards. But then I see it, and melancholy reflections gave way to joy.

'When did this come?' I said, waving the party invite at Mrs McG.

'Oh, I don't know. Ages.'

'Why didn't you tell me?'

'I put it there. Where they go.'

'But you should have said.'

But I can't be annoyed. There is more rejoicing in heaven at the sinner saved, and all that.

Figure of Eight

December 12. The world is changing. Budgets squeezed, belts tightened. The venue was new, and cramped. Many of my old writer friends hadn't been invited. Still can't quite work out why I've been spared the axe. Perhaps I'm viewed as 'staff', someone who can be relied on to chat with the shy new writers, the rising stars. Or they just forgot to delete me from the database. There are fewer writers, but there have been cuts on the publishing side, too. Everyone seems nervous and edgy. I spend most of the evening talking to people I don't really know. The only excitement seems to be around some quasi-tramp who wrote a book about his cat. Or perhaps the cat wrote a book about him.

I mean to be charming to a tall illustrator, and she takes offence. I might have mentioned her enormous feet. I can't seem to get drunk, no matter how hard I chase it. I try my old stand-by – the figure of eight manoeuvre. Basically, you just walk in a purposeful way in a figure of eight pattern around the party. It makes it appear as if you're doing something, rather than just desperately trying to find someone you know, or someone pretty, or someone… But there's no one.

And then the room begins to empty. Surely they haven't…? Could they really be going on to the pub without inviting me? Then someone in the coat queue mentions the pub, and I tag along. We're buying our own drinks, which has never happened before, not from the very start, like this. Or when I say 'we' I suppose I mean 'I'.

Downstairs there's a pool table, and a startlingly cool American writer of exactly the sort of dystopian trash I despise is taking on all-comers. My working class roots and misspent youth will, I know, stand me in good stead. She beats me before she even registered who I am, the pool balls clacking like a colony of jackdaws. At one point I try to lean on my cue, and manage to fall entirely onto the floor, like our collapsing drying rack.

I'm about to go home, when someone I half know – a publicity assistant, but not one who's ever worked on my books, so she probably doesn't realize how unpopular I am – says, 'We're going to grab a bite, want to come?' I eagerly accept.

I'm not quite sure who's the 'we' as we crawl through Soho. When we reach the destination – one of the Chinese restaurants where the rudeness of the waiters is part of the charm – I realize that my acquaintance has disappeared. I'm left with three other publicity people – each extraordinarily easy on the eye, as is their wont. I have to explain who I am.

'Multi-award-winning,' I say, and then add my jokey rider, 'two counts as "multi", whatever the cunts say!'

The publicity people are unamused by the line, and shocked by the language. For the rest of the meal they talk among themselves. I go to the loo, and when I come back, they have gone, and I am alone. Except, no, I'd just gone back to the wrong table. But it's home time anyway. I don't even get an air kiss from the publicity girls, which is pretty astonishing, as they'll normally kiss anything that looks even vaguely like an author, the way I've seen a tortoise trying to have sex with a bicycle helmet.

I decide that I need some kind of penance, that only through further suffering can my guilt – whatever it is – be expiated and redemption found. So I decide to walk back to West Hampstead. (Plus I seem to have mislaid my Oyster card…)

Two hours later I'm home. I take off my boots and find my socks are drenched in blood.

He Should Stop Going on About His Fear of Being Eaten by Bears

December 13. My Royal Holloway students handed in their course evaluation sheets today. You know, the modern university thing whereby the students mark their lecturers. It was anonymous, and therefore quite meaty. Generally reasonably positive, and anyway I'm quite good at accepting criticism. I enjoyed the parts of the form where, rather than just ticking boxes, they were supposed to write down actual words. I encouraged them to be inventive, viewing it as a creative writing exercise. These were my favourites:

'He has shit shoes and smells funny.'

'He waves his arms around like a biblical prophet, but nothing he says ever comes true.'

'Why doesn't he just comb his hair?'

'He always illustrates his points with passages from his own works. You'd think he was the only person ever to have written a children's book. Cunt.'

'He borrowed a fiver off me, and now denies it.'

'His eyes burn into you, like Jesus.'

'I would, if it was him or Michael Gove.'

'He should stop going on about his fear of being eaten by bears.'

Animal VD

December 14. Was vaguely wondering if other animals get sexually transmitted diseases... Not fish, I suppose – they just squirt forth their seed into the water, without either the delight or jeopardy of physical contact, as if I'd had a go at getting Mrs McG pregnant from the other side of the Finchley Road (which, believe me, is something you only try the once). But, you know, camels and ostriches and monkeys. Both possibilities seem faintly absurd.

Back in my PhD days I took quite an interest in mammalian genitals, and what they could tell us about animal – and possibly human – behaviour. For example, chimps have huge testicles, which reflect their reproductive behaviour. They live in loose clans and, essentially, when a female chimp is on heat, most of the lads get to have a go on her. Obviously the top male will try to bully his way into, er, pole position, but the females are cunning enough to elude and deceive. This means that sexual competition is at the level of the sperm – the chimp that can produce the greatest quantities of semen can flush out the opposition. With gorillas, things are quite different. They live in smaller, tighter family groups, and the alpha male is the only one to mate with the lady gorillas. As a result, though the silverback is physically magnificent in most respects, when it comes to the undercarriage, he's somewhat modestly proportioned. Humans, it turns out, are exactly mid-way between the chimp and the gorilla on the genital size graph.

Which means what? That we're both promiscuous and possessive? Or neither? Or something else altogether. Science hasn't got all the answers. Uninformed speculation, wild surmise, prejudice and whim are clearly the way ahead.

A Dapper Little Man (Not Heimlich)

December 16. There's a public lavatory in the scrubby green at the end of our road. It's not one of those impressive Edwardian constructions, with beautiful aqua-green tiles and sculpted urinals like Botticelli sea creatures, but a more utilitarian building, largely subterranean, dating from, I'd guess, the 1950s. Then again, it has an attractive decorative railing above ground, and it's the sort of thing you vaguely want to carry on existing.

I've never actually ventured within – it would be eccentric, given that I live five minutes away. I mean, leaving the house specially to use a public convenience might arouse suspicions…

Which leads me to my theme.

I quite often see a dapper little man (not, I hasten to add, Heimlich, my dwarf doppelgänger – this is just, stature wise, at least, an ordinary short person) standing just across the road from the toilet entrance. He looks to be in his late sixties or early seventies, very stylishly and strikingly dressed. Sometimes he'll be wearing a hat and cape, at other times a neat checked suit, with a silk waistcoat. His hair is thick and white, and occasionally reveals a subtle rinse, in purple or blue. And, yes, he does bear an uncanny resemblance to Quentin Crisp. I presume he's looking for action, but I've never seen anyone else around who might help to supply it. It – the lack of homoerotic opportunities – is probably because the council opens and closes the toilets in an utterly unfathomable way; I've tried to find a pattern – perhaps they're using the Fibonacci sequence, or something based on prime numbers, but I can't figure it. This random pattern of opening and closing makes the toilets on the green useless for cottaging purposes. It's like the way cicadas only breed every thirteen years, to confuse their predators.

None of this seems to have deterred my dapper little man. And I find something deeply poignant and, well, attractive about him. He has a severe and intelligent face, a look both wary and penetrating. I imagine that he had a life in the theatre. A dresser, perhaps, or the box-office manager, or something to do with costume design. (I suppose one shouldn't assume these things, and he might as well have been a postman, or accountant, although I couldn't really see him working on a building site or oil rig.)

And I always have an urge to go and talk to him, as I walk past with Monty. Once or twice he's looked me up and down, realized quickly that there's nothing there of interest to him and shifted his gaze back to the middle distance. Gays never think I'm one of them, which mildly offends me. It's a superficial judgement, based on my lack of style and inept personal grooming. For all they know I could be gay on the inside. But that's not the issue. I'd really like to talk to the man, find out his story (postman or dresser), buy him a drink (crème de menthe? dry sherry? pint of strong cider?).

But of course I never will. It's just impossible to imagine how it could be arranged.

'Er, excuse me… you look like an interesting little gay man, who must have endured terrible suffering and hardship in the bad years, and probably have all kinds of amusing stories about your theatrical friends, so could I buy you a cherry brandy?'

He probably carries a Taser for dealing with people like me.

The Absence of Suspicion Taken to Imply the Presence of Guilt

December 18. Had an odd sort of row with Mrs McG. I came into the bedroom, and saw her going through my phone messages. I've only ever been messaged by three people – her, my cricket team captain and my writer pal Arlo, who often has girl trouble and likes to talk things over with me. I don't really do phones. I don't like to talk on them, I often can't find mine, and I've never managed to learn a mobile number, mine or anyone else's.

Anyway, Mrs McG was scrolling down through the requests to get milk on my way home, or to bring a spare jock strap to the match. She looked up at me with one of her harder faces – not quite depleted uranium, but certainly tungsten.

I wasn't quite sure what I'd done, but thought it might be one of those cases to apply the fine advice offered up by the theologian Karl Barth (albeit in relation to God, rather than fierce spouses). 'Do not ask, "Is this right or is this wrong?" but just get down on your knees and beg for forgiveness.' Something like that.

But before I could get my speculative apology in, she said, 'You never even think of checking my phone, do you?'

I thought she was talking about some sort of technical check-up, IT being one of my household duties.

'I, er, it's working OK, isn't it. Happy to, you know…'

She wasn't listening.

'And just because you're too… because you're not, you assume…'

And then she got up and took Monty out for a late walk.

I knew I should have got that generic apology out earlier.

The Author Is Put in His Place

December 19. I'm at a book launch filled with London's literary and social elite, plus me, shambling around on my own. I feel I ought to attempt some rudimentary networking, but the beautiful people all know each other, so I concentrate on adopting diverse facial expressions, so the lads at the wine table might mistake me for a different person each time I go up for a refill.

Then, with relief, I come across an acquaintance I've always got on well with, in other contexts.

'So how are things at the *XXX Review*?' I ask, brightly.

'Oh, I'm not there any more. I'm now part of the re-launch of *XXX Magazine*.'

I suddenly think that it's time for me to ditch my Englishness, and try to scrabble up the greasy pole. There's a carpe here to be diemed (or the other way round).

'Are you by any chance looking for a columnist?' I see the light die in my friend's eyes. But I plough on. 'You see, people keep telling me that I'm quite funny on Facebook.' The eyes harden yet further, suspicion blending into contempt. 'And often, my Facebook updates are, er, roughly the same length as a column.'

I notice for the first time that he's got cruel lips. Not Jihadi John cruel, not Tamburlaine, ordering towers of skulls to be erected from the slaughtered children of a conquered town cruel, but cruel enough to get the job done.

'I'm afraid we already have a grumpy middle-aged columnist.' I'm beginning to sweat through the armpits of my blue velvet 'book-event' jacket.

'Ah, but I'm not so much grumpy as, er, *sad*. Sad is more, ah, poetic than grumpy. Anyone can be grumpy. But to be sad you need to be, um, profound.'

'But surely you must see that we couldn't have a sad columnist as well as a grumpy one? You *do* see that, don't you?'

His eyes flicker towards some beautiful publicity person, who might be a junior countess. It's my last chance.

'What about a fluffy columnist? I can be fluffy.'

As he turns away I try to mime someone being fluffy. I don't know why, but I hit on the idea of one of those old-fashioned burlesque performers who can rotate the tassels on their nipples in opposite directions by a subtle and sinuous gyration of the upper torso. But my friend has gone, and there's nobody left to see the performance.

Penguin Catheter Bags

December 20. Back at the British Library, there's an amusingly inept attempt to strike a seasonal note in the forecourt. A line of flimsy pine shacks selling festive tat doth not a Christmas Fayre make. Here you can buy fuzzy felt reindeer hats that would make any self-respecting Lapp go out and slaughter his herd with a claw hammer; there are catheter bags with a penguin motif; there are mulled underpants; a green orthopaedic shoe filled with sloe gin; toffee sprouts. There's also a sort of green grotto, guarded by a stuffed sheep with a bemused expression. You probably think I'm being whimsical, but this is the exact and total truth.

No one quite knows what to do with all this. The usual library crowd stare bemused at the gewgaws, like eunuchs in a sex shop. I guess it's possible a tourist might wander in, the way that a bumble bee will suddenly appear on a window pane in winter, and buzz forlornly until you let it out to die.

I suppose they're just trying to monetize the space, although that's more of a description than an excuse. Perhaps it's just me. Like most normal people Christmas makes me sad.

McGowan Festive Fun 1

December 27. We've travelled north, for our usual post-Christmas McGowan Family ordeal. My mum and dad are quite elderly now, but there are still supernova levels of rage, madness, love, hate and booze swilling around, especially when my sisters and brother are added to the mix.

It all began with a manic night at my sister Maggie's in York, with wigs, huge arguments, colossal makings-up, drunken revelations, two different roast beefs and a ham the size of three pigs, mad McGowans being kept in check by more or less sane partners, bottles piling up, children laughing, crying, laughing again, Monty doing his best to get his doggy brain around it all.

Then the usual surreality of my parents, like the Royle Family scripted by Beckett.

Me, shouting down the stairs: 'Dad, how do you turn the radiator on in the bedroom?'

Dad: 'You've got to turn it all the way round to "off".'

'To off?'

'Yes, that one only works when it's turned off.'

Four days of this…

Talc

December 28. Took Mrs McG into Leeds. She wanted to check out the sales at the swanky new Harvey Nichols. I stood around for a while, as she tried on shoes. The place was full of Yorkshire money: orange ladies, large men with tiny faces like anuses compressed into the middle of their huge, buttocky heads. Leeds has always been brittle, superficial, vain; less friendly than the other great northern cities. The kind of place where you can get your head kicked in for spilling a pint or looking at another lad's bird. We didn't invent football hooliganism, but we raised it to a kind of Platonic perfection, back in the late 1970s, bringing to it the clarity of line, the mastery of form and colour, of early Renaissance art. Everything that came after was mere decadence and decay.

'Got to get out of here,' I said. 'I'll be back in half an hour.'

She didn't mind. I was only in the way.

Outside, the streets had an odd mixture of the old and new Leeds. Students and the local bourgeoisie mingled with shell-suited smackheads and cold-eyed urchins, their heads shaved as a nit prophylactic. The street entertainment had changed. Back in my day, it was a shoeless tramp with a paint tin on his head who limped after you begging for the price of a cup of tea. Now there were steel bands, mime artists and a row of living statues, including a Venus de Milo, which, on closer inspection, turned out to be a genuinely armless man. I wanted to ask him how he got into the living-statue game, and if his arm situation limited the roles he could take, but I didn't want to put him off.

I slipped in for a swift one at Whitelocks (est. 1715).

Bad move.

The patterns in the faded flock wallpaper, every stain in the carpet, even the ancient nicotine shadows on the ceiling were the ghosts of my old friends from teenage drinking days. And though I thought I saw them among the heavy coats of the crowd by the bar, I was looking for a version of the way we were then. Now we wouldn't recognize each other, or what we're become. Nothing to do but dilute my beer with the tears of nostalgia and loss.

I remembered coming here in the sixth form, with Marc, and Beddy, and Allison Oxley, and Elizabeth Makin, and Christine Chillinsky. I was grievously in love with Elizabeth at the time, although you could probably argue that she had some weight issues going on. I remember when she sat down next to me on the padded vinyl of the bench, a little puff of talc escaped from the fabric of her skirt. She must have dusted her underthings, and the thought left me sick with lust.

I suppose I was in love with all of the girls. But other things were happening in my life and I never got up the courage to ask any of them out. Elizabeth or Allison, or Christine, or beautiful Carmel Byrne, who never came to the pub.

I went back and met Mrs McG.

'You OK?' she asked in a rare moment of noticing.

'Oh, aye, you know… Leeds.'

We went to find some happy-hour cocktails, and tried to get drunk. Well, I tried and failed; Mrs McG succeeded, spectacularly, and I carried her back, fireman-style, to the station, over my shoulder.

You've Got to Sneak Up on It

December 29. The lavatories here need a special flushing. The one downstairs (1973 extension, chocolate brown suite) you have to sneak up on, then launch a hefty buttock at the handle, otherwise it gives nothing more than a bronchial wheeze. The one in the upstairs bathroom (the 1987 redecoration, an iridescent pink, as of a diseased gum) is like something from the little house on the fucking prairie – you have to pump it while resting a steadying foot on the seat.

And I've forgotten my toothbrush, which is like someone backpacking round India and forgetting their Imodium. I've found some ancient, child-sized brush, and can only pray it hasn't been used on the dog, the toilet or some dentures.

It took me a few minutes to realize what was wrong with the bed in our room, but I got there in the end. My parents have put the foam mattress topper in the duvet cover, and the duvet under the bottom sheet. Mrs McG looks shell-shocked.

Not sure I'm drunk enough to cope with this. Might have to go back down and suck the insides from some more cherry liqueurs.

McGowan Festive Fun 2

December 30. Some McGowan family trialogue:

'Whose tooth is that?'

'How the hell should I know?'

'Has somebody lost a tooth?'

'Are you sure that's a tooth?'

'I think it's a hazelnut.'

'Has somebody lost a hazelnut?'

(The sound of a nut being crunched.)

'I'm not sure that was a nut.'

'Has anyone seen my tooth?'

McGowan Festive Fun 3

Me, shouting down the stairs:

'Mum, Monty's peed on the bathroom floor. What can I use to clean it up?'

'There's some shampoo up there.'

'Shampoo?'

'Yes, but don't use the Vosene. Use the Head & Shoulders.'

'Why?'

'We don't need it since your dad went bald.'

And more…

'You suit the extra weight – it makes you look less sly and vindictive.' (Said to me, that one, by my sister Moya.)

'Is there any fruit?'

'Yes, there's fruit.'

'Where…?'

[Points at the trifle.]

'Are the sheets clean?'

'Of course the sheets are clean. We've had the shower fixed.'

'Where is everyone?'

'Catriona's taking your dad down to buy milk. She didn't get dressed. But it's OK: she's driving carefully.'

Lots of love sloshing around. But quite hard for the non-McGowans to survive/comprehend. No one over the age of eleven has been sober since we got here.

Home

December 31. I've been a bit unkind about the ancestral Barratt house, and the McGowans therein. My parents are actually pretty amazing at eighty-six and seventy-eight, and the house is full of joy and energy, as well as chaos. And memories, of course. We've lived here since 1971, and every room has its associations, as well as the accumulated bric-a-brac of decades. Nothing has been thrown away, so every time you open a drawer or cupboard, a memory tumbles out – a toy, a book, a photo, a half-eaten pork pie.

There are paintings on the wall. Souk scenes, and curious portraits of oriental children that my dad brought back from his time in Iran, where he was working as a nurse in the 1950s. As kids, they fascinated us. We'd try to work out the story behind them, give names to the characters. My favourite was a village street. A turbaned man looked, to my childish mind, to be pushing himself along on a scooter. Now I see that he's holding a stick, and the scooter is just his shadow. But, as the paintings have lost their magic (their artistic worth is… limited), I wonder more at the life of my dad, leaving his tiny Scottish village, training as a nurse in Manchester, travelling to Persia. There's a wonderful photograph of him, in the big plastic shopping bag of photos, inoculating a child in some desert outpost. The child trying bravely not to cry, although the syringe is comically huge. My dad is calm and handsome, though already balding, in his twenties. At twice his age I have more hair. But that's about it.

Home tomorrow. Don't know how many more of these we'll have, so I'm bathing in the chaos, like Rider Haggard's She in the flames of youth, finding strength there, and new life.

The Last Failure of the Old Year, the First Triumph of the New

January 1. I was determined to finish my book before the year was out. I failed. So a whole year passed without a project completed, unless you count fixing on the new handle on the wardrobe door – the verb 'fixing' making the job qualify as a work of fiction, as it fell off the next day.

But six thousand words over two days has, at least, permitted me to type 'The End' on the first day of a new year.

Perhaps it's actually a good sign – a book finished on the first day of what will, surely, be a better year. I suppose the great benefit of being the author of your own woes is that you're in charge of the delete key. Plus you can type COCK and ARSE whenever you want.

Schrödinger's Sock

January 2. OK, so this morning I put a sock on my right foot. There was a hole strategically placed so my big toe stuck out in a grotesque manner. It had the look of a deformed peasant in a rustic scene by Pieter Breughel the Elder, or perhaps one of the more humanoid devils in a Hieronymus Bosch triptych.

So I took the sock off and, after pondering the matter for a few moments, put it on the other foot. Obviously the hole would still be there, but I reasoned it would be less conspicuous, the recession of the toes naturally preventing any protuberance or, er, *extrusion*. But somehow the hole was now exactly over my other big toe, which poked its head out, tortoise-wise. How is this even possible? It seems to go against all the laws of Nature.

I have a theory, but it involves Schrödinger's cat, and I totally hate theories that involve Schrödinger's cat, except for those devised by good old Norbert Schrödinger himself. I've spent most of the day staring at my toe and trying to come up with an explanation that doesn't involve quantum theory.

But of course it's impossible not to consider the whole affair as emblematic of my struggles with existence. I could be the toe, bluntly sticking out, cut off from the fellowship of his own kind, exposed, ridiculous, tragic. Or I could be the sock, unable to adequately cope with the modest demands placed upon it. Or I could be the whole shebang, the absurd irrationality of the world and my being in it, encapsulated by the shifting hole, forever popping up where it can cause the most humiliation.

Still Virgins at the End of It

January 3. Under instruction from Mrs McG, I've been doing my accounts. And we're staring a worst-case scenario in the face. Last year, it transpires, was an unusually good one – I had four new books out, and performed various other quasi-literary activities that paid quite well. But this year has been a stinker. And of course I have to pay last year's hefty tax out of this year's meagre income, not having put anything aside, being, you know, feckless. I'm like one of those foolish virgins in the Bible story who, er, well, they squandered something, didn't they, or did something unwise. I think oil was involved, or some other lubricant. The precise details escape me. Can't have been that bad, though, can it, if they were still virgins at the end of it.

So I'm going to have to tighten my belt. Or sell it on eBay, and walk around with my hands in my pockets as a way of keeping my trousers up.

Laces, Stains...

January 4. We went to a wedding reception this evening. Just before the taxi came to take us I found that my only decent 'wedding' shoes (by which I mean normal shoes, not trainers, or others serving some sort of orthopaedic function), last worn about four years ago, had no laces. I had a forlorn search for some, and even contemplated colouring in some string I found with a black marker pen. I ended up taking a lace from my football boots, cutting it in half and using that. It looks all wrong – as if I've fastened my shoes with a scorched tapeworm – but that can't be helped.

Also, my only semi-respectable suit had some curious chalky stains on the shoulder. Realized that it was sick from when Gabe was a baby.

Now It's a Thing

January 5. Printing out my just-completed book. Always satisfying to see a text for the first time in corporeal form. Until now it's just been electrical impulses or quantum burping, or whatever it is that happens on the inside of my Mac. But it's become a thing of ink and paper. To be lost now would take more than a power cut. You'd have to hack it to death with a Samurai sword, or go at it with a flame thrower, or spend the evening with a microplane grater, or laboriously Tippex it out, letter by letter, or bundle it into the washing machine, or run naked through West Hampstead, scattering it sheet by sheet, while singing the songs of Rodgers and Hammerstein, or soak it in milk overnight and bake it as a pudding or... Well, probably best to stay on Mrs McG's good side, till I send it off on Monday morning.

They Should Make Maltesers in the Shape of a Guillemot's Egg

January 6. Guillemot eggs are vaguely conical in shape, so they roll in a tight circle on their cliff-ledge nests, and don't tumble onto the rocks and surf below. They should make Maltesers like that, so when you eat them lying down off your jumper they don't roll on the floor and under the table with the telephone on it. I'm going to be writing to the Malteser people about this.

Like a Drunk Urinating in a Bus Shelter

January 7. Few things as depressing as job applications. You feel the despair and desolation wash over you like Bangladeshi flood waters. And then you realize that the only people qualified to give you a reference are retired, dead or hate you. And you imagine the scene as the panel look at your application. Some pimply wag in an unearned tweed jacket bends over in front of the Faculty and pretends to wipe his arse with your form. Another, senility offering some excuse, absent-mindedly blows his nose on it, or twists a corner and rootles in his ear with it, staring at the dark waxy substrate with baffled wonder.

So you close down the document, gawp at the wall for a while, until you realise that all the other things you're supposed to do are even more depressing. And then you hit send with relief but no hope, like a drunk urinating in a bus shelter.

Let's Keep the Woodpeckers

January 8. Planned a British Library day – arrived there and found that I'd forgotten to bring my laptop. So I cycled along to Regent's Park and ate my packed lunch – a limp cheese sandwich (that accidentally purchased half-fat Emmental) and a flask of miso soup.

I was feeling vaguely Larkinesque, as I contemplated my failures by some bed of lobelias, and then a green woodpecker came along to cheer me up. It was poking away at the grass a few feet from my bench. Such a handsome bird, with its green back and scarlet crest. And bigger than you'd think – the size of a jay. Then it flew away, with that characteristic heavy, effortful flight, as if it had necked a skinful of ale and a couple of meat pies.

And I was thinking that if you were starting from scratch, you'd definitely keep the woodpeckers, I mean, you know, if you had the choice of getting rid of the rubbish animals – the lice, the tapeworms, the mosquitoes. You'd have to be mad to say, 'Fucking woodpeckers, I hate them, let's bin them all, and keep the pigeons instead.'

Anyway, the day wasn't a complete write-off. It never is when you've seen a woodpecker. Or a fire engine.

The Man Obsessed with Monomania

January 9. Lots of people think that monomania means being obsessed with one thing (like Captain Ahab with the whale), whereas it actually means that you are mad in only one area of your life, and sane in everything else (like, er, Ahab and the whale). I suspect that most of us have monomaniacal tendencies. Mine concerns my persistent fear that I have tiny shards of glass stuck in my feet. I've taken myself, limping, to casualty a couple of times about this. At some level I know that I don't really have glass in my feet, and yet, at another, I surely know that I do, and it's just the incompetence of the medical profession that fails to confirm this.

And then last night I found a tiny sore lump on the base of my foot – exactly the kind of thing you'd expect to find when the skin grows over a splinter of glass. Now, I could go and get this looked at, but I almost prefer to keep it there, as pure potentiality. That little lump contains two incompatible states. Either it is splinterless, and confirms me as a deluded monomaniac; or it contains the shard, and I'm proved right, with the strong possibility that all those other fragments of glass are still in there, working their steady way to my brain, heart, lungs, and that one day I'll be on the bus, and a gurgling will emerge from my chest, and I'll stand up and spew blood all over the other passengers, and it'll teach everyone a lesson about ignoring my mild complaints about stuff.

Anyway, my point is that I don't really want to know either way, as each possibility is, ah, sub-optimal. So I'm going to think about something else.

Shoved Down My Bra

January 10. Had to go and perform today at a private Muslim school. I was concerned about this, as much of my act consists of pretty gross body humour, which I obviously wouldn't be able to indulge in. But I managed to find enough clean material to get me through, and it was actually very enjoyable – the kids, in neat, plump, happy lines, bought lots of books, and the staff were friendly enough, albeit a little wary.

The only difficult moment came when I offered to shake hands with one of the women teachers, and she reeled away from me as if I'd taken out my wedding tackle. But that was my mistake for not realizing the potential male–female skin-contact issues.

At the end, as I was leaving, I was handed an envelope. Have just opened it, expecting the usual cheque. It actually contained a fistful of used fifties. I feel dirty. But also strangely… gratified. From now on that's what I want. Used fifties. Shoved down my bra.

The Chaste Marriage

January 11. Going away to Ted Hughes country to teach at the Arvon Foundation. I've done it before. You live in a homely cottage with another tutor, in a sort of chaste marriage, like one of those brother–sister setups you find in Dickens, and spend the days blathering at young people, getting them to write poems about leaves or birdshit. It's quite well paid, but you earn your money. By the end of the week you feel you've Stanley-knifed yourself, opening up from neck to groin, and ladled out your viscera for the punters.

Whether or not it's fun depends mainly on how pleasant your fellow tutor is. I've just looked mine up. She's a rather beautiful poet. I have no plans to be distracted. I've told Mrs McG that she's hatchet-faced and Sapphically inclined. Just hope she doesn't bother to Google…

The Track Constrictor

January 12. Well, this is good. Got one of those dirt cheap advance first-class tickets, so I'm very much enjoying my train journey north, supplied with limitless free sandwiches and other fine things (crisps, cake, tea, love). A man keeps offering me free beer. So far I've rebuffed him. And as we pulled out of a station, somewhere north of Stoke, I saw a fantastically interesting piece of equipment. It was one of those bits of rolling stock designed to do unfathomable stuff to the track, and it had the most complicated machinery dangling beneath it, looking like the clustered mouth parts of a monstrous insect. I convinced myself that it was a 'track constrictor', designed to reduce journey times by shortening the line between London and Leeds.

If it were up to me I'd spend a year on this train, eating free sandwiches and looking at the fields, with Mrs McG and the kids occasionally popping in from standard class to say hello.

And now the joy of a pair of lapwings, flapping after a tractor in a muddy field. They used to be common as crows when I was growing up, but now you hardly ever see them. They're easily in my top five favourite birds.

And suddenly, a buzzard! How can the week not spiral down from here?

The Poet Is Beautiful

January 13. Well, yep, the poet is beautiful and, as I supposed you'd expect, sort of sad. The Ted Hughes Centre is exactly what Ted Hughes would look like if he were a farmhouse. It's set on the edge of a wonderfully grim valley, with iron skies and iron trees and sheep keeping their heads down, stoically putting up with everything. The kids I'm tutoring are from a state school in Heckmondwike – the grim Yorkshire town where the roughest of the McGowan cousins used to live, including Philip, who had Munchausen's and pretended to be a surgeon for a couple of years. But they're incredibly sweet and excited to be here (the kids, not the rough McGowan cousins – I've no idea where they are, or what became of them).

I plan to suppress my urge to crush their spirits and rub their faces in the horror of existence.

She Interpreted It as My Fear of Women's Pubic Hair

January 15. I had a feverish dream last night, which took the form of a more or less cogent fairy story. When I first woke up I thought it might be one I'd made up, but then I vaguely remembered that I'd read something similar to the kids when they were small. But it was still pretty intense, when I was in it.

A king has four sons and a daughter. He sends each son over the mountains to learn the way of the five weapons – bow, sword, spear, axe, cudgel. One by one, they fail to return. Finally, despairing of having a warrior to protect his kingdom, he sends his daughter. She learns the way of each weapon, and heads home. There is a short cut through the forest. She is warned not to go through the forest, because it is the realm of the ogre Sticky Hair. But she longs to get back to her father. She encounters the ogre, and uses each of the five weapons on him, but all are useless – they get stuck in his sticky hair. Then she attacks him with her left hand, which gets stuck; then her right hand, her left foot, her right foot – all become stuck in Sticky Hair's sticky hair. The monster is about to eat her, but she says that she has swallowed a thunderbolt, which will blow him apart from the inside. So Sticky Hair wisely declines to eat her. She sees the weapons of her brothers stuck in his hair, and follows the ogre back to his lair. She finds her brothers who have all been imprisoned by the ogre. She frees them, and they all go back to their father's kingdom, of which, in time, she becomes the queen.

I told the beautiful poet my dream in the morning, over our Weetabix. She interpreted it as my fear of women's pubic hair. I didn't think I had a fear of women's pubic hair before she said it, but now I definitely do.

The Man Who Uses Gel

January 16. On our afternoon off, the poet and I went for a walk along the valley. The sublimity of the scenery is intensified by the ruins of old mills along the river – they look like the remains of some lost kingdom in Middle-earth. Huge chimneys tower up from the trees, with no sign of what must once have connected them to the rest of the world. Anyway, one thing the poet said to me towards the end of our walk together has stayed with me, its resonant plangency thrumming through my very being.

'I've never known another adult man,' she said, gazing across the wooded valley, 'who uses gel.'

The Impossible Dream

January 17. When I go away, I like to take with me exactly the right amount of antiperspirant to last the trip. Now, obviously, this is close to an impossible dream, and the can will generally run out before the end, necessitating a trip to the chemist (fraught with danger and anxiety if you're in Ulan Bator, say, or Motherwell), or there'll still be some left, meaning I have to schlep it back, the dead weight of artistic failure dragging down my pack, and soul. But the ideal remains, the formal perfection of using up the last spluttering spray on the second, and final, armpit, and then the joyous rattle as the can hits the bin. It gives the whole thing the feeling of one of those Baroque fugues or partitas, or whatever they're called, that begin with a theme, and then meander around for a while, and then come back, the fat flautist so red in the face you think he's going to expire right there on the stage of the Wigmore Hall.

And this time I thought I'd done it. A long, tiring, but deeply rewarding week of teaching at the Arvon centre. The final shower. A shake of the can – perfect – the penultimate pit – another shake – almost nothing left, but almost nothing will be enough. And then… and then the final nozzle depression emits only that fatal afflatus, a gaseous cough. There is nothing left but the propellant. And so I begin the long journey home with one armpit perkily prepped, and the other undefended, helpless, dank.

All in a Day's Work for a Specialist Ironing Board Crash Investigator

January 18. One of my traits, or weaknesses, if you prefer, is to read significance into things that I know, rationally, can't have significance. The pattern of vomit splashes on the pavement, the shape of the moon, unexpected occurrences involving domestic goods, etc. etc.

Today I was given, by Mrs McG, as an early birthday present, a shoe rack. It is telescopic, so it can expand or contract horizontally to fit neatly into your wardrobe, should you have one.

'It'll help you keep your shoes tidy,' she said, a statement I found difficult to argue with.

I tried to show some enthusiasm, but the truth is that a shoe rack isn't in my top three most yearned for presents. It isn't even in my top three most yearned for racks.

Shortly after this, our ironing board broke, the legs shearing off, dramatically.

'Metal fatigue,' I said, stroking the torn metal like a specialist ironing board crash investigator. 'We won't know what really happened until we find the black box.'

These things usually occur in threes, so I'm keeping an eye on the heated towel rail in the bathroom, my heart filled with unease and foreboding.

A Little Down, the Day After

January 20. I had a party. It created, as one would hope, the brief illusion of popularity. There were enough people there (just), and many of them had travelled from several miles away. Some of them brought whisky, which seems to be the default gift for a man hitting fifty. Perhaps I'll acquire, this year, the moral gravity you need to enjoy good whisky. For now, it still just tastes like medicine.

But there's always a sadness to parties, isn't there? The party begins to die from the moment it is born. And when it's gone, it's gone forever. That party will never come back.

Rosie made Mojitos. It was kind of cute seeing a twelve-year-old girl professionally mashing up the lime and rum. She was the hit of the party. I moved from group to group, trying to be attentive, trying to give everyone that flensed sliver of my soul. But I couldn't summon up the panache and vigour. I didn't have a meaningful conversation, or even a humorous exchange, all evening, and my speech narrowly missed the mark.

But it's out of the way. Someone else's turn next.

O, to Be a Grebe

January 22. I had to get myself to St Mary's University in West London to speak to a group of creative writing students. I decided to leave the train early, and walk along the river from

Richmond. It's a journey I'd take a couple of times a week, a few years ago, when I was a writer in residence at the university. A pair of great crested grebes used to nest on a floating island of duckweed, and I marked the passing of the year by watching them successively court, brood their eggs and care for the young. Is there a more beautiful British bird than the great crested grebe? Too beautiful for its own good – it was hunted to near extinction so that the sunburst feathers of its lovely face and neck could adorn the hats of society ladies. And yet 'grebe' is such an unlovely word. I have a friend who is incredibly grebelian in terms of colouring and general elegance, but if I said to her that she was as lovely as a grebe, she'd most likely punch me. A terrible shame, really.

I was hoping they'd be there still, my grebes. And so they were (I'm going to pretend that it's the same couple, older now, but still together, still in love). In fact, there was something of a grebe-fest this morning, my old friends joined by a jaunty pair of little grebes. The little grebe cannot match the extraordinary splendour of the great crested, but they're the sort of bird that makes you smile, with their blushing cheeks and unnecessarily fluffy rear-ends. They're like a duck, given an anime makeover.

And I hate to anthropomorphize, but grebe pairs really do act as if they love each other. They have that rapt enclosure and completeness, the world beyond their love an irrelevance. The way they touch each other for no good reason. Delicate little nudges and caresses. And the way that, as they face each other, motionless in the current, their heads and necks come together to form a perfect heart. Ah, to be a grebe in springtime.

'Normally is Yugo Boss for more... stylish'

January 23. It being a while since I've enjoyed one of my clothes-shop humiliations, I decided to take back a shirt to

Hugo Boss in Brent Cross. It was rather a lovely shirt – a birthday present – but, in 'Large', just a little optimistically sized. I took it to the elegant Italian lady at the desk, and she helped me search for an XL. The last one in the shop was located, a process that involved most of the similarly lovely-looking assistants roped in to find a shirt big enough for the fat bloke.

In the changing room, I saw in the mirror that I had toast crumbs and other detritus adhering to my jumper, and I had my village idiot hairdo. Actually, it was more sci-fi than that – my head looked like a terminally damaged spaceship, from which the escape pods were being frantically launched.

I put the shirt on, and stepped out to find all the girls waiting. A sort of collective smirk emerged from them, as the buttons strained at my midriff.

The original Italian lady conversed with me, while the other girls tried to find something – anything – in my size.

'Normally is Yugo Boss for more… stylish,' she said in her beautiful voice. 'And more thin profile.'

She was stern but not unsympathetic. Finally, she added – and there was something deeper, more profound in her tone, something akin, I'd say, to love – 'And not so fat.'

Somehow an XXL in a different style was located – genuinely the biggest shirt made by Hugo Boss. Before I re-entered the changing room, a tiny Japanese assistant bowed and offered me an object. For a second I thought it was a tantō – the short sword used for seppuku, or ritual disembowelment – but then I realized that it was merely a longish shoe-horn.

The other thing that happened was shoe-related. I don't have many aesthetic principles, but one is that I don't like yellow things, and in my life I've never bought anything yellow that wasn't a banana. So I popped into the Russell &

Bromley sale, and saw, amid all the normal-coloured shoes, some yellow ones. I chortled to myself, and thought, of course they're reduced from £245 to £95 – they're yellow! – nobody wants yellow shoes.

It was only on the C11 bus back to West Hampstead that I realized that I had a shoebox from Russell & Bromley, and that it contained a pair of yellow shoes. It's the beginning of the end.

Plato's Head & Shoulders

January 24. I accidentally bought some anti-dandruff shampoo from a pound shop in Kilburn – an accident in the sense that I thought it was just ordinary, plain shampoo. But, abhorring waste as I do, I decided to use it up. And now, to my dismay, I find that this supposed anti-dandruff shampoo has *given me dandruff.*

This is, of course, a poor outcome, but now I'm confronted with a further dilemma – should I continue using the anti-dandruff shampoo in the hope that it will clear up the dandruff that the anti-dandruff shampoo caused? Or will this result in me having a head like a giant snowball made up entirely of flaky skin? This is precisely the situation Derrida discusses in the 'Plato's Pharmacy' section of *Dissemination.* At least I think it is – I've read only the introduction.

The Snotgreen Sea

January 25. Tomorrow I'm going to Bournemouth, to speak to some young people at the public library. I have mixed memories of Bournemouth. I went there for a weekend with a group of girls I was living with as a student back in the 1980s. It was a complicated and unsatisfactory period of my erotic history. I was, er, *seeing* two of the girls, each without the knowledge of the other. Of the remaining two girls in the group, one was in love with me, and I was in love with the other. It should have been exciting, but it – the trip and, indeed, the life – was stressful and debilitating. Then one night I set fire to my floppy, Morrissey-style quiff in a restaurant. The next day we were on the beach. It was the sort of bitterly cold day you get at the British seaside in May, with the sky looking like the victim of domestic violence. Showing off to the girls, I stripped down to my trunks, and ran across the pebbles to the sea. The second I hit the water I felt my testicles retreat to the safety and warmth of my abdominal cavity (is it true, I wonder, that sumo wrestlers are able to perform this trick, as Fleming claims in one of the Bond books?). I splashed about for a while, like an elephant seal being worried by a shark, watched not only by my girls, but by the four or five hundred people shivering on the Bank Holiday beach. I felt my body gradually become numb, until it lost all sensation, and my flesh turned from its habitual pale pink to the granular, white-flecked-with-blue of Daz washing powder. It was time to leave, or die.

As I jogged back through the crowd, I noticed that the people opened up before me to let me pass, their faces wearing a mix of disgust and amusement that, in the years since, I've grown used to, but was puzzling back then. Just as I reached my group, I noticed that there was something swinging down below crotch level. At first I thought it was a strand of kelp or bladder-wrack from the sea, and I grasped it. Only then did I realize the truth: it was a thick, braided cord of mucus, still attached to my cold-benumbed face. I was fully amid the girls by then, and they all recoiled from me in disgust. I half remember swinging the viscous, glutinous strand around my head and hurling it back into the snotgreen sea, like an Olympic hammer thrower.

Anyway, everything changed after the trip. Before that I still had a sort of dark glamour to me: I had a reputation as a player, as being just a little... dangerous. Post-Bournemouth I was the kind of person who set fire to his hair and ran from the sea with a trunk made of snot attached to his face.

That was thirty years ago, and I'm still waiting for the next phase. And perhaps my return to Bournemouth will prove the catalyst...

The Beer Is Only £2.40 a Pint

January 26. Oh Bournemouth. I've come back to you in a perfect storm of desolation. An out-of-season seaside town. A Fawlterian hotel, in which I have to move my single bed out of the way to reach the spluttering shower. The carpet is exactly the colour of a stain on another carpet, if you know what I mean. The sort of dappled brown that you can normally only achieve by vomiting over something else, waiting till the next morning, then haphazardly wiping it clean with a dirty dishcloth. I'm haunted by the terrible memories from my lost youth. The burnt hair; the snot-trunk; the desire draining from the eyes of the girl I loved. And there is that huge pile of work I both have to do and cannot do.

And now, seeking solace in drink, I've stumbled in to what seems to be the world's toughest gay bar, where I'm being stared out by people both much gayer and much harder than me. Smiling back at their confrontational, tight-lipped glares seems both the only, and the worst, option.

There is some consolation, however: the beer is only £2.40 a pint.

And am I consoled?

A little. A little.

I Found a Pair of Socks

I complained about my room – the one where I had to slide the bed out of the way to reach the shower. And so they've given me a perfectly pleasant double room.

But I've found a pair of socks.

I mean socks that aren't *my* socks.

And I don't know what to do with them. Should I hand them in at reception? For some reason, perhaps connected to the fact that the receptionist (the one who facilitated the room-change) is a ludicrously beautiful Slovakian (I'm guessing), I don't want to do that. It would feel somehow humiliating. Should I throw them out of the window? Boil them, using the adequate tea-making facilities? Or should I wear them? Perhaps the last owner died, and his soul is in the socks, and he'll take me over and make me do evil things. OK, I'm going to put these issues on one side, while I go and check out the pool.

Maybe she's Slovenian.

There Isn't a Pool.

Duck Breasts in Cherrie Sauce

In the hotel restaurant now. I'm the youngest person by at least forty years. On the menu there are '*egg's*' and (what I'm about to experience) '*duck breasts in cherrie sauce*'.

Despite my best efforts, I'm suddenly having a nice time.

Pretty Sure I Was Just Given Banana Flavoured Ice Cream as a Starter

I'm trying to clarify (the process muddied a little by the £2.40 lager), in my mind, the difference between Slovakian and Slovenian. Do even they know, the Slovaks and Slovenes? I suppose I'll never find out, unless I ask her, the receptionist, I mean. She probably gets it all the time. They shouldn't have given them such similar names. It was bound to lead to confusion. Similar places with similar names should be a basic cartographical no-no.

I wonder if she's still on duty.

With a Narwhal's Horn

January 28. Back from Bournemouth. The library events went quite well. I suppose Bournemouth might just be one of the last places on Earth where my style of capering and cavorting still constitutes entertainment. However, in the intervals between my performances, I became rather obsessed with the huge and somewhat obscene mural they have on the library wall. It depicts various nude and semi-nude figures in a Dionysian procession, accompanied by a menagerie of mythical and actual beasts. It's the sort of thing that might well intrude itself awkwardly and unbidden on the masturbatory imaginings of any teenage boy unfortunate enough to encounter it. The library staff viewed the mural with tolerant amusement, despite its potential for generating future perverts, of the sort likely to end up in a leather mask, locked into the case of a grandfather clock, with a narwhal's horn in their anus. Actually, they extended the same tolerant amusement to me, which is worrying.

The Author Is Disconcerted by an Incongruous Toilet Roll

January 29. I've just noticed that one of the rolls of toilet paper from a recently purchased Waitrose nine-pack is different to the others. It's five millimetres taller, and the central tube has a narrower, er, bore. I just don't see how this could happen. I'm finding it very unnerving. I've put forward various hypotheses. The fat tubes perhaps use Imperial measures, and the thin ones are based on the pre-Revolutionary Russian verst. But that doesn't explain why they've come to be mixed up in the same pack. One assumed that the different tubes must come from different factories... Anyway, it's unnatural and wrong, like finding a Bourbon cream in a packet of Jammy Dodgers.

One Day We Will All Speak Papuan

January 30. I'm very much a creature of habit. When I go to the British Library I almost always bring in a cheese sandwich, then at lunchtime go and buy an accompanying bag of crisps, a can of ginger beer and a cup of miso soup from the Pret over the road. (I like Pret a lot – the people there seem not to hate your guts, and to quite enjoy their jobs, which is cheering. Although that fades after a while, when you realize that they're not smiling at you: you merely happen to be standing in the way as they smile at the world.)

Then I go and eat in the semi-enclosed circular area in the library forecourt. It's about the size of a squash court, I guess. Though I'm not sure that squash would work in a circular context. You'd never really know where the ball would end up. Could be bloody anywhere. You'd go mad... It's usually nice and quiet there, and I can chew over my failures and disappointments in peace.

The only irritation is that there are a series of stunted pillars around the circumference, each topped with singularly inept statuary. These works of art consist of crudely carved human figures apparently copulating with large lumps of rock – of all forms of copulation, surely the least satisfactory. Still, it's a small price to pay for relative seclusion.

You can imagine my alarm, therefore, when, today, I found my circular refuge filled with high-spirited French teenagers. They played bongo drums, fooled around, laughed, joked and enjoyed themselves in quite inappropriate ways, totally ignoring my tuts and disapproving looks.

Then they started to sing 'Happy Birthday', not in French, but in English.

This made me wonder if all cultures sing 'Happy Birthday' in English – Inuit in their igloos, Highland Papuans in their huts, etc. etc. And then I realized that in thousands of years' time, when English is forgotten and the world speaks some other language, derived perhaps from one of the Polynesian dialects, or a version of Gaelic, that maybe people will still sing the words to 'Happy Birthday', without knowing what they mean. And I'm not sure why, but that cheered me up, a bit.

Big Bag of Old Shoes

January 31. I've got a Big Bag of Old Shoes, which I keep in the bottom of the wardrobe. I noticed today that it wasn't there any more, and I silently raged, assuming that Mrs McG had, at last, carried out her threat to leave it out for the bin men. The Big Bag of Old Shoes contained important historic shoes, such as my first pair of Camper trainers and my granddad's last ever pair of boots. He was a miner in Scotland, and cared a lot about his footwear. Part of the spirit of a man goes into his boots. So there was sadness as well as rage.

But then, when I returned to the wardrobe, I saw that the Big Bag of Old Shoes was there, where it had always been. I don't know how I'd managed to hallucinate its absence. I suppose that usually, with delusions, you imagine a thing to exist when it doesn't – a tumour, a ghost, a girlfriend, some incipient glory – so there's a certain novelty value in imagining a thing doesn't exist when it does.

Anyway, all this happened before Mrs McG got back from work. I silently apologized for the silent rage, which nobody knew about. And somehow that seemed fitting for the imagined loss of the shoes, although I couldn't tie it together to form a satisfactory paradox, or infinite regress.

Eggy-Bread Rondel

February 1. Had eggy-bread for lunch. Made it too bready, so fried an egg to go with it. The result was too eggy, so I had to make some toast to even it out. Made too much toast, so I was back to square one. This all seemed to sum up everything that's gone wrong in my life. And then for dessert, I found some old panettone, in a Quality Street tin. Does anyone actually like that stuff? If it's bread, it's trying too hard; if it's cake, it's not trying hard enough.

The Ballet-Dangler

February 2. My daughter got taken to the Sadler's Wells *Cinderella* the other day. On her return she asked me why everyone laughed when she referred to a 'ballet-dangler'. I had to explain that it wasn't the real name for a boy ballerina, but just an old McGowan family joke, coined by my dad.

Only later did I start to wonder what the proper word is for a boy ballerina. A ballerino? A ballerinum?

Mohican

February 3. Flicking through Eric Partridge's great *Dictionary of Historical Slang*, I found this: 'Mohican – A very heavy man who rides a long way on an omnibus for sixpence.' Seems odd that you'd need a special word for it… Also, delightful.

But We Both Know the Truth

February 4. When the post drops through the letterbox, Monty gets very excited, running panting to the door, emitting yelps and squeaks. I quite often do it as well, for the amusement of Mrs McG, if she's around. And then there are days like today, when I gallop to the door, panting, woofing, wagging my tail, and I remember that the dog and Mrs McG aren't here, and it's just me. So I feel a little silly, but also endearing, and I smile indulgently at myself. And then the bell rings, and the postman gives me something he's been unable to squeeze through the letterbox. He's heard my scampering dog impression. We don't meet each other's eyes. I look vaguely behind me along the hallway. 'Back, Monty, back!' I say, but we both know the truth.

In Small Things He Was True

February 5. You know how I'm obsessed with having invisible shards of glass in my feet? Well, I just found some glass in my foot. I showed it to Mrs McG – the glass, the foot, the works.

She was sceptical. She went to fetch her spectacles. She grunted her assent.

I have now proved that I have glass in my feet. This also proves that all the other unlikely things I say are true.

Dandelion Clocks

February 6. The other day in Waterstones, I came across a book called *Dandelion Clocks* by Rebecca Westcott. It rang a bell – the title, I mean. It turns out there are a few other books with the same or similar title, but that wasn't what was nagging at me. So I searched on my computer, and found that in 2008 I'd written about five thousand words of a novel (for adults) called *The Dandelion Clock*. I'd completely forgotten about writing it, but I did recall the incident that lay behind it. This was the brief synopsis I made, for my own purposes:

'With the world seemingly at his feet, young writer Michael Cruise Longley commits a terrible faux pas at his publisher's party and loses everything. As things fall apart, he retreats back to the small mining community he hails from. He had been a local celebrity, but is now in disgrace (a drug story in the newspaper). He is comically out of step with the locals, but eventually revives some old friendships. He begins an affair with a local woman. He contemplates a life of happy obscurity, but then commits another terrible faux pas, and has to flee back to the city.'

The pages I've found are quite funny. It begins with the disaster at the party. When I wrote it, there hadn't been any disasters. Perhaps by writing it, I made it come true.

Not sure why I stopped working on it. It's possible I just left it for a couple of days meaning to return to it, and then got distracted. Anyway, it's gone forever.

Mr Stobbs

February 7. Served my first detention for about thirty-five years. Worst thing is it was with scary French teacher Mr Stobbs.

Gabe had been permitted to take his French GCSE a year early, on condition he pull his socks up, homework wise. We (the parents) were supposed to ensure that he did. We didn't, and he hasn't, and so I had the job of going in for the dressing down. It was pretty humiliating. Mr Stobbs was impossibly old and grave. Fishing for an adjective, I thought *Victorian*. He didn't respond well to jokes. We'd let him (that's Mr Stobbs), the school, and ourselves down. There were long pauses. But if I tried to fill them, he would begin speaking again, talking over me. I blew my nose, more for something to do than anything else. But I must have breached some sort of a dam up there, and I had to carry on blowing for longer than I expected, my hanky filling up with runny snot.

'Sorry,' I said, into the hanky.

After one of the longer silences, I realized that Mr Stobbs had gone.

I tried to persuade Gabe to go to the pub afterwards, so I could get my composure back, but he didn't want to – even with the bribe of crisps and a Coke – in case we were seen. Not a great day.

The Author Is Compelled to Find a New Seat at the British Library

February 8. OK, so I've got the very last desk space in the British Library – a special one made for wheelchair users amid the grinding nerds in the Social Sciences reading room. I've never known the damn place so full. Not a seat left in Humanities 1, Humanities 2, or even Rare Books. I didn't even know this part of the library – the Social Sciences wing – existed.

I wonder if all the geographers and economists or whatever the hell they are can tell that I'm an artist just by my flamboyant typing style? I've got my back to the room, so I can't check them out, and for all I know they are pulling demonic faces at me and making lewd gestures.

Actually, on further reflection, I'm quite liking things here in the Social Sciences reading room. The staff are very friendly, and the users perfectly inoffensive. Most importantly, I've finished a chapter. And so I'm thinking that perhaps writing novels is really a social science, rather than an art. After all, I diligently observe human society in all its complexity and richness and then record my findings, helping to show the mechanical workings of that society, its economic underpinning, its gender and class relations. And what happens when a fat kid breaks wind when the teacher bends down. Yes, really I'm working in the tradition of Weber and Durkheim. They should make me a Professor of something, somewhere.

Just noticed that I'm sitting in seat number 00000. I think this means that I'm dead, and experiencing one of those oddly mundane afterlives.

Ah, well, it turns out that by moving vertically within this wing of the library, I went, in fact, from Social Sciences to Science plain and simple, and that's where I've been writing (the giveaway being the book on the shelf before me: *Atlas of Fetal Anomalies*).

But, now I think about it, isn't novel writing more akin to the sciences than either the arts or social sciences? Aren't

I an anatomist of the human heart? When I describe a sky full of stars, am I not a cosmologist? Don't I probe the subtle chemistry of love? The brutal physics of combat? And when I illustrate the digestive consequences of a diet rich in fibre, aren't I… oh shut the fuck up.

Let Go

February 10. I've learned to get by without much in the way of praise or encouragement from Mrs McG. The occasional curt nod after an adequately performed domestic function is all I get or, for that matter, expect. So when, this evening, she said how the comedian Stewart Lee reminded her of me I was pleased. I assumed she meant his darkly brilliant humour, mixing surrealism with trenchant social criticism. Then she added, 'It's the way you've both let yourselves go…'

Chocolatier

February 12. Came in late and could find nothing to eat in the house except some dark cooking chocolate. I loathe dark chocolate (I actually think that no one likes it – they just pretend to because they think it makes them appear sophisticated). So I mashed it up in my mouth with gulps of milk to turn it into home-made milk chocolate. Even as I was doing it, I felt myself to be failing in some fundamental way to be an adult.

The Sadness of Old Toys

February 14. My sister Maggie brought her children down from Yorkshire to stay for the weekend. Patrick and Veronica are still in their Lego years, so it was a good opportunity to pass on our long-neglected, expensively acquired stash. Gabe and Rosie sat with me, as we bagged up ruined fragments of our fallen Lego world, trying to match together the different epochs and empires. We recalled the endless hours spent making huge Star Wars kits, or re-creations of the Indiana Jones movies. We even played a little, assembling some of the tiny Lego people, half constructing an X-wing craft and sending it on a mission to blow up the Temple of Doom (Batman a sad victim of friendly fire).

'It's all right, Dad,' said Gabe. 'We got good play out of it.'

It was only with those words that I realized that my cheeks were wet.

Later on I found a lumpy carrier bag in Gabe's room, filled with a few pieces he'd kept back. A motorcycle; a man; a section of Lego wall.

A Hand Emerges from the Gloom

February 15. I've generally taken the view that when one door slams shut, another door does too; in fact, there's usually a tsunami of doors crashing shut, with a noise like gunfire in the background of a Syrian news report. But the same people who refused to interview me for a job they'd invited me to apply for have now offered me another job, without any kind of interview at all. So, this is a door that has creaked open. But does it lead into a glittering ballroom, full of light and sparkles, or to one of those subcontinental lavatories, where you have to stand amid the shit, while a hand emerges from the gloom to offer you paper, at ten rupees a sheet?

Heel Bar Hell

February 16. I had one of my experiences yesterday. I had to get out of the house, but had nowhere in particular to go, and so wandered around listlessly not sure what to do with myself.

Then I looked down and saw the state of my laces. The shiny acetate sheaths were long gone, leaving the ends to swish around like frayed kelp. Pondering for a moment, I realized that I'd never before purchased any laces, other than those that come with a pair of shoes attached. And then I thought of all my shoes – many with unmatched laces, cannibalized from other, dead or dying shoes. And there were entirely laceless pairs, perfectly wearable, but for the naked, lolling tongues.

Time to revamp my lace armoury.

I recalled that there was a heel bar down by the station, so I thought I'd go and buy a few pairs. Stock up. Never again have to time-share laces. And also help a local small-tradesperson. Plus, it still wasn't safe to return home.

There was a tiny Chinese lady in the shop. She looked a lot like Bloody Mary from the musical *South Pacific*. I asked her for laces.

'What size?' she demanded.

That stumped me. I held my hands apart, suggesting a sort of medium-sized lace.

'No, in centimetre!'

I really had no idea. So I pointed down at my foot. 'This long.'

The lady was too small to see over her counter. Then her phone rang. She put a big box of laces before me, while she took the call.

For the next few minutes there was much confusion, as I kept thinking she was talking to me, when she was speaking to the person on the phone, and vice versa.

I began to feel very claustrophobic in the tiny booth. Then another lady opened the door and entered. I literally had to squeeze into a corner to accommodate her. I imagined more people coming in, like one of those pointless *Guinness Book of Records* things. And I imagined never getting out of the heel bar, spending the rest of my life trying to decide between 100 centimetres brown, and 150 centimetres black.

So I grabbed a random handful of laces, I didn't really care how long or what colour, thrust them at the Chinese lady. They cost £2 a pair, and I had to scrabble in my wallet to get the money together, my elbows clanking against shelves of polish and suede cleaner, like an inept one-man-band, and with the owner and the new lady looking on disapprovingly.

Finally, I was out of there, gasping, the sweat drying coldly on my back. And I decided that buying laces is one of those experiences, like moving house and getting divorced and dying, that are really quite stressful, but beyond that I couldn't make much sense of it.

When I looked at the laces in my hands, I saw that they were mainly blue.

The Experiment

February 17. Mrs McG sprang upon me in the kitchen at lunchtime. I had a bagel in each hand, and so was unable adequately to defend myself. She proceeded to squirt some kind of noxious potion in my eye. I assumed she was then planning to bundle me out of the French window, and down to my death on the pavement, three storeys below, enabling her to cash in my old insurance policy for £2000. However, it transpired that she was conducting an experiment. She wanted, she explained, to see the effects of some anti-wrinkle cream, by applying it to one side of my face.

I could see her rationale – I'm quite a good subject for this, as I have more eye-wrinkles than Mr Miyagi from the original *Karate Kid*, and my recent laser surgery means that they are no longer concealed behind my glasses. Plus, nobody cares what I look like, so there's little to lose if it all goes wrong. So, we'll see shortly if it works – one side of my face may be like W.H. Auden's scrotum, and the other as smooth as old condom-face Cameron.

Becoming Vulpine

February 18. 'I had this dream last night…' – can there be a more dispiriting start to any conversation? Anyway, I had this dream last night. I was living in a bungalow in India. It was night-time, and I was standing by the open door of the bungalow, looking out into the forest. I felt something soft rub past my legs. I looked into the room and saw several beautiful (wolf?) puppies rampaging around. There was also a curiously feral-looking woman, with huge dark eyes and wild hair. She imparted to me the urgency of getting the puppies (I think there were also some feline creatures there as well) out of the house. The more I tried to get them out, the more they fought and squirmed. The woman became more frantic, scratching at me with long, dirty nails. Then I noticed that she was changing, becoming vulpine… That's when I woke up, deeply, to say the least, unnerved. It was 3 a.m., and I didn't really get back to sleep. I don't usually have dreams like this. Normally, I dream of being on the bus without my trousers on.

Les

February 20. Just listened to a very charming old episode of *In the Psychiatrist's Chair*, in which Anthony Clare interviewed the great Les Dawson. Dawson died a week later. I looked up his age – only sixty-two.

'The other day I was gazing up at the night sky, a purple vault fretted with myriad points of light twinkling in wondrous formation, while shooting stars streaked across the heavens, and I thought: I really must repair the roof on this toilet.'

The Many Faces of the Mugger

February 21. I bought myself one of those fitness bands. It tells me how many steps I've failed to take, and records my raised heartbeat whenever I hear something on Radio 4 that annoys me. It's also supposed to record my sleep patterns, but at the moment it seems to believe I'm slumbering all day, and running marathons at night.

The device itself appears at first sight to be a featureless black rubber bracelet, and I'm entertained by the thought that people might think it's an electronic tag, and I'm a potentially dangerous criminal – on remand for urinating in bus shelters, perhaps, or throwing stones at horses, or just doing some recreational mugging.

Thinking about this, I tried out a few mugger faces in the reflection from the Oxfam window. Blank-eyed psychopathic mugger; toothless crystal meth mugger; probably harmless schizophrenic mugger; coolly efficient professional mugger; casual weekend mugger; enraged revenge mugger. But then I realized this was all being observed by a startled shop assistant, and had to turn my final threatening grimace into an apologetic smile.

Hearing Secret Harmonies

February 23. Finding myself curiously charmed by the idea of the lost Mendelssohn song, unheard for 150 years. (They've been going on about it on the radio all morning.) I know they meant the manuscript, but I kept imagining the actual music, still existing in some Platonic sphere, tinkering away, awaiting its moment for rediscovery, like some Arthurian damsel in a tower. It's also quite a pretty song.

The Ur-fiasco

February 24. Shortly heading off for some school events in Llandrindod Wells, smack in the middle of Wales. It looks rather beautiful, in that wet Welsh way. I have to catch a little Ivor the Engine-style train from Shrewsbury, tooting through the hills as angry shepherds, their faces temporarily slackened with release, abuse their sheep, and bards declaim airily at haemorrhoid-coloured skies.

Alas, my own personal involvement with Wales has bordered on the tragic. My 1989 solo cycling expedition to Pembrokeshire was, I think, my ur-fiasco, the origin of all my future woes. Up to that moment – the precise mid-point of my life – you'd have described me as cool, or at least as not uncool. But from then on I was the kind of person who would bring one pair of shorts on a cycling trip, rip them completely in twain on the first day, borrow a gigantic pair from a massively obese American, flee the youth hostel in the middle of the night in order to avoid the intimate repayment of the debt expected by the American in return for the loan, get butted in the testicles by an enraged ram, lose his bike and almost his life over the edge of a cliff, and return home ragged, penniless, and so badly sunburnt that the skin on his ear peeled off in its entirety, retaining its ear-shape, a ghoulish souvenir he would take out to astonish people for many years, until it finally shrivelled away to the size of a small scab, which he fed to his dog.

Radical Faeries

February 25. Was reading the *London Review of Books* over my Cheerios, and came across an article on Kate Bush. It included the line, 'She has a huge gay following (queer pagans, radical faeries).'

This made me wonder if these two groups actually exist, and, if so, how they'd get on. It reminded me of Manchester Uni back in the 1980s, when you were either in the Revolutionary Communist Party (RCP) or the Socialist Workers Party (SWP). Of course there was Militant if you were right wing, or the Labour Party if you were a borderline fascist. Anyway, I was thinking that I'd probably be in the Radical Faery Party (RFP), rather than those sell-outs in the Queer Pagan Party (QPP). So, nail your colours to the mast – what are you, RFP or QPP?

Pasties Are Not for Sharing

February 26. One of the advantages of a long-term relationship is that you can safely offer to share something, in a spontaneous act of generosity, in the sure knowledge, based on your experience of the tastes of your partner, that the offer will be refused, and you can then bask in your enjoyment of both the object and the goodwill generated by your offer. However, even after nineteen years, this can go disastrously wrong. Hence today's 'Oh, yes, I would like half of that cheese and onion pasty' debacle.

The Intimate Massager

February 27. I was forced to take myself out of the flat for political reasons, and found myself sheltering from the tempest under the inadequate awning outside Robert Dyas on the Finchley Road. The window display was largely taken up with ugly and badly made items of kitchen equipment (a mincer, a mixer, a food processor, a giblet masher, a perineum fiddler, etc. etc.) all under the 'Hairy Biker' brand.

I thought this puzzling. I mean, who would actually want a Hairy Biker turkey baster or kebab rod? I've nothing against them, apart from the pathetic straining for eccentricity that is the ultimate mark of the bore, but... Well, if they can become a brand, then who couldn't? The Rolf Harris Babysitting Agency; Boko Haram Internet Dating; Anthony McGowan Sex Toys ('The AM intimate massager is shaped like a question mark, and is guaranteed to leave you vaguely unsatisfied with life, and prone to melancholic speculations about things that don't really matter very much').

I Long to Shred

February 28. Whenever I walk past a Rymans or WH Smith, I'm always drawn to the almost invariably heavily discounted paper shredders in the window. I don't know why this is – I don't really have anything to shred. Or perhaps that's it: I long to be the sort of person with important documents that mustn't be allowed to leak out. And I know that one day my resistance will collapse, and I'll buy one (reduced from £36.99 to £24.99). And when I have this machine, I'll feel obliged to shred things that probably shouldn't be shredded. Birth certificates, passports, contracts for the Taiwanese edition of my early novella, *The Bare Bum Gang Battle the Dogsnatchers*. And when I've shredded those, the iron logic of the shredder means that the shredding will continue, until I'm sitting alone, in an otherwise empty flat, on a giant pile of shredded matter, like a vulture on the bones of an elephant, feeling even then a vague post-coital dissatisfaction, because one thing will have remained unshredded – the shredder itself. No, two things. And so I slip out of my clothes in preparation for the final act of shredding.

SPRING

For Luck

March 1. 'You look sad, Dad,' said Rosie.

'What?'

'Sad. Are you sad?'

'No. Not really. Just had a bit of… I don't know, bad luck lately.'

Rosie went away. She came back a few minutes later.

'Put this on. It'll make it better. It's my lucky necklace. I was wearing it when Monty won his rosette.'

Monty had won the Best Trick category in the Queen's Park dog show. His trick was to 'stay'. Only one other dog was entered. I don't know what its trick was, as I wasn't there. But it can't have been especially impressive.

The necklace was one of those chunky, ethnicky ones, made from irregularly shaped blocks of wood. I'm wearing it now. I look like a 1940s *New Yorker* cartoon of a fat cannibal chief. But I don't mind, so long as it gets the job done.

A Metaphor Concerning Bees

March 2. It seems that most of my life, at the moment, is spent guiding huge bumble bees safely out of the window. And yet I still find dead ones on the carpet, exhausted by their futile efforts against the glass, able to sense freedom but unable either to reach it or to understand the invisible barrier that stands in their way.

The Perineal Tear

March 3. Disastrous morning so far. Going up to York for some interviews, and general media whoring. In my usual mad panic, but things tolerable till I threw my leg over my bike to cycle down to the station. Colossal rending sound as my newish trousers split asunder. No time to change. So, must spend all day in the media spotlight with a hole in the arse of my trousers. The only consolation is that it's what we connoisseurs of the trouser rip know as the 'perineal tear', so it's relatively unobtrusive. Until, that is, it grows… I expect by the end of the day I'll have two trouser legs joined only by willpower and buttock tension. Oh, and I missed my train, so sitting now in the slow stopper, grinding my teeth in despair.

In York, with Fresh Trousers and Old Memories

March 4. An update on yesterday's trouser ignominy. Things did, inevitably, spiral down, trouser-wise. I was sitting there in my sundered pants being interviewed by a nice man from the local York press, and I was thinking I'd got away with it, as the tear was only visible to anyone crawling around on the floor under the table, and the truth is the only person likely to be crawling around under tables at events like this is me. But then, contemplating an answer to a gently underarmed question, I over-vigorously dunked a thin ginger biscuit in my latte. This set up a series of waves in the cup, inexplicably amplified (chaos theory?), and for which I tried to compensate with judiciously counterpoised cup-tilting. But I got things slightly wrong, resulting ultimately, via a faulty feedback loop, in a catastrophic spill of almost the entire cup all over the crotch zone of my trousers. It was pretty appalling, really. The embarrassing thing is that it must have looked exactly as if I'd done it deliberately, perhaps to get attention or sympathy.

I did a couple more interviews in my drenched, stained and scalded condition, then went off and bought some new trousers from Gap, for thirty quid.

I had some free time before my train home, and wandered around. It's pretty, of course, but York doesn't have the same kind of resonance for me that Leeds does. There were a couple of school trips. An occasional date with a girl. But there was just enough to trigger a nostalgia surge.

I sat on a bench in the gardens of the Castle Museum, and thought about the time I'd come there thirty years before, with M. She was my teacher, and we were in the middle of an intense affair. Secret, of course, which is why we'd come to York, where we were not known. We kissed recklessly on the grassy bank below where I now sat. Pregnant bank. Swelling up to rest the violet's reclining head. I must, surely, have recited 'The Ecstasy'. Our eye-beams twisted and did thread our eyes upon one double string. I was studying Donne, and had forced dozens of lines into my head. Like loading bullets into a magazine, ready to be fired out on the day of my exam.

Later we wandered around the Shambles, and she bought me an old copy of Tennyson's *Poetical Works*. It was that kind of affair. I have the book here, now. At the time I thought it was rather fine, with its red leather cover and gilt edging. But now I see it's a cheap Collins edition, and the leather is only embossed card.

And inside the front cover:

To my dearest,
with fondest memories
of the Summer of '81.
Te amo.

A Small Regret

March 5. Just saw one of our greatest living actors, Simon Russell Beale, sitting outside a café here in West Hampstead. My definition of a play is 'a theatrical occurrence that you wish was over forty minutes before the end', but I've never seen Beale in anything without wanting it to go on forever. I nearly went and paid homage, but, well, I suppose a chap has the right to a quiet morning coffee without someone with mad hair and odd shoes (long story) bothering him.

Sex Talk for Authors

March 6. Just got an email from the Society of Authors inviting me to a 'Sex Talk for Authors'. I was intrigued by this, imagining the different forms that it might take – help writing sex scenes, perhaps, or, more literally, a seminar on how to write sexy dialogue. And then I wondered if, rather than 'professional', it might be 'recreational'. I'd go along, and some foxy author would talk mucky to us for an hour. Or maybe give us practical tips on sex talk to help us pick up people in bars, and keep them entertained, during/after a perfunctory coupling in a motel.

Anyway, I was happy to sign up for any of these. Then I saw that it was actually a 'Tax Talk for Authors'.

Watermelon Placement Issues

March 7. So, I bought this watermelon. Huge it is, weighty enough to destabilize my bike so much that I nearly fell under a bus. Anyway, I got it home, and now I don't really know what to do with it. Nobody wants to eat any watermelon at the moment, and I just don't know where to put it. It looks faintly absurd in the fruit bowl, like finding a fat naked man sitting in your sink. And if I leave it on a counter or surface, it'll roll off and kill Monty. I could put it on the floor, but, again, that seems wrong. I mean, how would I explain it if someone came in?

'Why is there a watermelon on the floor?'

'I, er, well, I don't really know… I didn't want it to kill the dog.'

They'll think I'm an idiot. I've a feeling it's going to haunt me forever, always there, mute, massive, accusing. In the end they'll bury me with it, the two of us locked together in the last embrace. I really wish I'd never bought the damn thing.

The Owl of Minerva

March 8. Rosie's going to be a flower girl at my brother's wedding, later in the year. The hairdresser for the day has been in touch asking for 'some ideas'. I've suggested 'the owl of Minerva flies only at dusk' and 'ontogeny recapitulates phylogeny'. Interested to see what she comes up with.

Chips and Curry Sauce

March 9. Today I taught an abysmal session at Royal Holloway, on writing horror. During the course of this I discovered, a little to my surprise, that I have no interesting views whatsoever on this subject. It was a little like finding out, halfway through a hot date with a perfectly attractive woman, that you're gay.

On the way home, I developed a craving for that student stand-by, chips and curry sauce, the dish that had kept me sustained through six years at Manchester University. Very few southern chip shops offer this, so imagine my delight when I found that the self-same chip shop that failed to adequately deliver on the promise of cheesy chips had precisely what I was after.

And they were good, although chips and curry sauce is a hard one to mess up, once you've actually committed to it. So I stood in the rain at Egham station, eating them with the little wooden fork that subtly enhances all chip-shop experiences. I was anxious to finish before my train arrived. No one likes to be trapped in a carriage with a chips and curry sauce eater. But the highly efficient insulating quality of the thick greeny-brown sauce, flecked with the darker raisins suspended in it like fat bluebottles, meant that the chips stayed painfully and ungorgeably hot. I couldn't dump them – hunger and the misery of the unsatisfactory lecture made them more essential to me than my dignity.

The only seat was next to a jabbering, sockless loony, which gave me some comfort. We could keep each other company, in our anti-social behaviour. But then he sniffed, ceased his jabbering, and turned to me. His face wrinkled in disgust at my polystyrene tray of delicious filth, and he gathered his plastic bags full of old newspapers and moved further down the carriage.

When I got home I had a stunned nap, from which I emerged thinking it was tomorrow.

Oh yes, I forgot to mention that when I popped into the office at Royal Holloway, the departmental secretary handed me a shirt and a pair of glasses that I'd left in the disabled toilet last week.

'Yours,' she said, as she passed them over, accomplishing this task without looking at me. She gave me no chance to explain. She probably thought I'd been trying to have sex with the hand dryer.

I'm Hungry All the Time

March 10. Due to my progressive and inexorable engorgement, I've decided to go on the 5:2 diet (the one where you eat as much as you like for five days a week, and fast on two). So far I'm finding it pretty tough. I'm irritable, listless, possessed by a disabling ennui, my skin looks grey and pitted, and I'M HUNGRY ALL THE TIME. It's going to be terrible when I get to one of the fast days.

DIY Gel

March 11. I burnt my hand a couple of days ago trying to teach the children how to play safely with matches. It developed into an impressive blister, which burst this evening on the crowded train from Richmond. A little confused about what I could do with the puddle of clear fluid cupped in my palm, I first rejected the idea of lapping it, the way Tarzan would drink from a pure jungle pool, and then decided to use it to smooth down my unruly hair. Although in one sense this is clearly gross, in another it… no, I can't go on.

Pathétique Symphony

March 12. Wandered aimlessly round town, haunted by lost presences, the places I used to go when I first came to London, back in 1989. Tower Records in Piccadilly; The Bar Pelican on St Martin's Lane; a dive on Swallow Street that I now can't even remember the name of, but where girls carried shot-glasses in bandoliers, like beautiful banditos. I've fallen out with nearly all the friends I had then, my university gang. My fault. If I could go back I'd find a much more enjoyable way to fuck it all up.

Probably a mood thing. As someone said to me recently, 'When it was raining it was the pathetic fallacy; when the sun shone it was irony.'

Life-Art-Life

March 13. Yesterday morning I sliced up a mango for my daughter's breakfast. She declared that it was unripe and sour, and refused to eat it. I was then confronted with what to do with the mango. The options were: just eat it myself in its unripe state; throw it away; do something innovative with the fruit.

Then, almost at the same moment, a thing to do with the mango, and a joke about it, shaped itself in my mind. It took the form of the sentence: 'I made a mango salsa; then I forced a pomegranate to do the foxtrot.'

I was moderately pleased with this joke, though I don't doubt it's been made before. I told it to Mrs McG – not in the way of telling a joke to an audience, but more in the subtly different sense of saying, here's the joke I made, what do you think of it?

She gave a grunt that I took to be of approval.

But then, with the joke exposed, albeit in this half-hearted way, I felt uneasy. There was something inauthentic about the whole process. It had to be validated, turned from the realm of linguistic opportunism into real, lived experience. So I made the salsa. It was quite nice.

Michael Jackson Rides Again

March 14. 'Dad, you can't go out with just one glove on.'

'What?'

I look down. It's true. I'm wearing one glove. It's one of those Thinsulate ones. The woolly outside has fuzzed and frayed, making it look as though I've inserted my hand up the anus of a startled cat.

'I can't find the other one.'

'It looks stupid.'

I think about mentioning Michael Jackson, but I'm not even sure my son knows who he is. The world has moved on. And, besides, it would hardly count as a justification.

'I don't care,' I said, defensively. 'At least I'll have one warm hand.'

'You just can't. No one wears one glove.'

'I'll keep the bare hand in my pocket as I cycle along. Happy?'

'No. You'll fall off, again.'

Outside I took the glove off, furtively, making me feel a failure in at least four different ways.

Or Possibly Laos

March 15. I've always liked the sound of the great book fairs that punctuate the publishing year, held at Bologna, Frankfurt and London. Writer friends have told me that they are, in fact, stupendously boring, unless you happen to be one of the 'buzzy' authors, who travel around with an entourage, in a whirl of camera flashes and popping champagne corks. I'm not one of those. But I thought I'd have a poke around the London fair, just to see. And perhaps it would be a Wonka World of magic and splendour, with rides and acrobats and elephants, all made of books. And I thought there would at least be some pretty PR types, from the half dozen publishers I've had over the years, and they'd be nice to me, and perhaps invite me to one of the famous after-parties.

So I arrived at Kensington Olympia, with just the right amount of expectation. A tingle rather than a throb. Sure, it probably wouldn't be amazing but… it might!

I'd printed out my pass at home. There was something wrong with it, and I couldn't get through the barriers. Rather than faff about waiting for it to be cleared, I picked up a large cardboard box and walked in with it, adopting the traditional workman's limp.

I wandered around in the vast hangar for an hour, rather bewildered. Pigeons had got inside, and fluttered heartbreakingly in the rafters. There were stalls set up, but many of them were supplying utterly mysterious goods and services that had an at best tangential relationship to books. Men in suits and women in clickitty heels hurried by. A Middle Eastern gentleman stood to attention in dark glasses and a colonel's uniform, fringes of braid like golden birdshit on his shoulders. I'm sure there was an Angolan delegation selling cashew nuts. Or at least their stand was adorned with plastic foliage, and posters showing smiling cashew-shellers.

An announcement came over the Tannoy, pressing people to go to the session on religious publishing in South East Asia. I resisted the temptation. I walked past glass-walled side rooms with people attending smaller seminars. Flip charts. PowerPoint. The anxiety in the eyes of the salesman.

There was a café, and I saw a couple of people I half recognized, but they were in the midst of Important Doings, and so didn't have much time for me. My translator friend Danny rushed through. He was going to be speaking about Brazilian literature, if I was free…?

It was time to go. I tried to snaffle some complimentary stuff, but all I got was a bottle of water and some leaflets about the Bible in Vietnam. Or possibly Laos.

Nobody invited me to an after-party.

I wandered out again, not understanding anything that had transpired within. On the way I picked up the box I'd put down, and left it in the lobby for the next person with flawed documentation.

The Sports Hairbrush

March 16. I'm in Exeter to visit some schools. Exeter seems like a very fine city to me. I never managed to find the seaside, but they have a perfectly adequate, if somewhat squat, cathedral, as if constructed on some distant Earth colony, on a planet with much greater gravity. Nice pubs. Friendly locals, too. But then I did have a hairbrush-related fiasco to drag me down…

When I set off this morning I deliberately didn't bring a hairbrush with me. I've never actually owned a hairbrush, relying on the tonsorial generosity of parents, siblings, girlfriends, spouses, etc. to supply, by their excess, my want of hair-brushing paraphernalia. And I knew I'd have a couple of hours to kill in Exeter, and thought I could use them up by buying a hairbrush.

Anyway, when I got here, time was running out, and I couldn't locate an obvious hairbrush shop. I found myself outside Sports Direct. So I went in and asked a bemused-looking assistant if they sold hairbrushes. The second it was out of my mouth I realized the folly of this question, but there it was, out in the open.

'What do you mean?' asked the assistant.

I did a brief mime of someone brushing their hair. I couldn't stop myself. I saw the assistant look over my shoulder. He thought this was some sort of practical joke.

Then I said, 'Like a, er, *sports* hairbrush.'

I suppose I was thinking that there might be an Adidas hairbrush, or a Puma, or a Slazenger… I don't know. I'd had a long journey, and I wasn't thinking clearly. 'It doesn't matter,' I said. 'Just forget it.'

Then I walked away. After that I looked in Tesco. They didn't have any hairbrushes, as far as I could tell. I nearly bought a washing-up brush, which I think would have worked, but then thought, what if they have cameras in the room (I've long feared this), and someone – a young local girl, perhaps – sees me brushing my hair with a washing-up brush, and then that same person serves me my full English in the morning? It'd be too terrible for both of us.

In the end I found a 99p hairbrush in Poundland. It's not been sports tested, but I think it would stand up under match conditions. The gauge is a touch narrow for me: it uses the Napoleonic four-centimetre standard, whereas I prefer the old Imperial three-inch measure. But it has a cushioned bed, and an adequate tine density. All in all, I'm satisfied.

Hard Labour

March 17. Well, that was a tough day. I woke up at five, which always happens when I'm in a strange bed without my special pillows. Picked up at quarter past eight for an event at a school. Some chat from me, then ten presentations from various schools, all of which I had to stay alert for, as I had to summarize/praise them all. Then another turn from me, and a Q&A. 'Sir, if you were a tumour, what sort of tumour would you be?' etc. Then a half hour break for lunch, followed by a 'creative' session with forty Year 8s and 9s lasting from 1.40 to 4.30. I'm not a bad talker, when I get going, but three hours of it nearly killed me and left them looking like the film I'd seen recently of a new global warming-related oceanographical blight called coral bleach.

More of the same tomorrow and the day after. I know it's not like a real job but, still, I feel like I've had all the juice sucked out of me, and not in a good way.

Egret En Croûte

March 18. I'm at The Mill on the Ex, sitting in the garden, looking out over the river. There's a snowy egret picking its way through the shallows, somewhat disdainfully. Seeing its elegance here is like bumping into a supermodel at a Tesco Metro. Unlike the egret, I passively await my food. I've ordered either *mackerel en suite* or a *bathroom en croûte*. Only time will tell which.

Before dinner I strolled around town some more, and I came across the Royal Albert Memorial Museum. This is now, officially, my favourite museum. Excellent local history, but also brilliant ethnographic matter (obscene Polynesian war clubs, Eskimo walrus ivory harpoons, etc.), poignant stuffed animals, ichthyosaurs, a display case of Neanderthal hand axes, a room full of erotic objects from around the world (huge phalluses, Ancient Chinese porn, rude Peruvian vases…). And then at the end, in case the Meso-American anal-sex figurines have got you worked up, a poster displaying a stern injunction against masturbation. Everything you'd want, really, and compact enough to get round in an afternoon. Worth the trip to Exeter all by itself.

Lord Jizzmond

March 19. My dad gave me an old jumper of his last year. It was hand-carved on one of those dour and dismal Scotch islands – Mal, or Muck, or Bumm – the Protestant ones, where old men shake their sticks at you and sexually abuse puffins in the long winter nights (i.e. from September to June). The sort of place where Mrs McG's ancestors bayonetted most of the locals, so they could bring in the sheep that would eventually provide the raw material for this knitwear atrocity.

It truly is a hateful garment. It makes me look like I've been badly modelled in cold mashed potato. The torso section is massy and shapeless, yet the arms curiously mean and attenuated. It's almost impossible to move sensibly in this jumper; it has both great inertia and irresistible momentum – getting going, stopping, changing direction – all require a titanic act of will.

I just walked Monty wearing this clumsy glacier, and I suspect the sight was rendered comic, given that Monty looked like he was wearing a miniature version of the same jumper, i.e. his usual scruffy white pelt. Two lady joggers sniggered. Some children threw stones.

And then, as I turned for home, who should I see but Heimlich, my dwarf doppelgänger.

In truth, I'd become a little worried about him. He never looked well, and one understands that dwarfism brings with it complex health issues. And then there were his pursuers, with their dogs and whips... And of course I wondered what my fate would be, if anything terminal happened to Heimlich. The connection between a man and his dwarf doppelgänger is an intimate one...

So it was with some relief that I saw him hurtling towards me along the Finchley Road. And then for a moment I felt another surge of weirdness – that feeling called by Freud, paradoxically, 'unheimlich'. You see, he was wearing a similar jumper to mine, in the same shade of dirty white, mottled with brown, like a meth-head's teeth, and it was as shapeless and intractable as the one I was wearing.

And now I thought that my chance had come – that I could use the similarity of our awful jumpers as an excuse to stop him and engage him in discourse and so discover if we were truly the same person. Or at least to check in case he had the other half of this amulet…

But as he drew closer I saw that it was an off-white hoodie, rather than a giant, cable-knit prepuce, like mine, and so, rather than smiling at him, or holding out my amulet, I looked away, vaguely ashamed.

The worst thing is that in all the excitement of the dwarf, Monty failed to do his business, and so I'll have to take him out again later.

Needless to say, the family still don't believe in Heimlich.

'Why would a dwarf wear a hoodie?' asked my daughter, as if that was some kind of knock-down argument.

'There are no laws about what dwarves can wear,' I replied. 'Not in this kingdom.'

It was as if I'd blundered in from a different sort of book. I am Lord Jizzmond, Defender of the Small Folk. My weapons are the axe and the skipping rope.

Chicken Pie Meltdown

March 20. Fucking dinner party, will you do the cooking darling, chicken fucking pie, four burners going, deboning fucking chicken, whole bunch of bloody celery, just how many fucking leeks has she bought, Jamie fucking Oliver, well fuck him, I'm going off-piste, Campbell's soup for the stuff in the chicken pie that's not chicken, too early to get drunk, not even time to have a shower before going to a film-world meeting in sweat-stained rags, no thyme/time, or what's this in the freezer? Could be thyme, could be chopped-up gangrenous ear, pastry, pastry, if I had a gun now I'd execute this fucking pie, mafia style, two to the head, one to the heart, send them a message they'll understand.

How to Scorch Off Your Own Pubes

March 21. Tonight I fell off my 5:2 diet into a lake of leftover Prosecco. It means that now it – the diet – is looking like the score from when my old school football team in Leeds used to play the Southern Softies: 11–1. Or possibly, 15–nil. And Prosecco is such a terrible drink. I don't know how or why it's become the thing to serve before every dinner party. It tastes like the sort of aftershave you'd win in a school-fete tombola, diluted with Tesco diet lemonade. It'd be more humane just to stab your guests in the throat with a broken bottle of Hai Karate or Denim. I much prefer good old Cava. It may produce an acid belch that, if directed downwards, could scorch off your own pubes, but at least it doesn't taste like something you'd serve at a dolls' tea party. Anyway. Anyway.

I Interfere with Dolphins

March 22. My bad luck with jumpers continues. I've only got one OK jumper – a black cashmere bought in the M&S sale last year for twenty-nine quid. Well, it's vanished. Either the moths have eaten it down to nothing, or it's at the bottom of the laundry basket, and I'm not going in there, not for any money. So my choice for cycling to the British Library was stark: wear the huge mashed potato thing, sculpted by mental patients on the Hebridean island of Bumm; or the black polo neck, bought for me fifteen years ago by Mrs McG, in the vague hope that I might bring her some chocolates (which I don't suppose means anything to anyone under forty...).

Obviously, I couldn't go the potato route. And I've always regarded wearing a black polo neck as tantamount to saying to people, 'Oh, hello, nice to meet you, I'm a pervert.'

'What sort of pervert?'

'Oh, you know, I interfere with dolphins, mainly. The odd porpoise. Pilot whale, if I can get one.'

Plus, every Yorkshireman has a dark fear that, having been tricked into wearing a polo neck, he'll find himself eating a curry (the hottest on the menu, of course, Yorkshire bullshit machismo being what it is) in an airless room, and dying a horrible, red-faced, sweaty death. So I took the third option, and cycled jumperless through the chilly streets.

Capricciosa, Il Mio Amore

March 23. I go down to my locker in the British Library basement, to recover my lunchtime sandwich. I'm number 351. At 352 there's one of those beautiful raven-haired Italian PhD students named, I expect, after a classy pizza – Fiorentina, Marinara, Capricciosa (though probably not Meat Feast).

A brief look passes between us, and with it comes the knowledge that something extraordinary could happen were it not for the fact that, on my part, I'm happily married to the lovely Mrs McG, a woman with an almost infinite capacity for revenge, and on hers that she doesn't want to.

Then I open my locker, and out flows a deafening miasmic stench, as if a hyena had shat in there.

It's my cheese sandwich – some noxious French stuff, soft as bronchitic mucus, left over from our dinner party on Friday.

Capricciosa's face wrinkles in disgust. I think about trying to explain the sandwich, the cheese, the dinner party, but she's already reeled away. She's probably assumed that I store my soiled underpants in the locker.

I lunch alone in the desolate sunshine of the courtyard, even the pigeons shunning my crumbs.

Another Sandwich Fiasco

March 25. On my exotic travels again, I found myself sitting on a bench in the middle of Coventry eating a foot-long Subway sandwich. I'd never had one before, and I was interested to explore this part of our culture. At the start of the, er, process I had a large, loose sticking plaster on my thumb. By the time I'd finished the sub, I noticed that the plaster had gone. It took me a second or two to realize that I'd eaten my own plaster, incorporated, somehow, into the sandwich. I found this distressing. Usually, when I'm on one of my downward swings, I look for some marker that indicates that I've reached the lowest point. Truly, I hope that this is it.

Not a Natural Anthony

March 26. The lady next to me in the British Library is reading a book that at first I thought was titled *Entering Women*, which afforded me some amusement, until I realized it was actually called *Centering Women* – a worthy goal, doubtless, but not quite the thing to keep me awake on a somnolent library day.

But now I've just noticed the name of the author – Hilary McD Beckles. I wonder how you're supposed to pronounce it? McDbeckles? Or is the McD short for something? Or an acronym? I can't settle down until I find out. Plus, why don't people just have normal names any more?

(A voice from my childhood has just come back to me – I think it might have been my old dinner lady/playground assistant, Mrs Walsh – saying 'He's not really a natural Anthony, is he, bless him.')

Chips, with Uranium

March 27. Great – the Marlborough Mansions communal hedges haven't been strimmed for nearly a week, so they're giving them a good old go now, with the volume turned up to eleven. You'd think they know that I have a shitload of work to do, plus a hangover. I'm off to the park to sit hunched over on a bench, a bag of chips leaking grease and vinegar onto my lap, with a heart as heavy as depleted uranium.

Three Annoying Things

March 28. 1. There's something stuck between two of my back teeth. I flossed for hours, but it's still there. I can't see it, or really feel it, but I know it's there, it really is. And I've got a feeling that it's conscious and... changing.

2. I've had some new photos done to replace the absurd one that's on the internet, and which makes anyone who books me on the basis that I might look like it weep or guffaw. The new photos are excellent, except for the fact that they look like me. Or at least a Dorian Gray-like portrait of my soul. So there, staring out with filmy eyes is a narrow-lipped, dissolute, shabby roué, on the lookout for a countess to fleece.

3. Nobody liked the pan-fried mackerel I made the family for dinner. They didn't like it because it wasn't very nice. And there, glistening unwanted in the pan, grey stripes on paler

grey, exuding a vague aroma of failure and helplessness, it looked even more like me than the photos.

Let Me Give You My Card…

March 29. You know how charity begging letters now often come with a printed sheet of sticky labels with your name on them, to be used, presumably, as a return address thingy when you post a parcel? Well, I'm wondering if it would look cheap if I stuck them on bits of cut-out cardboard (cereal boxes, etc.), and used them as business cards. (At the moment I have sheets of these things from PETA, The Macular Society, Cancer Research, The Smile Train and The Distressed Perineum Fund. Just throwing them away seems a terrible waste.)

Piss from a Stone

April 1. 5.15 this morning found me wandering the (near) deserted streets of West Hampstead in my pyjamas, attending to the gastric emergencies of an unwell dog. No chance of getting to sleep after that, so I did three hours on my novel, which was like trying to squeeze piss out of a stone – managed half a page (of piss). Then stumbled across pictures of Palestinian toddlers with lumps blown out of them by Israeli missiles, which helped to get things in proportion, if not exactly to lighten my mood.

Croissants and Oranges

April 4. Walking Monty this morning, I was tempted by the offer of a coffee and croissant, for £2.20, at my local non-chain café. Unexpectedly, the sun was glinting on the wet streets, so I sat outside, and immediately felt part of the community. West

Hampstead has lots of residences for people with psychiatric problems, and the seats outside the café were full of the usual jabberers, ranters, mumblers, and others silently spinning around their own private anguish. Sockless, in my pyjama top, worn under my unattractive anorak (or Ragnarök, as I've started to call it), I felt quite at home.

Anyway, the croissant duly arrived. It was OK – the typical British croissant, assembled from flakes of psoriasis, held together with lard, and inflated with some kind of methane-like gas. But the taste of it took me back, in clichéd Proustian-style, to Liverpool in 1987. I had a Scouse girlfriend, then – and as everyone knows, Scousers make the best girlfriends. Her mum lived in a terraced house in a poor part of town. But just along the way there was a bakery, run by a Frenchman and his wife. He made croissants like none I've ever tasted – denser, less flaky, more cakelike, and yet still delicate, and evanescent on the tongue. You wouldn't dream of adulterating it with jam or anything else. I always wondered how a croissant maker of such genius ended up in that tough part of Liverpool. I should probably have asked him. I expect he's dead now, and only a few oldtimers even remember the glory of his croissants.

I was thinking about the croissant, and that ex-girlfriend, when the man at the next table took out a big bag of oranges and peeled one. He tore it open with his big, grimy hands, and offered me half. I said I had to get going. But as I left I was hit by a surge of self-hatred. I should have taken the orange. But now it was too late.

The Uses and Abuses of Clingfilm

April 5. Things you find yourself saying: 'You people, you don't understand clingfilm; you don't respect it. You shouldn't be allowed to use it.'

I Am Umbilico, Volcano Lord of Fiji

April 6. I have to produce a short biography. As usual, the problems of striking the right tone when writing about oneself loom large. One has to pick a path in between insincere-sounding self-loathing and insane egomania ('I'm useless and evil: you should hate me' / 'I'm the greatest living writer: you should worship me like a god, as the winged serpent, Quetzalcoatl, or as Umbilico, Volcano Lord of Fiji'), not to mention the major issue of trying to choose some photos that a) do actually look like me, without b) making me look old enough to remember the invention of the bicycle.

And all this with the kids on the rampage about the house, and Mrs McG giving me the evils for not doing the things I'm supposed to do, and doing the things I'm not supposed to.

I have dozens of these things – the short biogs, I mean. Paragraphs produced over the years for websites or festivals or for journalists. They all seem fine at the time, but very soon become deeply embarrassing. And it's not even that they are embarrassing in the same way. One will be strident and stentorian, like an Ulster Unionist bellowing in your ear and spraying you with noxious yellow spittle. Others are timid and fawning. Others eager and puppyish. Each one could, with the exception of the books published, be for a completely different person. Of course none gets at the essence of me. For that, rather than words you'd need a picture of a void, shrugging.

The Shite-Hawk

April 7. Not really enjoying *H is for Hawk*, Helen Macdonald's story of training a goshawk, mixed up with a bit of lit-chat about T.H. White. The writing is incredibly laboured and mannered, as if she's said, 'OK, I'm known for my wonderfully poetical prose, so I'd better not let anyone down.' So a forest is 'washed pewter with frost' – which seems wrong visually as well as conceptually muddled; and 'ankled' is used as a verb to describe the way a deer moves. Why? It forces you to try to imagine what it might be like to walk on your ankles, perhaps because you've had your feet amputated by the Taliban, and in that moment, the deer escapes. It's the awkward detail that takes you not closer, but further away, like a curious wart on the nose of a Sistine Chapel tour guide.

Almost every phrase smacks of an hour of pencil chewing. I suppose the aim is to make the world seem new and fresh, but the effect is the opposite: everything is either dry and dead; or unpleasantly moistened, like the boiled sweets offered to you by an elderly aunt, with that unsettling knowledge that she's already had a good old suck on them.

The trouble is that the modern vogue for nature writing has attracted purple prose stylists, who think at last they'll get their chance to unleash those sunsets and thunderstorms on a hitherto unwelcoming world. As ever, the test is humour. There isn't any.

It's also made me think of how, as kids in Leeds, we'd use 'shite-hawk' as an insult. A shite-hawk was the British name for the black kites circling over rubbish dumps in India, but I've a funny feeling it may go back further, to when kites were scavenging in the streets of Elizabethan England. And I like the thought of that – our urchin insults reaching back to ring in Shakespearean lugs.

I Use a Few Drops of Bile to Bring Out My Natural Sweetness

April 8. I know, what with the barbaric massacres around the world and tidal waves and earthquakes, one shouldn't complain about trivialities, but I'm really annoyed about people talking about 'bringing out the natural sweetness' of things that aren't, in reality, sweet at all. Rhubarb. Onions. Potatoes. Turnips. Hydrochloric acid, and so on. I'm just waiting until a TV chef says, 'A few sprinkles of sugar bring out the natural sweetness of the salt.' And I've detected the first signs of the reverse of this: 'a splash of wine vinegar brings out the natural tartness of the honey'. There's only so much a person can take…

Bum Silo

April 10. I was surprised, yesterday, to receive a remittance advice, stating that I'd been paid a reasonably large sum by a company called Babcock International. I had no idea what this might pertain to, so I had a quick Google, and found out that Babcock are the forty-second largest defence contractor in the world. I wondered briefly if the money might relate to the new type of tank I designed when I was nine, which had two gun turrets, and tracks along all four sides to aid manoeuvrability; or that maybe I'd done some freelance espionage, and then forgotten about it; or that it was because I'd agreed to be cyborgally transformed into the Super-soldier of the Future, with rockets firing out of my anus, an impermeable Kevlar exoskeleton, etc. But then I had a look through my old emails, and found that Babcock also manage the school library service in Devon. Which, in its way, is odder than me firing missiles out of my anus.

Bored of the Rings

April 12. Went to Camden market this morning to buy a new wedding ring – my third in the past two years. The trouble is that a) wedding rings are the sort of objects that are very easy to misplace, and b) I'm very good at losing things, creating scientifically perfect conditions for the denuding of my finger. If this one goes the way of the others, I may have to resort to some kind of Prince Albert type arrangement, or perhaps a set of those neck rings sported by certain Burmese tribal people.

Mrs McG, of course, thinks I deliberately lose them because I don't want to be married. But by that logic the fact I keep mislaying my wallet means I don't want to be rich.

And now I think about it, it's probably another example of projection.

He Limps Away

April 13. Like most authors, I spend a lot of my leisure time going around bookshops turning the few copies of my works I find there so that they face outwards onto the indifferent world. It's the nearest I get to a marketing campaign. And of course I've given up even vaguely hoping that I might make it on to one of the tables from which people actually choose books. We have a rather wonderful indie bookshop here in West Hampstead, but it's a bit small for me to get away with the book-rotating thing and, anyway, they know who I am. (In fact, I suspect that they retrieve my books hurriedly out of deep storage whenever they see me stumping towards them along the street, and return them thence once I've passed safely by.) So I usually target the Waterstones in the O_2 Centre on the Finchley Road, or the posher one up in Hampstead for my activities.

Anyway, the other day at the Hampstead branch, I took things a stage further. I saw that my teenage books were on the bottom shelf, where only someone crawling on the floor, as if under barbed wire, might spy them. So I thought I'd rearrange things, swapping my books with those on the top shelf, which turned out to be by Sophie McKenzie. I took three or four minutes to achieve this, making it all look trim and neat. Then, surveying my work, I had a pang of guilt. I've met Sophie and she is one of those awfully nice people; no, more than nice, good, as well as being an excellent writer.

So, with some reluctance, I swapped them all back again.

Then I felt that prickling sensation on the back of my neck. I turned around to see a black-clad sales assistant eyeing me suspiciously. I made some kind of incomprehensible mumbling noise by way of explanation, and then moved away. After a couple of steps I started to limp. Not sure why I did this, but it may have been some form of disguise, or perhaps to signal that I wasn't quite right in the head.

Anyway, I'm assuming that there's a six-month staff-turnover, so it should be safe to return in October.

Knickers

April 14. Mrs McG gave me strict and detailed instructions about the kind of knickers I was supposed to buy from the M&S in Brent Cross. It was a double-strike mission, as I also had to find my daughter a swimming costume. As well as the written instructions as to number, colour, size, etc., Mrs McG also gave me a (clean) pair of the target knickers, to act as a template, or perhaps like one of those Dulux colour charts. She went off to do something unfathomable, while I was left with Rosie, in the harsh light of Brent Cross. We're going on holiday tomorrow, so I was dressed in my otherwise unwearable, semi-disposable clothes – a sweatshirt from 1996, smudged and grimed and graffitied by age and chilli sauce, and a pair of trousers that looked like they'd been shot out of a cannon, during the final stages of a siege when all other ammunition has been exhausted.

Anyway, as I knew it must, there came a time when I was wandering around the M&S underwear department, holding up the old knickers to various potential matches, trying to work out if they were the same. It was strangely difficult – like comparing different recordings of a Bach cantata, especially if you don't really know what a cantata is.

Perhaps in my paranoid and nervous state I imagined the stares, the suspicion, the outrage, from the other shoppers – who knows?

Rosie was no use – she wouldn't permit herself to be associated with the mission, but hung back and pretended to be part of various other families (ringleted Orthodox Jews, fully veiled Muslims, an Apache war party, and so forth).

Finally, assistance was sought, and (reluctantly, I perceived) given. A plump Asian woman, who pursed her lips disapprovingly. And now I'd found what I was looking for, I was taken over by a force way too powerful for me to control. I took the knickers – the new ones, still attached – no, crucified – to the small plastic hanger, like some blood sacrifice – and slowly brought them towards my pelvic area, as if checking them for size and cut. And then a small wiggle.

I suppose I may have intended this as a sort of attempt at humour, but there was no comic brio in the performance, just a kind of doleful perseverance. The assistant cracked no smile, but took the pants, firmly, back from me, and hung them up.

I wandered away, and found Rosie (she'd insinuated herself into a group of Tongans). I told her I'd buy her whatever she wanted if she went and got the knickers for me. She did it, and I hurried off to pay on a different floor.

When I met up with Mrs McG half an hour later, it transpired that I hadn't bought the right number of knickers, so she went back to stock up, rendering all I'd been through utterly futile.

I slumped on a bench outside the Apple Store, inert until it was time to get the bus home.

The Pipes Are Calling

April 17. Bought a new washing machine – the catchily named JLWM1200 from John Lewis, delivered to us on Tuesday. Actually, now I think about it, washing machines seem always to be given meaningless strings of letters and numbers, rather than sexy names. I wonder why. Wouldn't surely the Electrolux Knicker Glide or the Bosch Sudmeister sell better than the R27498FX/2 or PPP474/H?

What I particularly liked about this model is that it was the cheapest one they had.

And I can now confirm that it does, actually, clean your clothes rather well – you could eat your dinner off my underpants.

There's only one small worm in my cherry. When I was trying to fix the old machine, I got it into my head that there might be some sort of blockage in the pipe into which you plug the concertinaed hose thingy at the back of the machine, to carry away the dirty water: that touching human soup of life's exudations, secretions, accidents.

Anyway, the bit of bamboo that I used to poke about in the pipe broke in half and fell into the hole. And then some more bamboo that I used to try to fish out the first bit of bamboo also fell in the pipe.

Despite trying for an hour, I couldn't get them out, partly because I'm not bendy enough to get into the right position, and partly because it's just really hard to get sticks out of pipes in difficult to reach corners of your utility cupboard.

The John Lewis men came round to install the new machine, and I meant to tell them about the bamboo, but I just couldn't do it. I knew they'd think less of me. I'd become, in their eyes, not a fellow horny-handed toiler, practical, and cool under pressure, but the sort of person who lost bits of bamboo in the plumbing.

And so they're still there, those two lengths of bamboo. And I think about them all the time. They come to me in the night, like Banquo's ghost, or Hamlet's dad, or Lucy Westenra, imploring, yearning, fatal. And I'll never be free of them.

The Escalator Down

April 20. At the British Library there's a short, pointless escalator down from Humanities 1 to a sort of mezzanine, where they have exhibitions. I say pointless, but I suppose it's of some use if you have mobility issues, or are bone idle, or have a sense of entitlement ('… and they just expected me to walk down those stairs. Me!').

Anyway, this escalator always causes me problems. I pause at the top of it, and think, how can I ride down on that, when there are normal steps right next to it? How lazy, how foolish, how unhealthy, what a waste of electricity. And so I'll move to the stairs. And then I think, well, the escalator is running all the time, and me walking down the stairs won't change that. And then, well, that escalator has used up a certain amount of the Earth's precious resources. Not much, maybe – only a puffin's worth, say, or a hedgehog – but that's still something. And if I walk down the stairs, then that puffin has died for nothing. OK, perhaps a puffin puts it too high – maybe just a woodlouse or a moth. But I hate stuff going to waste. And so I'll move back to the escalator, for the sake of the moth. And then, about halfway down, I'll remember that there's a compromise – that I could ride and walk at the same time, and so I take one step, and because the escalator is so short and pointless, it's a step that takes me on to the mezzanine level with a vaguely unpleasant jolt. Sometimes the closer you look at things, the harder they get to understand.

There Should Be More Felt

April 22. I sprang up at six this morning, meaning to start the week off in an efficient and businesslike manner. But no sooner had I swept yesterday's desk-filth onto the floor, and settled down with my mug of tea, than a series of huge random crashes began to resound, accompanied by a grim metallic grinding, with any remaining aural space taken up by the steady background rumble of a diesel engine. Yes, it was skip-lorry time. Is anything more hateful to the writer than the sound of a skip being emptied? I am filled with inchoate rage and despair. And now it's been going on for HOURS.

There should be a new rule saying that skip lorries (and skips) have to be made out of felt. And now I think about it, wasn't it the case that more things used to be made out of felt, in former times? Hats and, er, trousers, perhaps. Or am I just getting it mixed up with the world of Fuzzy Felt, in which *everything* was made out of felt – trees, dinosaurs, the sky…? And if that infinite parallel universes thing is right, then there must be a universe in which everything truly is made of felt. I could get some work done there. But, in any case, there should be more felt.

The Many Laminated Signs

April 23. I quite like working in the Swiss Cottage public library. It definitely has a buzz – it's full of 'revising' schoolkids, chattering and flirting, fat chemistry text books open and ignored before them. And the old folks who've popped in for a potter (or a Potter). Nannies parking their pushchairs while they gossip. An angry solitary eccentric, researching an ancient, private grievance in the legal section. A vagrant reading the *Financial Times*, every word on every page. Even a middle-aged writer or two, getting himself out of the house, nursing a latte in the café, as there's nowhere else to sit in the whole building, a little nervous lest the forbidding Eastern European lady in charge observes and then confiscates his yogurt-coated peanuts and raisins, illicitly bought off the premises in contravention of the regulations set out on the many laminated signs.

Quern

April 24. I venture out at the crack of dawn tomorrow on my first visit to Vienna, where I'll be doing my thing at a couple of swanky 'international' schools. Looking forward to immersing myself in the full Austrian cultural experience – the Walls' Viennetta, the Mr Kipling Viennese Whirl, er, Wittgenstein, etc. etc.

I've always liked the idea of Wittgenstein designing a house in Vienna for his sister – the classic, rarefied intellectual engaging with the material world, having to concoct window catches and doorbells, as he did. Many years ago, I worked for the Manchester University Archaeological Unit, taking various exhibits out to junior schools, to show them what archaeologists 'do'. Stone Age axes, made out of resin; quern stones, made out of resin; a medieval hat, made out of resin, that sort of thing. The touring schedule had plenty of gaps, so I initiated a side project to help pass the time. My plan was to build a model of a dig, showing the various layers of historical evidence as you went deeper into the earth. I taught myself carpentry to build the frame, invented new chemical compounds to stand in for the soily matter of the dig, used industrial levels of PVA glue to bind it all together. It took me eight months. It was tremendously hard, and profoundly satisfying. I'd turned myself into a different sort of a person: a craftsman, leaving his material imprint on the tough matter of the world. It even looked a bit like an actual dig. People came from across the university to look at it in my basement workshop.

Eventually it was ready, and it was time to load it into the van to take it on the first school visit. It took four of us to lift the monster. It didn't fit through the doorway. It didn't fit through the window. Shortly after, I left the Unit, destined for London. It's still there now, I imagine, in that basement, a thing of curiosity and wonder to anyone who comes across it.

And now I think about it, it was probably the first of my great failures, the first time I'd tried something challenging, something noble and good, and utterly fucked it up. Perhaps if I'd measured the damn doorway, my life might have been different…

Ah, and now I check the agenda, it seems I have twelve events over three days in Vienna. And being the second sweatiest man in children's publishing, I'll need a clean shirt for each event. That's twelve shirts, plus whatever I require for the evening revelries (waltzing and other typical Viennese delights).

I don't think I have twelve shirts, not without delving into the novelty section of my wardrobe. I suppose I might be able to find enough, and organize it like some kind of cull. No, like Amundsen's assault on the Pole – the way, I mean, he ate his dogs as he went along, in that most un-English fashion. So I could wear a shirt (perhaps one from my old bullfighting outfit, or one from my short-lived and ill-conceived line-dancing phase), and then discard it, gaily. There may be some Austrian down-and-outs who'd appreciate a purple nylon dress shirt, or one of my old kaftans. Yes, it seems we have a plan.

Broccoli and Bestiality

April 25. At Heathrow, and nothing too bad has happened yet, apart from a mildly disappointing muffin. But then life's most fundamental message is that everything is mildly disappointing. Except sushi. It's odd – if the eighteen-year-old me had been given a dossier about the old me, the me now, I don't think anything much would have surprised him. Some things would have pleased him (writing for a living, marrying someone quite hot, two healthy children, not being bald); some things would have saddened him (the fact I've spent my life splashing about in the shallows, never quite making it out onto the open ocean; the way nobody really fancies me any more; being largely unrecognized outside of a tiny group of specialist librarians). Anything much, that is, except for my liking for sushi. Being from the North, I like my food not only cooked, but burnt. Not really sure how the raw fish thing happened. But it gives one a little hope that you can grow. In another thirty years I might have developed a taste for broccoli, or bestiality.

The Pants, the iPad, the Lavatory Pan, the Pee

April 26. Three authors are abroad, visiting an international school, in a beautiful old European capital. Their hotel is out of the historic centre, and a little short on character, but perfectly pleasant. Everything that needs to work works, and the bar is cheap. Two of the authors visit the third in his room, before the three of them set out for a night of competitive anecdotage. Their intention is to chivvy him along a little, but they also have that urge to make sure he hasn't been given a slightly better room than theirs.

He opens the door to them, shirtless, and dank from the bathtub, but decently draped below the waist. There's no awkwardness: the authors have bonded on the trip. One of them offers up, for the second time, the observation that the German word for nipple translates as 'breast wart'.

And then one of the authors, conscious of the attentions of a temperamental prostate, asks to use the bathroom. What confronts him there takes a moment or two to absorb. Before the lavatory there lies a pair of underpants, squinting up into the bright fluorescence of the recessed bulbs.

And upon the pants, an iPad.

There is insufficient room for the visitor to attend to his micturational needs. Does he edge the little sculpture away with his loafer? Does he attempt to pee crosswise, from the side, risking collateral damage, or casualties from friendly fire?

I'll leave you to conject. Anyway, he emerges, looking thoughtful. He decides that the least embarrassing thing would be to mention the bathroom ensemble. There is a moment of silence. It's impossible to know how this will turn out.

But then, something unspoken passes between the authors. Some understanding that human frailty and vulnerability have been captured by the pants, the iPad, the lavatory pan, the pee. And with this comes the knowledge that this frailty and vulnerability are not the markers of the absurd and the ludicrous, but the sublime: that we are not brought low by such things, but exalted. The eyes – pale blue, dark blue, hazel – moisten. Had one of the writers not still been naked from the waist up, there might have been a Tellytubby-style group hug. But these are three English authors (although one claims to be five sevenths Irish), and so they go to a bar and get rat-arsed.

All Were Either Left Blank, or Defaced with Scrawled Penises

April 27. Just got my latest (and last, as I'm stepping down) set of feedback forms from my Royal Holloway creative writing students. Makes interesting reading, so I suppose I can take credit for that. Samples:

'Doc, you are a cool shambling giant of bullshit.'

'The lecturer on this course achieved good attendance. Physically.'

'MAAAAAN you have BAAAAAALLLLLLLS of steel to stand there and say what you say, lookin like you do.'

'Sir, you is well hot, and only needs to shed a few flabs…'

'The course content was relevant to a course entitled "Writing for Children". For any other course it would have been less useful.'

'I can read your mind. ZZZZZZZZZZZZZZZZSHSHSH SHSHZZZZZZZSST – that was me doing it.'

'The best thing about the course was when you said making a book was like making a cake, and then you ate that book.'

In felt tip I had added an extra section to the form, which said: 'If your lecturer were a Greek God, which Greek God would he be? Tick one.' The options were 'Apollo', 'Zeus', 'Artemis', 'Demis Roussos' and 'Herpius' (Greek God of out-of-fashion STDs). Sadly, all were either left blank, or defaced with scrawled penises.

My Mouth Was Giving Birth to Some Small, Gelatinous Foetus

April 28. I brought back some wine from Austria. Rather than a cork or a screw-top, one of the bottles had an interesting stopper made from glass, with a little rubber seal. The glass had a tiny, rather beautiful salamander embedded in it. The whole thing looked like a small crystal mushroom. Anyway, I drank the wine, lying in bed, while Mrs McG was at one of her yoga sessions. After the wine was all used up, I played with the glass stopper, rolling it around my fingers. I then conceived a desire to put it in my mouth. I was convinced that this would be somehow satisfying. And it was. The cool weight of the glass, the faint tang of the grassy white wine, the gentle clicking against my teeth. I tongued it, playfully, the way a sea lion balances a ball on its nose.

And then the bedroom door opened, and Mrs McG was there.

'What are you up to?' she asked, with no more than her usual suspiciousness.

Of course I couldn't answer, not least because my mouth was full. Obviously, in retrospect, I should just have spat the glass stopper out and made a joke. But being surprised like that made the whole thing seem furtive, and faintly filthy, as if she'd caught me in the midst of an auto-erotic moment.

'Nothing,' I said. Or, rather, 'Nnnngth Nnnnnnngth.'

'Are you eating something?' she said, after a scrutinizing pause.

'Nnnngth.'

'Well, what's in your mouth?'

'Nnnngth.'

She came round to my side of the bed, and put her hand out.

'Spit.'

I looked up at her, imploringly.

She was implacable.

I let the glass mushroom slide out of my mouth and into her hand. It looked like my mouth was giving birth to some small, gelatinous foetus.

Mrs McG looked at the stopper, and then over at the wine bottle.

'Thanks for saving some for me,' she said, and then left the room.

Tiny Tear-Shaped Amber Nuggets

April 29. Barely recovered from Vienna, I had to make my way to Cornwall for the Kernow Youth Book Award. It's the final chance for my latest (and possibly last – one never knows…) novel, *Hello Darkness*, to win anything. Basically, I only became a writer so I could put on a posh frock and go up and accept awards, exulting over my conquered enemies and rivals. And I have several undelivered acceptance speeches prepared over the years, as well as a victory dance that I choreographed for the Young Minds Book Award in 2009.

I love a long train journey but, due to an administrative muddle, I was confronted with the ultimate nightmare scenario: five hours on the train, my Kindle and iPad both out of gas, no back-up book. So I decided on a radical solution – to see if I could make it the whole way to Cornwall without having a single pee. Eccentric, you might say, but the alternative was to swallow my own tongue from boredom. And it sort of worked. The journey became an epic, multi-part adventure, like *The Lord of the Rings*, except inside my bladder. Towards the end I became slightly delirious, and began to hallucinate, as if on a bad ayahuasca trip. I became a shaman, and walked with the spirit animals. I found the origin of all things, and also the end thereof. It was horrible. But I made it. Afterwards I went to the loo, but it seemed I'd gone too far, and all that emerged were three tiny tear-shaped amber nuggets, of the kind you expect to contain a fossilized mosquito. But I think it was worth it, assuming I can survive the dialysis long enough for them to find me a new kidney.

And the other thing that happened concerned an interesting yokel I encountered while changing trains in Plymouth. He was sitting on a bench, grinning at a patch of platform near his feet. As I passed, he looked up at me and said, his voice full of joy and wonder, 'Thurn beam mapples.'

'Pardon?' I said.

'Thurn beam mapples,' he repeated, more emphatically.

As I tried to work out what he meant, he became agitated, and this time shouted angrily, 'Thurn beam mapples!'

I was looking in my pockets for a pound to give him as a way of ending the conversation, when I found myself swept away by the tide of people rushing for the Truro train. But as I left him behind I regretted not having taken a different course. I could have agreed straight away, that, 'Aaaargh, thurn beam mapples.' I think that would have made him happy. Or I could have confronted him, and engaged in a deeper debate, asserting on the contrary that 'Thurn baint not beam mapples, thurn beam nartichokes,' or some such.

Anyway, it left me feeling dissatisfied, and something of a failure.

I'd Stopped Paying Attention

April 30. It turned out I was the only one of the shortlisted authors to attend the Kernow Youth Book Awards ceremony. The organizers were very grateful, and charming. I came, quite literally, last. Not sure who won. I'd stopped paying attention.

Afterwards I did a couple of events at a local school. The kids were really gentle and tried to comfort me about the humiliation. But humiliation isn't the sort of thing that can be comforted. In this, humiliation approximates not to guilt but to shame, and can only be hidden, not expiated or forgiven.

The Death of a Teacher

May 1. The news reached me through my sister, who'd heard it from a friend who still had a connection with the school. A teacher stabbed in the classroom. A name: Mrs Maguire. It took me a moment or two to find her in my memory. Which was odd, because so much of that time is clear to me, clearer than last year, than last week. And then I had her. The thing was that she was a teacher I always thought of as Miss Connors. The blonde bob. The smile that took in her whole face. That way of listening with her head held at an angle. The flashes of fire, when riled by some act of impertinence. And I felt a pulse of grief and astonishment, followed by a slower wave of sadness. Yes, Miss Connors, then Mrs Maguire. She was my form teacher, and I loved her for a few months, in 1976, in Leeds.

It wouldn't be true to say that the press photographs of Corpus Christi brought more memories back. They'd never left me. True, the building was smarter now than it had been back then, when its stained concrete and broken glass made it look more like a Bulgarian nuclear reprocessing plant than a school. But the geography hadn't changed: the redbrick of the surrounding Halton Moor estate, the brown, winding beck – then a virtual sewer with nothing alive in it but rats and a corrosive green scum that dissolved the shopping trolleys and dead cats dumped there – now, I'm told, a haunt for newts and sticklebacks. The tussocky green field beyond the fence, where travellers would appear and disappear according to their unfathomable ways, leaving odd things behind them – a three-wheeled pram, a defrocked deckchair, buckets. Loose stuff, the things you'd get by shaking Leeds and seeing what fell out.

It was by the side of that field that I was dropped off on my first day by my dad. Back then parents didn't spend years discussing where their children would go to school. My dad drove past Corpus every day on his way in to work at St James's Hospital, so that's where I was sent.

I'd been brought up outside Leeds, and attended a tiny village junior school, so that first day was a major shock. The chaos and confusion, not knowing where to go, or what to do, shoved and cuffed by hard kids, yelled at by teachers. I was in blazer and tie and carefully pressed trousers, my hair neatly parted, but most of the other kids were wild, some filthy.

Leeds back then still had the eleven-plus. Most of the Catholic kids who passed it would go to St Michael's or Cardinal Heenan, for the boys, Mount St Mary's or Notre Dame for the girls. But some – those local enough to walk – would go to Corpus where they were streamed into the top classes, 1M or 1L. The others were dumped in 1J or 1G – the hard kids from the local estate, mainly. The ones already deemed failures. My local education authority had already got rid of the eleven-plus, so I never took it, but as far as Corpus was concerned, I'd failed it. So, here I was in 1J, among the disturbed, the idle, the uninterested, the mildly psychotic. Of course there were kids there who had plenty of intelligence, and some from that class have gone on to achieve fine things, overcoming those early handicaps. But others hated being there, and sweated a mixture of boredom and ferocity.

And Miss Connors was our form teacher. She must have been twenty-three or twenty-four. Not long out of teacher training college. Blonde, neat, very pretty. And yet she had authority, even then. She controlled that class with a combination of humour, kindness, decency, but also an intense fierceness, when required, matching their ferocity with her own. And, in truth, it was required quite often.

There was a pervasive feeling of violence at that time in the school. Breaktime scraps were common. You'd hear the cry of 'Fight! Fight!' and look around the playground, locate the knot of eager spectators, and gather round to watch two warriors thumping, kicking, biting. Bullying was endemic. The usual rituals of teasing and humiliation, of course, but also old-fashioned batterings. The hard kids preyed on the weak, the quiet, the studious. That should have been me, but I escaped. I was tall for my age, and good at sport – then, as now, a way out of the zone of the persecuted.

At the time I hated the bullies, the meatheads. They ruined school for a lot of the kids, made it a place of horror and fear. Now, I can see how this all flowed from that environment, that background, the desperate poverty of Halton Moor.

Some teachers responded to the violence with brutality of their own. Corporal punishment was a daily ritual, administered with a sort of dull thoughtlessness, or sadistic relish, depending on the tastes of the teacher. Even a good kid like me could be slapped across the face for talking, thwacked on the knuckles with an iron-edged technical drawing ruler for forgetting their homework.

There were other teachers who rose above this – and they remain heroes to me. A music teacher called Mr Bloodworth, who shone with a charismatic joy; Mrs Freeman, a brilliant, dedicated, witty teacher, impossible not to love; Mr Kaisermann, who taught drama and who could make even a Leeds lad suddenly understand, however fleetingly, a line of Shakespeare, see its beauty and resonance.

From what I gather, Mrs Maguire became one of those – loved, respected, dedicated. But when I knew her she was still young, so young it seems to me now. Hardly more than a girl, trying to control a class full of kids for whom the kindest word you could use would be unacademic.

And what I remember most about her was her determination to get the best from us, to put into our heads what we needed to get through, to get by. And that caring, that intensity, could at times spill over into fierceness, goaded by some jackass, or when she came across bullying or unkindness in others.

But it isn't the fierceness that I remember when I think of her. I think of her face, always on the verge of a smile. Her consideration. The way she listened when you spoke to her, and tried to answer, rather than fob you off. I remember her personal kindness and consideration for me. I could easily have had a terrible time in class 1J. I was an outsider. I was different. My parents, lower middle class. I didn't have the hard Leeds accent, so like a hammer hitting rock. And I was brainy. My hand was always up in class.

But she looked after me, and I got through. Others she helped more, those who had greater problems to overcome. For forty years she did this, week in, week out. And she had earned the right to spend another thirty years thinking about the good that she had done, the lives transformed.

Media commentators on education tend to have been educated privately, or at grammar schools. They go into a modern comprehensive, and emerge a little shell-shocked by the noise and turmoil and apparent chaos. They compare things with their own civilised schooling, the rows of neat boys and girls learning Latin, and they see a pattern of decline. However, anyone remembering what a secondary modern was like, the brutality, the violence, the lack of resources, could not help but see modern state schools as sublime oases of calm and contentment. I've visited perhaps a hundred state schools as an author over the past ten years, and even the ones deemed to be failing, struggling with difficult kids from deprived areas, seem relatively gentle places, now. I recall talking to a group of teenagers at a school in Derbyshire. They self-identified as emos. I asked them if they got any stick, expecting a litany of bullying, beating, intimidation. 'They, er, sometimes shout out "emo",' one lad said. There was a general muttered agreement. But bullying? No, not really.

And the best of them contain within themselves a genuine ideal of what a comprehensive education can achieve, education seen as a way of bringing us together, rather than separating achieving sheep from failing goats.

But I want to return to Mrs Maguire, who I first knew as the beautiful, young, earnest, funny, wise, exciting, fierce Miss Connors. The world we're in now, the world of Halton Moor and Corpus Christi, is a better world than it was in 1976. It's better not because of the politicians (or, for that matter, writers), but because of people like her, who spent their lives with their hands thrust into the world's cold loam, bringing on each generation, through sheer willpower and love.

A final memory. At a parents' evening, I'd just had a good report, and was basking in the glory. I was still loitering around when the next group approached Mrs Maguire. A shy girl and her meek parents. After a while, Mrs Maguire asked the girl what she wanted to be when she grew up. She was from the Halton Moor estate, a place of narrow horizons and stunted chances, thwarted hopes.

'A teacher, Miss,' she said. 'A teacher like you.'

Trouser Music

May 2. For reasons I can't go into now, I've just been trying to find the Latin for 'trousers'. I thought it might have some link with pataloon/pantalon, and so, in my search, I came across a musical instrument called the pantalon – essentially a hammered dulcimer of monstrous proportions, the undamped strings of which would resonate sympathetically when any one of them was struck.

I instantly formed a powerful urge to hear the pantalon, which, played by its inventor, Pantaleon Hebenstreit (according to the *OED*, Louis XIV transferred the name from the player to the instrument), was something of a craze in the early eighteenth century.

Alas, with the demise of the original maestro, the instrument fell into neglect, and none now survive. And so we'll never be able to hear the lost trouser music of the pantalon.

Snip They Went

May 3. I've found that trimming my eyebrows is a highly cost-effective way to look a bit younger, a bit more with-it, and less Gandalfy. So I was snipping away, when I noticed the scissors I was using. They were rather interesting, with a slight curve to the blades, as if they were peeping round a corner. But sharp, and with a nice positive action. Snip, they went, as all scissors should.

And then I thought, still snipping, of the last time I'd used these scissors. It was when I'd trimmed the dried, nuggety dangleberries from Monty's arse.

The Glory and Sadness of Life

May 4. My daughter's Siamese fighting fish passed quietly away in the night, pining, perhaps, for the battles he never fought. Great wailing and lamentation in the McGowan household. Of course I got the blame, despite being the only person ever to clean out his tank. A flowerpot funeral will follow later in the day. I'm preparing my speech.

The fish episode was not my greatest work as a parent. We got them to stave off Rosie's yearning for a dog, in the unsatisfactory way you'll stave off a craving for a muffin or Bakewell tart with a stick of celery.

The fish – goldfish and guppies and other delicate, long-finned creatures – died slowly, leaving in the end only the fighter. He was beautiful, shimmering through his tank in a purple ball gown, like an old-fashioned drag queen. I did my best to keep him alive, changing the water, buying filters and heaters. But it was all in vain. And Rosie stopped caring after Monty came along to love her.

Until death came to remind her, and us, of the glory and sadness of life.

A Few Minutes of Doing Nothing

May 5. The five minutes after the kids go off to school and the flat is empty are the best of the day, aren't they? And you think, well, I can afford a few minutes of doing nothing, surely? I mean a literal nothing, just leaning back in your chair, and emptying your mind, and letting the quiet settle on you like the dust and dark of the sepulchre. But then you remember all the things you have to do and, even worse, the things you know you'll never do, weighing you down, heavy as a bad pasty. And then you see your big toenail, manky now for five years, and you realize that perhaps it isn't manky, but just the toenail of an old person. And you also notice that the sole of your foot is wet and the knowledge dawns that somewhere in the flat the dog has pissed on the carpet.

Look in the Pot, Please

May 6. Lying in bed, listening to the radio before the chaos of the morning commenced, I heard the announcement that they've just discovered a Viking treasure hoard, including a metal pot, 'the contents of which have yet to be examined'. Well, that shows a fundamental lack of curiosity. Look in the fucking pot, guys, for heaven's sake.

The Naming of Invertebrates

May 7. On the radio they just mentioned something called the depressed river mussel. I now have a new favourite animal.

And just now, researching the depressed mussel, I've come across the Boring Millipede (*Polyzonium germanicum*).

Wish my job was naming invertebrates.

More divertingly named invertebrates: the poetry of the Scarce Four-dot Pin-palp (*Aplota palpella*), the pleasing specificity of the One-grooved Diving Beetle (*Bidessus unistriatus*) and the Small Dark Yellow Underwing (*Anarta cordigera*). Crucial not to confuse that with the Small Pale Yellow Underwing... And who wouldn't love the Wormwood Moonshiner (*Amara fusca*), or the Dingy Mocha (*Cyclophora *pendularia*). But I think my favourite is Ron's Diving Beetle (*Hydroporus necopinatus subsp. roni*) – fucking great for Ron, getting that recognition.

Giant Pecker

May 8. The woods around Golders Hill Park are lovely at the moment, full of birdsong and flowers and little glades where the sunlight pours in with an almost artificial intensity, as if packed with E numbers. I was walking along with Monty this morning when I heard the sort of chirruping racket that always signifies a nest full of gaping beaks. I stared up, not expecting the satisfaction of actually seeing anything. But there, on the trunk, was an almost Platonically perfect hole. And a second later a greater spotted woodpecker emerged. It saw me at the foot of the tree, and almost immediately started up a raucous alarm call. I backed away a little, not wanting to disturb the nest. But the woodpecker followed me, hopping closer along the branches. And then it was joined by its mate, and the two of them now were yelling at me to clear off.

I imagined an undignified scene, as I fled through the woods, the woodpeckers hot in pursuit. The thorny undergrowth claws and tears at my clothes rending and stripping them from my loins. And then I fall, face down. The enraged male lands on the back of my neck, jabbing with murderous intent at the base of my skull. The beak finds and punctures the carotid artery, sealing my fate.

As I begin to fade out of consciousness I realize how this must look. These woods are a notorious gay pick-up place. My torn clothes… It'll be assumed that there was some kind of… encounter. I imagine the headlines: MULTI-AWARD-WINNING (YES, TWO COUNTS AS MULTI) CHILDREN'S AUTHOR FOUND DEAD IN GAY HAUNT. POLICE INVESTIGATE.

So, as my final act as my eyes dim and the last of my strength fades, I scrawl in the dirt a defence. *Pecker, giant pecker…*

Guilt

May 9. My newish washing machine is leaking. Frustratingly, I can't work out precisely (or even roughly) where it's leaking from. It's like when your spouse is annoyed with you and you've got no idea why, or what it is you've done, this time.

Doing Useful Work

May 10. I saw an interesting character yesterday when I went to visit Mrs McG at the London School of Economics. He appeared to be homeless, and had a general Rasputin-like air that rather drew the eye. Whenever a plane went overhead he pointed a device of some kind at it – it looked like one of those toy sonic screwdrivers you can get. He then carefully examined the device, as if taking a reading. Then he wrote down whatever it was in a notebook. It was all rather fascinating. And admirable, in a way.

I hope if I'm ever in the same situation I manage to keep busy, like that, doing useful work, and don't give in to despair.

The Last of the Rhinos

May 11. Just read a sad story about the probable extinction of the northern subspecies of the white rhino. I looked it up on Wiki, as I knew the southern white rhino was doing rather well. Anyway, I came across this sentence: 'It spends about half of the day eating, one third resting, and the rest of the day doing various other things.'

I became somewhat obsessed by the casual 'doing various other things'. It seemed a curiously human way to spend one's time. I imagined the rhino flicking listlessly through the *Metro*, or popping into the Oxfam shop to see if there were any interesting books in, or standing by the sandwich toaster contemplating, and ultimately rejecting, a cheese and onion toasty, or trying to find the remote for the telly, giving up, and randomly pressing the buttons on the side of the screen, hoping something might come on, or listening to a feature on the lesbian bee-keeping community on *Woman's Hour*, or knocking over the athlete's foot powder in the bedroom, covering up the mess with his pyjama bottoms and making a mental note to get the hoover out for it later on, or just gazing out of the window, trying to work out where it had all gone wrong.

I was sorry for the rhinos and I suppose we'll have used them all up, soon.

Bloomsday

May 12. This is what happens when I commit myself body and soul to a day of work. First I wait around for two hours for the washing machine man to come, anxiously fretting the whole time in case the washing machine would refuse to leak while he was here, or, even worse, that it should prove to be some obvious thing, like me forgetting to shut the door.

It was an obvious thing.

The bamboo sticks I lost in the pipes trying to fix the last problem had blocked the outflow. The man was quite nice about it. He had a slight Leopold Bloom air to him, and let me off the call-out charge. But I then spent three of the worst hours of my life taking the pipes apart, cleaning them, and then trying to reattach the bits I'd dismantled, all the while squeezed into a teeny-tiny space between the back of the machine and the wall, with a gaping window offering the entertaining prospect of a dramatic death plunge should I overbalance in my exertions. I was covered in the grey sludge from the pipes, which had a queasy, organic, almost maritime richness to it, like duck shit mixed with whale spunk.

There seemed to be endless possible ways of putting back the three bits of pipe I'd taken out, and an almost infinite number of rubber washers. Cool reason got me nowhere. Rage, tantrums, brute force, got the thing roughly assembled. During the first trial run, water spurted out of every joint, like those scenes from films set in New York where the kids cool off under a spraying hydrant. I tried hitting the pipe with a fucking big spanner like they do in submarine films, when a depth charge goes off. It works in submarines; it doesn't work with washing machines.

Finally, I worked out that one particular rubber washer needed to be held in place with another rubber washer. For some reason this doesn't lead to an infinite regress, with that washer held in place by a further washer, and so on. Three literal hours of that. Then I had to answer some questions for the Society of Children's Writers and Book Illustrators conference. And that took us up to now.

Anyway, this is where I spent my morning and much of the afternoon. It was an epic battle of good against evil. I can only pray that the seals hold.

Further Domestic Adventures

May 13. There's something, I find, almost uniquely dispiriting about changing the battery on the smoke alarm. The first stage is the two days of infuriating bleeping, which we try to ignore, putting off the horrors to come. Then I crack, and go off and buy a battery, and the installation ordeal commences. One has to operate at extreme altitude, well beyond one's natural range. This involves climbing to the top of a highly unstable pagoda-like arrangement, made up of a chair, a, er, pouffe, and a wooden box (specially claimed off a skip for exactly this purpose).

I usually get the kids to watch this, so they can at least have a last memory of me as I tumble to my death, providing them with an amusing anecdote for their later years.

Mrs McG occasionally makes an appearance at this stage, propping me up aggressively with the hard end of the mop, which isn't actually that helpful, especially as she's sharpened it roughly with her Bowie knife, like the stakes used to protect the archers at Agincourt.

And then the tiny instructions on the alarm, which tell you to insert a screwdriver (can never find one, so use a potato peeler or toenail clipper or some such) and 'push away'.

This 'push away' invariably confounds me for a good ten minutes, as I try to pry the cover away from the ceiling, before I remember that 'away' means away from the direction the screwdriver enters the slot, and parallel with, not away from, the ceiling. The kids are usually crying by this point, through the combined power of anxiety and boredom. With the cover finally off, I see that I've bought the wrong kind of battery, so we have to rewind a few steps, and endure another two or three days of bleeping. Then back up I go, this time alone, and complete the job.

Sometimes the alarm ignores the new battery and carries on bleeping. That's when I start looking for the hammer, realize we haven't got one, and bash the fucker off the ceiling with the milk pan.

But the pain and inconvenience aren't the real issue. The real issue is that the failing of the alarms is another biennial marker, another notch whittled into the mop handle of life, each one taking me closer to that sharpened, terminal end.

The Cab at the Door

May 14. I've been spending most of my free time, lately, in a strange place, a land of ill-fitting dentures, and frayed collars, and failed moustaches, and commercial travellers, and complex undergarments, and inept seducers, and women driven slightly mad by the knowledge of their unattractiveness, and people called, unironically, Cyril and Enid and Albert, and men striving to achieve a mediocrity that is just beyond their reach, and things given a lick of brown paint to brighten them up. It's V.S. Pritchett country, and it feels like home.

I remember when Pritchett was a name – the two huge volumes of his *Complete Essays* and *Complete Stories* came out in the early 1990s. He was commonly regarded then as the Greatest Living Man of Letters. Now he's dead and forgotten. The stories are astonishingly good (especially *The Camberwell Beauty*), and the essays interesting, but his masterpiece is *The Cab at the Door*, the first of the two volumes of his autobiography. And one wonders how many people will ever again read it for pleasure. Seventeen? Twenty-two? Or perhaps I am the last of them.

A Sprocket for the Socket

May 15. Having recently had an interesting discussion on the subject of 'bricolage', i.e. bodging a job by employing a thing to do a task for which it wasn't intended, I realized that I actually had the perfect example of this before my eyes. We have these fancy taps in the kitchen, but they're rather badly designed, and so the handle bit regularly wears out its, er, socket, meaning I have to pay £30 to get a new sprocket for the socket (or whatever it's called).

Part of the problem is that the design puts a lot of pressure on the joint. So, I decided to save the money, and employ a small bolt, in place of the handle. This has various advantages. It works. It was free. It annoys Mrs McG, who thinks it's essentially ruined our house, by making it look like it's made of old screws. Crucially, it's actually better than the original, as it exerts less pressure on the joint. This means that it will last forever. It'll be like the silicone breasts of starlets, still pristine, they say, after the body has decayed.

So, post-apocalypse, when everything else in our flat is rubble, or dust, or just loose atoms, my little bolt will still be there, doing its job, annoying Mrs McG.

Sticky Fingers

May 16. Went to a book launch last night. I didn't really know anyone, apart from the very charming author. This situation – me at a party, where I'm not tethered by pre-existing social ties – has, historically, led to both my greatest triumphs and darkest hours. But this was OK. The only person I offended was the book blogger I accused of being a saddle sniffer, because of the way he hangs around the writers of teen books for girls. Quite late in the night, one of the publishing people (I think she might have dealt with foreign rights) scuttled away and came back with a clinking drinks trolley, full of the sorts of liqueurs and obscure spirits people bring back from places like Madagascar and Wolverhampton. Today's fuggy memory of what followed includes me finding the opportunity to unleash that old joke, 'Liqueurs? No! Lick your own.' But that might just be wishful thinking. I suspected the foreign rights lady may have had a soft spot for me, but at one point her dentures slipped a little, and the shame of it sapped her erotic energy. I cycled home with my fingers sticky – not from any kind of illicit activity down the cavernous bloomers of the foreign rights lady, but from the thick deposits around the necks of the various peach, cocoa and mulberry flavoured drinks bottles from which I'd swigged.

No Eye Deer

May 17. Came across a forgotten folder on my hard drive. I've sometimes bragged that almost every word I've written has been published. This turns out to be a MASSIVE lie. The folder was full of projects I started and never finished, and subsequently totally erased from my memory. There were five thousand words of a trilogy about evil mermaids, who copulate with human males, then eat them; there were ten thousand words of a death-row thriller I'd abandoned; a jokey Zombie apocalypse (two thousand words plus lengthy synopsis). Other things even less formed. All wasted. But at least I used to have ideas. Now I don't even have ideas about ideas. (What do you call a deer with no eyes? No eye deer.)

Icon, Sign, Index

May 18. I know writers are supposed to be good at noticing things: we're expected to be observant, Sherlockian in our perceptions of minutiae. A twitch of the eye, the first bud of spring, the blood under the nail. But I'm not like that. I walk around in a daze.

This is not because my mind is set on profounder matters, but rather my gaze settles on the middle distance, on the approaching dust cloud that signals my doom. Yes, I think that's it. The philosopher C.S. Peirce distinguished between three sorts of sign. The first is the 'icon' – where the sign resembles that which it signifies, like a painting of a face or a tree. Then there is the 'sign' proper, in which the link between the physical element – the sound or the shape of a word – and the meaning it conveys is entirely arbitrary and conventional. Finally, there is what Peirce calls the 'index'. With an index, there is a physical connection between the signifier and the signified, a hand stretching across the chasm of meaning. So, a blush is an index of your embarrassment. The burp is an index of your indigestion. The bang an index of the explosion. And that dust cloud, which marks the approach of your pursuers...

Anyway, this habitual inattentiveness to the appearance of things means that when, for whatever reason, I'm made to look, to see and to feel, the world can seem startling and unexpected and new and strange. But that's only because I haven't noticed it before banging my head against or treading in it.

So I find myself today on a wifi-less train, somewhere in darkest Suffolk, and decide to pass the time by self-consciously noticing things.

My train has a name: *The Vice Admiral Nelson*. Why not *The Admiral Nelson*, or *The Lord Nelson*? A sign at a station reads: 'Colchester – home of Colchester zoo.' Well, where the fuck else would it be? There is a slice of fossilized cucumber on the plastic between the seat cushions. I don't have the right sort of implement for flicking it out, so I move seats. A lady gets on and sits opposite me. I've taken my glasses off, so the world is a blur. She reaches down into her dress and does something dramatic to her bust – some sort of rearranging manoeuvre. By the time I've put my glasses on, she's stopped. She's mediumly pregnant. Don't know if that has something to do with the business with the bust. She has one of those faces that always looks to be on the verge of taking offence. She's on her phone: 'The reason I'm late is because Phil cut himself shaving and we couldn't get it to stop.' She pronounces 'no' with a strange 'yuh' sound at the end. It sounds like 'nigh yuh'. If things had worked out differently I could imagine being married to her. It would have been terrible. A scruffy field planted with saplings, protected by white plastic sheaths. They look like untended war graves. A small mountain of cars at a scrap metal yard. Only the one at the very top is still roughly car-shaped. Almost looks like it was driven to the top, and left there. The others are all squashed. Wonder if it's like a compost heap – they rely on the weight of cars on top to compress the ones in lower strata. A magpie pecking at the eye of a dead rabbit. Thinking how seldom we see dead animals, apart from roadkill. Unlike the Serengeti, where you can't move for carcasses. An unexpected factory amid the scruffy fields. It has the strangely futuristic look of a space port. What does it make? Fertilizer? Beer? Condoms?

Jack Curtis, Bodyguard

May 19. Just dropped my daughter off at a party in a tall house near Sloane Square. The door was answered by a ravishingly dressed Sikh butler, with jewels in his turban. As he turned away after admitting Rosie, I saw a scimitar swinging from his belt. A couple of other girls arrived at the same time. As far as I could tell, they were delivered by their drivers, rather than parents. I was wearing my only waterproof item of clothing, a sort of camouflage jacket (actually quite a trendy garment that I received as part-payment for writing a script for a fashion show, but that's another story…). So, I decided that I'd pretend to be Rosie's bodyguard – not one of those Russians in monkey suits, but a former SAS man, a down-to-earth, rugged, take-no-bullshit character. Called, I don't know, Jack Curtis. Dryly humorous. Probably having it off with his charge's mother, i.e. Mrs McG, who had grown sick of her fuddy-duddy, unmacho husband. Enabling me to cuckold myself. Anyway, that's what I was thinking on the tube on the way back. Bit worried I might have been acting part of this out, as no one sat next to me on the otherwise rather crowded train. Adjusting the scope on my sniper rifle; twisting my stiletto into the back of one of the assassins; taking another out with a single punch to the throat. That sort of thing.

In That Way It's Exactly Like Love

May 20. You know when you pour your hot water over your two teabags, and then wander off and forget about it and only remember later on when the tea is a tepid black slurry, and then you add some milk, take a swig, wince, and then fill the cup up with fresh hot water? That's my favourite kind of tea, that is. But I've found you can't deliberately recreate these conditions. It has to come as an accident. In that way it's exactly like love.

Manly Alchemy

May 21. Had to use my special glue again – the one you need to create by mixing two different, er, pre-glue glue-like substances together. I can't tell you how satisfying I find this. Like doing an especially manly form of alchemy. For someone not naturally gifted at the mechanic arts, this really is as good as it gets.

Party Blues

May 22. I spent an oddly melancholy night at the *Guardian* Children's Book Awards. It should have been fun. Nice party, lots of OK booze and really very good nibbles. But, well, one felt that the world had moved on, and left one somewhat behind. The room was very now, but I was, I don't know, maybe 2009. Like some trudging mollusc on the beach, the tide has overtaken me; and if I turn, it will pass me again, as it goes out. Best to press on. Perhaps a rock pool. Perhaps a child's bucket. Perhaps a gull.

Orange, Purple, Month, and...

May 23. This morning's key discovery: nothing rhymes with 'whelk'. Except 'elk'. Which is no bloody use.

The Whelk

1.
Between the sand and water trod
A melancholy gastropod.
Alone and lost and blind is he,
Forlorn on land, confused at sea.

He trudges first towards the dunes
Ensnared by bladder-wrack balloons,
Then overtaken by the tide
He turns to find a place to hide.

But gone for good his mollusc luck, it's
Not the laughing children's buckets
Or friendly frond-filled rock-pool home,
Refreshed by salt spray, flecked with foam.

No haven, his, no larder full:
Spied, rent, gulped, shat-out, by a gull.

2.
If it's not clear, that whelk is me
The world of books, well, that's the sea;
The gull is death, the dunes old age,
The rock pool a mythic living wage.

Or maybe, no, the dunes are peace,
The surging waves my sweet release;
The rock pool's where the peril lies,
Crab-clawed, envenomed, made of eyes.

Or, the sterile bucket's hell,
Soft flesh decaying in the shell.
But now, I think, the whelk's not me,
Nor I the shore, nor yet the sea.

Benign, oppressed, demure and dull?
My talk's a screech: I am the gull.

And Our Fingers Touched

May 24. Cycling back from teaching my Faber class, I hit the crowds streaming out, post-gig, from the Roundhouse in Camden. They were a curiously gentle lot, with their beards and long hair, and I amused myself with the thought that they were all auditioning to be Fleet Foxes' second triangle player.

And just then, in a moment of extraordinary synchronicity, Fleet Foxes' 'Tiger Mountain Peasant Song' started playing in my headphones.

As I reached Chalk Farm station, the crowd was flowing over the crossing. I went into a slow weave. A kid – he looked like a sixth former, or maybe first year uni – smiled and put his fist out to do a fist bump with me as I cycled by. Then he saw how old I was, and transformed it into an open hand gesture, and our fingers touched, in something not quite a handshake.

I was almost unmanned by it, the whole thing, I mean. The music, the softly moving crowd, the gentleness of the young man. Though I don't really like Fleet Foxes any more.

Shoe Goo Good Voodoo

May 25. I've got a good news story for a change. I bought something called 'shoe goo' in order to protect the toe-end of my new cricket bat. It's a sort of liquid rubber that hardens post-application. Its official use is for mending shoes with holes in. Well, I thought I'd have no further use for it after smearing it on my bat, and anticipated having to stare at it for years on the shelf, as it hardened in the tube, until I'd finally throw it away sometime in late 2027. But now I find that my trainers have, in fact, developed a hole. A hole I can now fix with my shoe goo! I don't think I've ever had a shoe with a hole in it before. It's pure synchronicity – the second time in two days (after the Fleet Foxes). And two examples of meaningful coincidence can't be a coincidence. I can't help but think that now everything is going to slide into place.

Ups and Downs

May 26. I planned to cycle over to a school in Islington. However, a quick check showed that everything that could go wrong with my bike had gone wrong in the two days since it'd last been mounted. The tyres were flat. The breaks were jammed – those at the front stuck on open, those at the back clamped around the wheel rim like Romulus and Remus on the teats of the wolf. So it took me a grimy, dank and cold hour to coax it back to its normal state of clanking inefficiency.

I soon wished I hadn't bothered. I hate cycling across, rather than down into, town. It's only then that you become aware of the topology of the old river valleys, flowing down into the Thames. Which means that you're always either going up or down – there's barely a yard on the level. And you can't enjoy the down bit, because of the approaching up. It's like the short-lived agreeable warmth when you wet your pants – the pleasure is always, from its inception, intercut with the anticipated cold, clammy sequela.

But things went OK at the school. I was paid on the day, in actual used notes, which inevitably makes one feel furtive – it's impossible not to glance over one's shoulder, as the bulging envelope is passed to you, as if I were a drug dealer, or one of those Turks who sell trafficked human livers to rich American dentists.

Blue Shoes, Two Pairs, Of

May 27. A week ago I had a dramatic and rather upsetting trainer cull, initiated by Mrs McG's 'one in, one out' policy (which, I don't doubt, she'll eventually apply to husbands). It was triggered by my purchase of some strikingly unattractive, electric-blue Nikes. They're the sort of trainers that are supposed to emulate the feeling of running in bare feet, so you can re-establish contact with the Earth's energy fields, or some such, as you leap leopard-like across the savannah, or through the jungle. And to that end, you aren't supposed to wear socks with them.

I went out in them sockless for the first time today. I found it a curious experience. It feels, frankly, a bit kinky. Admittedly, on the kinky spectrum, it occupies the section right next to 'not kinky at all'. But for someone of my restrained and conservative tastes, it feels a bit like wearing ladies' underwear, or attaching the old nipple clamps.

And the other thing, which I admit is a bit eccentric, is that I've actually got two pairs of these. I can't fully explain the rationale for this… No, actually, of course I can. They were an internet bargain, and I wasn't sure if I was a 10 or a 10.5, so I ordered both, meaning to send one pair back, but knowing all along that I never would, and that I'd shortly be owning two pairs of identical trainers, only one of which fitted me.

Anyway, I was thinking, as I was walking around, that if I went to Waitrose again tomorrow, people would think, 'Oh look, there goes that man wearing an odd combination of a tweed jacket and ludicrous blue trainers.' But what they won't know is that it's actually the *other* pair that I'm wearing. And so the other thing I'll be wearing is a smug expression, as I'll know that I've got one up on them. And if you say, well, no one cares what shoes you're wearing, or even noticed you, then I'll answer good, because it's none of their business; so, in a very real sense, I'll have won that one, too. A good start to the week, I think.

Undoubtedly Expressive

May 28. Was crossing the Finchley Road this morning, with Monty, when I was startled by a loud noise – a sort of honking bark, or barking honk. I looked up to see two motorcyclists, side by side, sharing a joke as they waited at the lights. And then I realized why they were laughing in such a strange way: it was because, I deduced, they wanted the other person to be able to hear that they were laughing, through the muffling effect of their helmets. It was laughter as a performative/ communicative, rather than expressive, act. In other words, the loud, mechanical laughter was the product of a generous social impulse, not the expression of some 'inner' mirthfulness.

This rather chimed with my conception of creativity as essentially communicative, rather than expressive, and so it pleased me.

Monty, however, was greatly startled by the noise and shamed himself on the crossing, in a gastric act that was, undoubtedly, expressive.

Bubbles

May 29. Realized today that I just don't have the right equipment for taking part in a Serious or Intense conversation. It's not just my words, but also my face, which undermines whatever I'm trying to say. It's like trying to do the *Iliad* in limericks. Or perhaps like those cheap amplifiers with a 'Tone' control that doesn't actually make any difference to the sound. So, even when turned right up to ten on the gravity scale, my voice still comes out tinkling like a 1950s toothpaste advert. Are bubbles really only one molecule thin?

Like a Giant, Delicious Flake of Dandruff

May 30. I was just making this toasted cheese sandwich, when a thin slice of cheese (a wafer, really) that I'd just, er, sliced fell off the kitchen unit. I looked for it on the floor (mmmm… floor cheese), but there was no sign of it. It had literally disappeared. Then I thought it must be stuck to me somehow. Or to have worked its way inside my clothing. Nothing. All very mysterious. My fear is that I'm going to be gesticulating tonight at my Faber class, and the wafer thin slice of cheese is going to fall out of, or off me, like a giant, delicious flake of dandruff. Don't know how I'll explain that to the class. Would it be gross to eat it? Today is proving exceptionally problematic.

SUMMER

The Moon Starts to Go Wrong

June 1. There's a really unsatisfactory moon out tonight. It's just a fraction less than a half moon, and it makes everything feel slightly wrong, like when you know you have a migraine approaching. And the trouble is that, by tomorrow, it'll be just a bit more than half a moon. Someone has badly misjudged this. Pity, as it's otherwise a good night for gawp-ing at the moon.

I Had a Lover's Quarrel with the World

June 2. Did my best to shrug off my manflu by going for a walk with Monty and Mrs McG in the lovely West Hampstead graveyard. I was collecting names for future novelistic use when I came across what appeared to be my own gravestone. It was a simple and rather beautiful piece of slate with, carved in deep, sharp letters,

> TONY
> I had a lover's quarrel with the world

Spent the rest of the walk composing appropriately mordant epitaphs for myself, an activity in which Mrs McG partook with startling enthusiasm.

> Beneath this stone
> There lies poor Tone;

Once flesh, now bone,
He died alone.

Etc. etc.

Alpha Male Blues

June 3. One of my main jobs as the alpha male of the family, the rampant silverback, the protector and provider, is to blow down any length of tubing we encounter in our day-to-day lives. Any cardboard tube longer than a toilet roll: scaffolding, drainpipes, those curious concertina-like lengths of plastic hosing you find coming out of the ground on building sites, that sort of thing. To lay aside my habitual modesty for a moment, I'm very good at this. I can produce a variety of tones and effects, from a plangent musicality, not unlike an oboe, through a faintly comic didgeridoo, all the way to a bone-shaking, biblical horn-blast.

So I was quite pleased when my daughter's new violin bow came in a nice long tube. I expected to produce something like the sound envisaged by Wagner when Wotan prowls around the stage: sonorous, deep, majestic and yet unsettling: a sense of masculine power only just constrained by the bonds of reason and civilization.

However, in front of the whole family, all I managed to emit was a feeble honk, like the last dyspeptic belch of a disappointed man, dying in a nursing home, in Slough.

At this point my son stepped forwards and took the tube from my unresisting hands. He then blew upon it, and the entire flat resounded. It was like a trumpeting mammoth. The rest of the family broke into applause, and I trailed to my study, defeated, alone. The baton had been passed. The old silverback was defeated. And yet I felt, co-mingled with the gloom of perished glory, that spark of pride. I'd taught the boy well. My work was done.

Not Away, but Towards

June 4. I was thinking back to schooldays, doing some psycho-archaeological research for my current project. There was a kid in my year, picked on, persecuted, really, just because he looked a bit odd, with his large lips and goggly eyes. I never joined the tormentors, but I never quite had the guts to stick up for him – he wasn't one of my friends, so I wasn't prepared to risk a beating on his behalf, or even the other, less tangible danger of acquiring some of his loser/outsider taint. Plus, there were other kids who had it much worse, and he was never entirely alone – he had a little group of friends, someone to talk to at break, someone to say 'are you all right?' when one of the hard kids gave him a dead leg, or daubed shit on his schoolbag.

But over the years I've worried about him, and hoped he was OK. So I just looked him up on Facebook, and found him, still up there, in Leeds. Rather handsome, now, in middle age, with four smiling kids. Things worked out for him, it seems. His resilience and fortitude saw him through.

And then I remembered how, on the last school sports day of our lives, he made a bid for glory in the 1500 metres, not pacing himself, but sprinting from the outset, somehow marshalling his gangly limbs into a semblance of athleticism.

And suddenly the school saw him for the first time, not as a victim, nor yet quite as a hero, but just as a kid, an actual kid, and began to cheer and yell, and I pushed myself to the front of the crowd and screamed him on (we were in the same House, for sports – St David's) and it looked like he was going to win, but he was caught, just on the line, by the year's champion runner, Martin something, Gilpin, perhaps. And the yells turned into a sigh, because we knew that something amazing had almost happened.

So he lost that one, but he didn't stop running – not away, like some of us, but towards.

A Slice of Danish

June 5. Mrs McG has gone to deliver a paper at a conference in Copenhagen. She had her highlights done before she went, and bought a new outfit. A cool, clean, simple, efficient outfit, of the sort a hot detective in a Scandi crime drama would have worn. I told her that I also used to deliver papers, but my round got taken off me by a bigger boy, who pushed me in some nettles and then put dog poo on my bike saddle. She didn't find it amusing, even though it's true, sort of.

I'm generally too self-absorbed and complacent to feel much in the way of jealousy, but I'm feeling a spidery tingle of it now. I suppose she'll go down well with the handsome Danes and Swedes and Norwegians. They'll sense an affinity, and want to crack open that icy reserve, like an egg. Er, an egg made of ice. Yes, that's it, an ice-egg, with a hot liquid centre. And, OK, that hot centre would melt the ice shell, so they'd have to get a move on. But I expect it'd be worth it. For them.

A Mnemonical Ditty, for Søren

June 6. I was toying with some Scandawegian names to pin to the rugged Viking types I was picturing Mrs McG cavorting with ('Noo, I vill be squeezing the titty, ya? Yew hooled onto m'beard.'). Sven, of course. Perhaps an Eric, although the associations there are problematic. And then Søren came into my head, and where there's a Søren, there's sure to be a Kierkegaard knocking about, too. Which reminded me of a rare conference I attended, back when I was still vaguely in academia. There was a German philosopher present, who was an expert on Kant. He pronounced Kant precisely as a normal person would say 'cunt'. When I mentioned Kierkegaard, which is something that can happen on those sorts of occasion, he snorted with derision. 'Ha ha, nein, nein, nein,' he scoffed, as if verbally telephoning for the philosophy police. 'Es ist nicht pronounced *Kierkegaard*, but like this: *Kiekegooore*.'

My inability to pronounce Kierkegaard soon became the talk of the conference. Complete strangers came up to me, and leered in my face: 'Go on, say it, say "Kierkegaard" in your funny way.'

It was all quite humiliating, and contributed to my decision to leave academia. Well, that and my inability to get any job interviews. But I resolved that at the very least, I'd learn how to pronounce the bastard's name. So I composed this little mnemonic ditty:

Autodidactly inclined,
I've struggled long and hard
To comprehend the complex mind
Of Søren Kierkegaard.

But now dismay, wrapped up in shame:
I've been told by a bore,
That 'Kierke-guard' is not his name –
It's Søren Kierke-gore.

Later, Hungry, He Ate the Moon

June 7. The series of shit moons has now come to a climax. It's as if someone had vaguely heard of the concept of a full moon, and tried to model one out of moon-coloured play dough, by just roughly rounding it off in his hands. And then he lost interest in the project, and went and sat in the cold on the bench outside the new little Waitrose in West Hampstead, and drank a can of Uruguayan lager, bought as part of the Crap Beers of the World promotion at the local no-name off-licence. And then he remembered the ill-formed moon in his pocket, and held it up to the dark sky, and tried not to despair.

Later, hungry, he ate the moon.

I Imagine

June 8. Oh, yeah, I should say, Mrs McG's back from her Scandi adventure. She seems… changed. I think the conference went well. The successful delivering of a paper can do wonders for your self-confidence. I imagine.

Exactly the Right Amount of Careful

June 9. Fell off my bike last night, on my way back from a book launch. Four hours in casualty were enough to establish that I didn't have any broken bones. Luckily, my skull absorbed most of the impact, protecting my otherwise vulnerable limbs. What happened was a dramatic brake failure on my new bike, followed by a spectacular sliding crash into the side of Domino's Pizza on the Finchley Road. I spent about ten minutes lying on the ground, during which time one of the Domino's men came out and asked me if I was OK. When I said 'fine' he went back inside and made some more pizzas.

Not quite sure how I got back home – suppose I must have remounted my bike. Mrs McG drove me to the Royal

Free, where I sat around with the other drunks and nutters, got X-rayed, had my wounds dressed (ear, leg, arm) and then wandered out, hoping to find a taxi. There weren't any, so I walked home, which took about an hour.

I suppose I should be more careful. But the fact I'm still alive suggests I'm being exactly the right amount of careful. And it's not as if I exactly live life on the edge.

We All Secretly Believe Ourselves Immortal

June 10. One of my proudest boasts is that ours is a zero-food-waste household, for the simple reason that anything that's about to be thrown out becomes my dinner. Well, tonight came the ultimate challenge. I found a piece of fish at the back of the fridge. None of us were sure where it came from or how long it had been there, though Mrs McG said she vaguely remembered taking something out of the freezer 'about a week ago'.

I had a quick sniff, and it was definitely fishy. I wouldn't have given it to anyone else, but I didn't like the thought of that noble cod giving up its loins for nothing. So I made a kind of improvised ramen, with miso paste, noodles, onions, ginger and a tin of water chestnuts that were already in the flat when we moved here, sometime in the late 1990s.

Anyway, it wasn't very nice, and the fish definitely had a certain… sweetness that you don't really expect or want in your seafood. I've never tasted that ammonial rotted shark that the Icelanders eat, but perhaps my cod loins were nodding in that direction. So now the waiting begins. I think the McGowan granite constitution can take it. But then, right up to the moment we perish, we all secretly believe ourselves immortal.

Nobody Really Likes Radishes

June 11. The big success of my window box market garden was the radishes, the last of which I've just picked. They grow quickly and abundantly, and they look like actual radishes that you might buy in a shop.

The downside is that nobody really likes radishes, so I end up eating them on my own, in a joyless act of self-sacrifice. But I've always been concerned about the leaves. I had a vague notion that they might be edible. The internet suggested that they were, but needed a bit of preparation. I opted for radish-leaf pesto. Got quite excited, making it. It had a lovely vibrant colour. What do you call it…? Yes, green! It looked like the best sort of Italian deli pesto. Then I tasted it. Fucking horrible. Bitter and vaguely metallic, as if I'd taken some spinach and rubbed it around a car engine or the derailleur on my bike.

Oh well. More joyless eating. It'll probably be good for me.

I Don't Know Why I Even Bought It

June 12. There's a lovely communal garden behind our flat, full of half hidden terraces, and secret footpaths through the shrubbery. The perfect place, in fact, to drink, on a sunshiny day. And some friends of ours from across the way have invited us out to do just that.

Now the only problem with the going-out-to-the-garden-to-get-drunk plan is that I'm wearing a clean, but startlingly unattractive, shirt. Blue, grandad collar, short sleeves. Whenever I wear it, Mrs McG makes her joke: 'Oh, that reminds me, I must book a check-up.' And it's true that it makes me look like a down-on-his-luck Australian dentist, eking out his twilight years working in a clinic at a detention camp for failed asylum seekers. But if I go and change it – given that it's quite clean enough for garden drinking – that makes me a certain kind of person – an unnecessary shirt changer for vanity purposes – that I don't really want to be.

So: to change (and look less like a dentist), or to keep my integrity (and look like a dentist)?

Truly, life is full of insoluble problems.

Unless I put a jumper on…

Winner of the Silver Medal in the Baltimore Design Awards

June 13. Just bought a new wallet. Was trying to work out how many I've had over the years. Definitely fewer than ten, despite my carelessness. And generally, I've worn them out, rather than losing them. Oddly personal thing, a wallet. And think where they live: next to your heart, or thrust deep in a trouser pocket, nuzzling your genitals. I'm sure, like the bicycle in Flann O'Brien's *The Third Policeman*, the exchange of molecules presupposed by Brownian motion means that a wallet takes on much of your personality.

The best wallet, though, the one I loved the most, I did lose. It was a gift from one of my rich American uncles – Tony, or Tommy, I think, rather than Jimmy. Neat, and beautifully designed, in pressed black leather. Despite its suppleness, it seemed to have an almost military snap to it. There was a little card that came with it, saying 'Winner of the Silver Medal in the Baltimore Design Awards', or something like that. I kept it in one of the credit card slots, not having any credit cards. And there was a photograph of M. Not as she was then, as that would have been too dangerous. But her at my age, or a little younger. Sitting in a garden, somewhere, smiling up at the camera. Not beautiful, perhaps, but pretty, so pretty.

It must have fallen from my blazer pocket as I ran down the hill after school to the Leeds bus station. I have a feeling

I even felt it, felt it slip gently down my body, and onto the grass. But I didn't recognize the sensation for what it was, as you never do, when you're losing something.

When I reached the station, I realized that the wallet and my bus pass and the photo were gone. I went back and searched, but of course it had been picked up and pocketed – it contained a five-pound note, earned on my Saturday job, pumping petrol.

I wonder if it's still in use, somewhere, that little wallet, Silver medallist in Baltimore. They wouldn't have kept the photo, of course. Unless they too were captured by that pretty face, and the dark hair. But there's no comfort in that. Leeds, so much to answer for.

The Healing Pasty

June 14. Generally, when brought low by depression or drink, or just the general Sadness of Things, I indulge in a cheese and onion pasty luncheon. And then I always think, as I did today, that it would be nice if you could buy things in units of one-and-a-half. Because, really, what I want is one-and-a-half pasties. One pasty isn't anywhere near enough, unless you're Mahatma Gandhi, and two, frankly, is excessive. That final half pasty feels like duty rather than pleasure – like... well, you can insert your own example, which will probably be less smutty than the one I was going to use.

So today I thought I'd try something cunning. I bought one cheese and onion and one amusingly Mediterranean spinach and feta cheese pasty. I did this thinking the novelty would fool my system into enjoying the whole shebang – a bit like when you think it might be interesting and refreshing to kiss someone upside down for a change (and, from my experience, it is, but not enough to make it worthwhile on a regular basis, or in social situations).

And the second reason for going down the spinach and feta route was that it would count as a vegetable, transforming the whole meal into a positive nutritional exercise.

Anyway, I performed the experiment, and I'd have to declare it a moderate success, in the admittedly somewhat specialized, McGowan, sense of not being a complete disaster. And it's had the bonus of helping to settle things down after the manky-cod loin fiasco of the other night.

So, I'm saying, green shoots, green shoots.

Huge Bottom

June 15. As part of my regular series in which I discuss CHEESE, I'd like to talk about Västerbotten, a cheese from the country of Sweden. It's as if parmesan and cheddar were trapped in a loveless marriage, but still managed, probably as a result of some *Who's Afraid of Virginia Woolf*-style hate sex, to produce a beautiful cheese-child. And the pain half concealed behind the cheese baby's eyes should make eating it a troubling process, but it isn't – it slips down very easily. Anyway, it's a deep, meditative, philosophical and profound cheese, but not without a sense of humour – like reading Ibsen to the sound of Sibelius, while Strindberg does armpit farts in the background.

Amusingly, 'Västerbotten' is Swedish for 'huge bottom'.

A Man with a Mullet Going Mad with a Mallet in Millets

June 16. Went to a little drinks party for the Faber Academy tutors. It was fine, although none of the other tutors had the faintest idea of who I was. I'm used to that – there's a fundamental asymmetry at work. Most children's writers read adult books, but few adult writers (unless compelled by their reproductive mishaps) go the other way. So I swallowed down my ego, with as much beer as was necessary.

One sweet moment was provided by finding out that one of the tutors was exactly the same age as me. It was deeply strange and rather wonderful. She's from Cornwall, I'm generic northern, but we had precisely the same frame of reference. Everything I knew, she knew – I mean telly, music, books – the important things. In fact, her knowledge not only encompassed mine, but overhung it – like a maple leaf placed over a sycamore – as she remembered various ITV kids' programmes that I never watched. We even completed each other's Half Man Half Biscuit quotes. There's a man with a mullet going mad with a mallet in Millets, etc. etc.

It all made me think how much texture, how much richness, you lose, when you're just a few years apart in age. I don't think anyone born after 1966 or before 1964 will ever quite get me, or truly understand what the fuck I'm on about.

It also generated a very slight erotic energy – one based not at all on physical attraction, but purely on the fact that we were epistemologically conterminous. I understand that something similar passes between siblings raised apart, who meet as adults. I suppose this quasi-erotic component of our discourse may have passed her by, as she limited her flirtatiousness to agreeing that I would have made an excellent *Blue Peter* presenter, in the lean years after the departure of John Noakes.

Roy Hattersley's Lover

June 17. Wandering aimlessly around West Hampstead, I found myself before a bookshelf in the Oxfam shop on West

End Lane. I looked blearily at a small paperback – a 1970s Pan. Two figures scantily entwined. We could only see the back of his head, but she looked to be having a nice time. The title appeared to be *Roy Hattersley's Lover*, and I found myself overcome with the mirth of despair. Then I blinked and saw it was, obviously, *Lady Chatterley's Lover*. I expect it's overwork. Truly, I am spent, like the eggy husk of an old and rather disappointing firework. The sort that it's perfectly safe to return to. Not that anyone would bother.

Most of Them Appear to Be 'Breast'

June 18. There's a young woman sitting opposite me in the British Library, and whenever I stare vacantly ahead of me, which I spend quite a lot of time doing, as part of the cogitative process, she's doing roughly the same sort of thing. So then our eyes meet embarrassingly for a moment. And then I let my eyes dip to avoid the naked stare, but it turns out she's got a very low-cut top on, so I obviously have to avoid that, which means I have to look away at an angle, say to about ten o'clock, which is uncomfortable and annoying and not at all conducive to the Act of Creation, so then I'm forced to start typing again, but without the ideas being properly cooked.

Rubbish, really. And I've already eaten my lunch, so there's nothing to look forward to. I have written a thousand words, though.

And, reading through, most of them appear to be 'breast'.

I'll Have That

June 19. Just went down for some milk to the new Micro-Waitrose in West Hampstead. They have some needlessly complicated self-service stations there that cause great confusion among members of the easily bemused community. Today, for the first time, I decided to pay by cash, having scooped up a fistful of miscellaneous coins from the bowl in the kitchen. I searched for a slot of some kind, hoping it would be like the telephone boxes of my youth, when there'd be a satisfying amount of resistance before your money went down, as if BT didn't want your money. Rather than the expected slot, you have to put your coins on a little pressure-sensitive conveyer belt that then moves it towards a fringed cavity. Before it reaches what you assume will be the drop into the machine's innards, a little wizened plastic hand shoots out and grabs your coins, one by one, and a witchy voice says, 'I'll have that, I'll have that.'

I complained about this to the man standing there, who looked a bit like Lenny Kravitz.

He just shrugged his shoulders and said, 'Headquarters', like that explained everything.

The Sea, the Sea

June 20. 'We invite applications from creative writing candidates who are fascinated by the sea, and the science of the sea, and who have demonstrable skills in writing poetry. Their task will be to explore the role poetry has in speaking up for the intertidal zone and the world beneath the waves.'

I'd quite like to have a crack at that post – after all, I've recently written poems celebrating anchovies, the manatee and the joy of harpooning mermaids. Except, of course, it's in Hull, and I can't see Mrs McG moving there, just because the beer's cheap and there's a couple of decent curry shops in town.

Plus, well, 'fascinated' would put it a bit strongly. I'm more *quite interested*, in the sense that I don't actively hate it. And it would probably come out in the interview.

'So, Dr McGowan, tell us about your fascination with the sea.'

'Ah, well, cod and chips, great. Peeing over the side of the cross-Channel ferry, love all that. Getting pulled down by a giant octopus, tentacles wrapped around me, the gnashing chitinous beak… can't reach my Tarzan knife, ungowa, ungowa, but the dolphins can't hear me, aaaggghhhhh, gurgle… gurgle… – not so much.'

An Empathy Thing for Things

June 21. I found some reddish crystals in an unmarked container under the sink. For some reason I formed the idea that they might be bath salts, and used them as such on several occasions. I've now lost faith in this hypothesis. It's been pointed out to me that I've turned slightly pink, and so has the bath. Also, the 'salts' haven't performed any of the invigorating or rejuvenating functions that I was vaguely hoping for. I still don't know what the crystals are – rat poison, drain unblocker, incense, carpet deodorizer have all been mooted. The only consolation is that I didn't act on my initial impulse to see if, once in solution, they were intended as mouthwash.

I suppose it's all part of my compulsion to use things up. I can't pretend this is a life-affirming desire to drink down the whole of life's bottle, yea unto the dregs. It's more a fear, I think, of loneliness. Not, I should stress, my own. I like being alone. Being alone frees me from the need to be Anthony McGowan. No, it's an empathy thing. An empathy thing for things. The thought that there is some small, sad, unused portion, ignored and unloved. And my job is to love it, until there's none of it left.

Mrs McG takes a harder line on these matters, and so I often go through the recycling cupboard, checking for a smear of shampoo, or a usable film of toilet cleaner.

Money Issues, Toothache, Athlete's Foot

June 22. Here's something I've learned: whenever I'm stuck on a plot (or something else literary), planning and mulling never solve it. All that solves it is writing through it, i.e. the act of solving a literary conundrum is always writing it, never thinking it. The solution arrives through the practical work of the fingers, not through abstract thought.

And I wonder if life is the same – life's problems aren't ever solved by thinking about them, but by living through them, and that often the lived solution will be quite different from any you could have arrived at *a priori*. Not quite sure how (or if) this dovetails with my other theory about problems, which is that they come in two sorts (of course): the sort that get better if you don't think about them (love issues, stomach ache) and the sort that gets worse if you don't think about them (money issues, toothache, athlete's foot).

Right, back to work – another thousand words to hammer out before the library closes at eight.

The Midnight Feast

June 23. I came across a curious sight this morning as I walked Monty: a dumped black bin liner, its bloated abdomen neatly sliced, and the guts strewn over the street. And then a trail of bulging white nappies, like spineless albino hedgehogs, leading to a dense knot of indestructible rhododendrons. I followed the trail and saw a sort of nest, thick in the clump. And here the nappies' locks had been picked, and they lay unfurled, like brown flowers, their butterscotched interiors open to the eye. And I saw at once what this was: a vulpine midnight feast of baby shit.

Reductio ad Absurdum

June 24. Just watched Spike Jonze's *Her.* Best film I've seen all year. Incredibly well written, but it's the acting that makes it sing. However, it's slightly dismaying how uninterested the film maker is in the structure of society in the future, i.e. the economics, politics and social system. The only problems are personal problems – whom will I love; who will love me. It's a profoundly conservative view of art. The politicians and bankers will never be made to quail by a kooky romantic comedy. I hold with Adorno on this: any art that eases the pain of existence simply pads our chains. The only permitted laughter is the bitter laughter of rage and despair. I suppose the logic dictates that the same goes for food. And probably shoes. Every time you shake that stone out of your shoe, you make it less likely that you're going to overthrow the system. Same when your underpants get twisted up your crack. Leave them there, lest you settle into complacency.

Ballocks: I hate it when I get trapped into *Reductio ad absurdum.*

Laughter and Weeping Must Take You by Surprise

June 26. Everyone is in a heightened emotional state because of a big row over housework. The kitchen is silent, although the air still resonates with the last of the guttural shouts, the last of the wails. Some instinct – or perhaps just the need to do something… anything – causes him to put his foot on the pedal of the kitchen waste bin. The mouth opens and he peers in. And there, in the dark heart, he finds a pair of lady's shoes. He takes them out.

'What was wrong with these?' he asks, mystified by the idea of throwing away shoes.

'Look at the soles,' she says, patiently, as if to a child or an idiot.

He looks. What he sees reminds him of a rotted corpse, with gaping holes and frayed flaps of white, rubbery skin. And as he contemplates the shoes, he senses everyone watching him, waiting for his next move.

The pressure is intolerable. He turns the shoes the right way up, hiding the horror below. He notices the laces.

'But these are fine,' he says, and begins to pull the laces from the eyes.

'What are you doing, Dad?'

It's the youngest one, her own eyes red from the traumatic hoovering dispute.

'Laces,' he says. 'Perfectly good. I have shoes without… I need… Starving children in Africa, and we throw away perfectly good laces.'

One lace is hopelessly frayed at the end. He hides it from the family, like an inept conjurer. He hides it, also, from himself.

Half an hour later he hunches over a pair of his own shoes, newly laced in old, unsuitable, frayed, discoloured laces. He considers weeping. But who ever thought, 'Yes, now is the time to weep,' and then weeps? Laughter and weeping must take you by surprise, if they are to take you at all.

All the Pestos

June 27. My Frankensteinian explorations into the pesto dark zone continue. Tonight I've made pesto from spinach. It tastes like pesto. So far I've chalked up radish leaves, rocket, iceberg lettuce and now spinach. I'm beginning to think that you can make pesto out of almost anything, and it will end up tasting like pesto.

Next, the green cardboard from a shoebox, bedroom curtains, asbestos.

Another Chocolate Teapot

June 28. I've been reading a little on the history and theory of children's literature, and I was struck by how everyone seems to accept the familiar Philippe Ariès theory, that childhood didn't really exist as a concept before the early modern period (roughly the seventeenth century), and that children were dressed and treated (and exploited) as small adults.

I've never found this theory particularly plausible, and after encountering it in a naive form in various collections of writings on children's lit, I thought I'd look into it. And it transpires that Ariès's theory has been extensively criticized by other historians, and can only be sustained (if at all) in a highly modified form. And yet writers on children's lit carry on as if it's unambiguously the case that childhood is a modern invention. This always happens whenever a concept or idea is wrenched from one area of knowledge and hammered into another, whether it's Heisenberg's Uncertainty principle, or chaos theory or evolutionary psychology. These borrowings almost always turn out to be variations on the theme of the chocolate teapot.

The Decline of the British Bicycle Manufacturing Industry

June 30. There's another big publishing party tomorrow, this one at the Serpentine Gallery. That was the venue for my first ever publishing do, a HarperCollins party, back in 2003 (I think). I was unpublished, and there as a sneaky +1 – Mrs McG was the official guest. I knew not a soul in the book world, and felt somewhat overawed. The first person I bumped into was a very well-known literary novelist, surrounded by a giggling crowd of sycophants of the kind I've always coveted, but never quite attracted. He wasn't one of the better-looking authors at the party, with a face like a ballsack coarsely manipulated into the rough approximation of a visage. But he had a certain not unimpressive queenly presence, which the acolytes feasted on, the way certain ants suck the sweet liquor extruded from an aphid's anus.

The author looked me in the eye, as I tried to squeeze past on my way to the bar, and set out explicitly what his preference was, and suggested precisely how I might like to gratify it, as the sycophants rolled around at the Wildean brilliance of it.

I don't suppose it was a serious proposition – he was just trying to discommode a young whipper-snapper. It had the opposite effect. After years of Civil Service tedium, followed by more years of solitary study at the British Library, it suddenly felt like the Literary Life had just come and given me a big wet kiss. I could have embraced him and his handmaidens.

Sadly, the subsequent years have never really delivered on that early promise.

Later on I met Alan Sillitoe. We talked about the North, and the decline of the British bicycle manufacturing industry.

Dormice Factoids

July 1. Some things I've learned today in the library: the best bait to catch an edible dormouse is bacon dipped in brandy; the Minorcan giant dormouse is extinct; until recently there were no dormice in Ireland, but they have spread rapidly since 2010, delighted by the abundance of hedgerows. So, I think I've got the dormice covered, fact-wise.

But I'd still love to see one. And a harvest mouse. Playing in the construction sites and waste ground as kids, we often came across dead mice and voles, which always received from us a Christian burial. A crisp-bag shroud, a few dignified words. There were even more dead shrews, as few predators will eat a shrew. Those we treated with less reverence, and more fear. There's something evil-looking about a shrew – that long nose, those sharp, crude little teeth. There's no mercy in a shrew. The densely furred little body would be flicked away into the long grass with a stick, though we might find it again a week later, dancing with maggots. Then we'd bury it, although without ceremony, in a plague pit or pauper's grave, like Mozart.

Smeared with Swanshit

July 2. Well, the party – which took place in the Summer Pavilion at the Serpentine – was a fine affair, full of people who were interesting, accomplished, amusing and beautiful. And yet I felt rather like someone putting his hand out for a taxi, only to find each one has the light dimmed. I think you hit an age when every party leaves you feeling empty and desolate. For me that age has come.

I suppose the main problem is that the books I've written for this publisher have only done quite well, and they are the kind of publisher for whom 'quite well' counts as really not very good. I have a sense that, on this tight-run ship, I have been invited up from my cabin for a stroll around the deck. A kindly mate will suggest I come to the rail and take a look at a school of porpoises, or an exultation of flying fishes, and then I will feel a sharp pressure between my shoulder blades.

So I wandered from group to group (I've abandoned my ship metaphor now – don't be imagining rigging or salt sea spray), never feeling a part of anything, drinking too much and shunning the vol-au-vents. My best friend on the editorial side is now rather high up, and was too busy hobnobbing with the gods of children's publishing to waste time with me.

My writer friend Arlo was there, ravenously hunting for love, but that made him an unsatisfactory companion, especially as he's a lot more famous than me, and whatever kindness was on offer went his way.

I had one interesting conversation with an editor, who kept her mobile phone in the top of one of her cowboy boots, like a Derringer, and I thought she was very cool. She's in charge of a famous imprint for younger readers. She seemed to be dangling before me the possibility of a job, and I eagerly suggested some possible titles: *A Short History of the Vest*, a picture book version of Derrida's *Of Grammatology*, with flaps to lift and tabs to pull. You know, trying to be funny to hide my excitement about the idea. Anyway, doesn't matter, as I can't remember who she was, and I don't suppose I made a very coherent case, and it may not have happened anyway, as I had quite a lot to drink and was in a state of heightened emotion.

And then at the end, as the party broke up, I tried to take a shortcut to the pub, and found myself utterly lost in the desolation of Hyde Park with not another living soul around. And eventually I thought that I could find my way out if only I could pass across a stretch of duck-infested water, and I waded out half a mile or so to my knees, and then further to my waist, and finally to my neck, and then realized I didn't know which way was the shore, and at that moment a line of geese and swans drifted by, and I watched them for a while, and they beheld me with godlike indifference, which made me think they might be sleeping. And then I saw there was a sort of island in the darkness of the lake, and I briefly considered living there, forever, on duck and swan. And then I bestirred myself, and found that I was on the nightbus home, damp to the armpit, and smeared with swanshit.

Bad Pasty

July 4. Just had that rarest and most distressing of experiences: a bad cheese and onion pasty. It had been left too long in the warming cabinet – overnight, I suspect. The outside had, essentially, calcified. The filling had the texture of lava the second before it solidifies. I took a few bites, then stared at it sadly, for a while, before falling back on alternative sustenance – the second cheese and onion pasty I'd bought. It was a good one. Then I began to feel a bit sorry for the first pasty. After all, what was I but a stale pasty, left to desiccate in life's warming cabinet. So I ate that one, too.

X-Ray Vision

July 5. The author finds himself at a book award party. He's not sure why he's there, as he hasn't been shortlisted. Or longlisted, for that matter. It's probably the free drink, but that wouldn't explain why he was invited. It's midweek, so perhaps they've had trouble filling the room. He joins a group of vaguely familiar figures, but they drift away, leaving him alone with a young woman professionally attached to one of the shortlisted authors. Editor, perhaps, or publicity person.

'Sorry about my sweaty face,' he tries. 'I had to dash to get here before the wine ran out. I don't want to have to resort to swigging the dregs from abandoned glasses, again.'

She doesn't seem very interested, and conversation dries up. She makes those little movements that indicate someone is about to bolt, but hasn't yet worked out where.

'I've had my eyes lasered,' he says, hoping to keep her so it doesn't appear that he's totally friendless at the gathering. There's a pause while she takes this in.

'Oh, that's nice,' says the woman. 'Did it work?'

'Quite well. But there are some side-effects.'

'Really?'

'Hmmmm, yeah... There's some X-raying.'

'What?'

'You know, just mildly. I can see through... things.'

He expects that she'll laugh at this, and the tension will be relieved, and she might even stay until the speeches begin, at which point he can sneak out. Instead she holds the book she's carrying – the shortlisted one by her author – higher up, covering her chest area.

'No! I wouldn't, er, use it on...' But now he can't stop himself. 'I mean, I'd never use it, my ability, I mean, all the way, down to the skin. I'd go as far as the bra and then stop. No further. Or use it for detecting hidden weapons. See that man over there, the tall one with a beard? He's got a tomahawk strapped under his arm.'

The young woman looks over, a little sceptically. But she hasn't ruled it out.

Then his one friend in the room appears. The woman takes the opportunity to slip away. As she leaves she carefully places her leather satchel behind her, covering her bottom.

'Did you tell her about your X-ray vision?' asks Arlo.

'Well, er, I may have mentioned it.'

'You should keep quiet about that.'

Please, Sensei, NO!

July 7. I have a new Faber Academy course beginning tonight. My fifth. Each time I start a new one I find that my notes are entirely incomprehensible, so I have to start from scratch, reinventing the wheel. (Lesson 1: avoid cliché.) The one constant is my tomfoolery, my capering and prancing around, trying to get everyone to like me. Well, I thought this time I'd go all austere. At the beginning of the session I'm going to have ten minutes of silence, during which I stare them all out, one by one. If any of them challenges me, I shall arm-wrestle them into submission. Then I'm going to make them sit and watch me peel and eat a hard-boiled egg, with my nails sharpened to points. And I'm going to get them to call me Sensei, or Master. And rather than going to the pub with them afterwards, I'm going to chase them out of the Faber building with one of those Kendo sticks.

'Yah! Yah!'

'Please, Sensei, no…'

The Flensing Knife

July 8. It didn't work. I sweated blood (remember Lesson 1) to make them like me. I smiled too much and laughed too hard, like an extra in a party scene, desperately trying to catch the director's eye, and so ruining the take. I coaxed them down to the Museum Tavern, buying all the drinks, until I was left alone by myself, still grinning my fool's grin.

I wish that either I didn't care so much about being liked, or that I was better at making people like me. At the moment it's the worst of all possible worlds (see Lesson 1). I'm a cowardly sadist, a hot air balloonist afraid both of heights and balloons, a monkey who abhors bananas, a finicky dung beetle.

Mrs McG was waiting up for me when I came in. She has the sort of face suited to disdain.

'Where have you been?'

'The first night. I was trying to… I feel guilty about… They pay a lot of money, so I feel I owe them, er…' There was a slight pause while I tried to think of the right coinage for a debt of this sort. 'Slices of my soul.'

I mimed cutting sections of my soul away. To begin with I used an imaginary flensing knife, of the sort formerly employed in the whaling trade, long and flexible. Then, unsatisfied, I switched to an electrically powered bacon slicer, moving my soul methodically back and forth, making a nice job of it.

In both cases, rather than my soul, I suppose what I was slicing was more in the region of my liver. At some stage during the performance I realized that Mrs McG had gone to bed. I followed shortly after, although I lay awake for some time, going at my liver/soul with, alternately, the flensing knife and the bacon slicer.

Stolen Soup

July 9. A British Library day. As usual I brought a packed lunch, and, as usual, it was a sandwich and a flask of miso soup. I wheeled my bike through to the new covered bike park they have there, and, on a whim, left my sandwiches and whatnot in my rucksack, which I locked to the bike frame. At lunchtime I went to fetch it, intending to eat my sparse repast in the refreshing cold of the courtyard.

But then when I picked up the flask, it seemed disconcertingly light. I opened it, and saw that it was empty. Someone had come along and drunk all my soup. I thought that was an extraordinary thing to do, but consoled myself with the thought that they must have been really hungry, and at least they'd left me the sandwich, and the empty flask.

I decided I ought to put the rucksack in the lockers in the basement of the library, and then got in a lift to go back up to the second floor. There was a young woman in the lift with me. She had a neat, studious look to her, with a small element of craziness, which seemed just right for the library. A little befuddled by her presence, I accidentally pressed the 'LG' button rather than '2', which caused a delay, as the doors closed, then opened, then closed again. I smiled apologetically at the woman.

I noticed her shoes – they were like desert boots, but with a high heel.

'Nice shoes,' I said.

She half smiled and, encouraged, I added, 'If I were a woman, I'd wear shoes like that,' which was actually true – they looked both comfortable and stylish.

She didn't smile, this time, but looked away, and I panicked in case she thought that I was telling her that I liked to dress up in women's clothes. I thought about explaining that I didn't, particularly, but instead said, 'Someone just stole my soup,' thinking we could have a light-hearted discussion about that.

But as soon as the words were out of my mouth, I realized what had really happened. I'd obviously just forgotten to make any soup, and absent-mindedly put the empty flask in my bag. That took the wind out of my conversational sails.

The doors opened on the first floor and a man got in. Even though the woman obviously wanted to go up to the second floor, she got out. It was probably my worst ever British Library lunch hour.

A Failure to Perform in the Hairdressers

July 10. I have a stressful social function to negotiate tomorrow and thought I'd better get my hair cut in order to give more of an impression of mental stability. Rather than my usual artisanal shearing, I decided to go somewhere swanky and get it, er, *styled*. I was quite prepared to bite the bullet and smash through my usual £8 ceiling. Anyway, I picked on a place in West Hampstead, and got as far as opening the door, and smelling that strange smell that only hairdressers have – perfume, hairspray, burnt hair, longing – and approached the counter. I was wearing some hapless combination of tweed and corduroy, and I'd considerately picked off the identifiable food remains from my jumper.

I deliberately hadn't done anything with my hair, so they could experience it in its natural state.

I had to wait a while for the lady behind the counter thingy to notice me. She was very pretty, but had so much foundation on that I imagined that the face beneath it must be unnaturally small, about the size of a satsuma.

And then I opened my mouth and realized that I had no idea what to say. I mean in the sense of what to ask for. What sort of style. How short or long, or if I wanted something technical doing to it, highlights or straightening, or reinforcing with carbon rods, or whatever it is that happens at hairdressers. I felt the panic begin to rise, and my face was coated in sweat. So I walked out again, without saying a solitary word.

And it just occurs to me that you have to make an appointment anyway, at that sort of establishment, so no good would have come of it.

I've decided to settle for trimming my sideburns, and using a black marker to colour in my three grey hairs.

All Problems Are Slow Punctures or Fast Punctures

July 13. Few things are more dispiriting than a slow puncture. I used to say that all problems can be divided into the ones that get better if you ignore them, and the ones that get worse. But now I think I prefer the puncture metaphor. All problems are slow punctures or fast punctures. The fast punctures are more dramatic, and call for immediate action, and pretty well fuck up your day. But the slow ones destroy your soul. Each morning you return to your bicycle filled with dread and foreboding but also, and this is the thing that really kills you, hope. Will the tyre still be jauntily firm, and ready to go? Will it be utterly flaccid and useless? Or will it be somewhere in between, just about able to get you through your ride, but without giving any real satisfaction?

And you put off doing anything about it for days, weeks, years. But, ultimately, the solution to both the fast and the slow puncture is the same: you sell up and buy a new house, and hope someone might have left a usable bicycle behind them in the garage, even if it's a Chipper from 1975, and you look like an idiot riding it.

The Moon Improves

July 14. The moon is wondrous tonight. She's leaning back and laughing at the universe. And not some tight-arsed, sardonic laugh, but a whole-hearted, welcoming, Rabelaisian laugh, inviting us all to join in. Good work, moon, good work.

Pearl & Dean

July 15. I recently shifted my allegiance from the Oral B to the Philips Sonicare dynasty of electric toothbrush. Oral B had never let me down, but I just felt in need of a change. I wasn't actively regretting my disloyalty, but nor did I think it had much improved my life.

And then, just now, as I was brushing my teeth in the bath, I discovered that if you cup your lips around the stem while the brush is on, and make *wow-wow-wow* type noises, the effect is like that of a primitive vocoder, or that autotune thing Cher used. You can't really make any articulate sounds – all I managed was a decent stab at the Pearl & Dean advertising jingle you used to get at the cinema, the one that went *ba-ba ba-ba ba-ba ba-ba ba-ba-ba-ba-ba.* I suppose it's more like an electric kazoo than anything.

Still, though, it's better than not being able to do it, and I strongly believe that you should suck what sap you can from the dry stick of life.

Dismayingly of Liquorice

July 16. I have a not particularly attractive Levi's shirt that has three buttons on the cuff. I always wonder what terrible flapping sleeve calamity must have happened to the designer for him to have taken such precautions against the cuffs coming undone. And as one of my hobbies is rolling up my sleeves, then rolling them down again, and repeating this process randomly throughout the day, the excess of cuff buttons looms large in my life, at least while I'm wearing this shirt. I suppose I could just fasten one or even two of the buttons, but that seems like a waste. They're there, so I have to use them, the way you'd eat some wine gums you found on the floor, even if you didn't really want to. Or the black midget gems, from the olden days, that tasted not of blackcurrant but, dismayingly, of liquorice. Yeah, you'd eat those, even though you hated them, as you'd paid 5p for a quarter. Bastards.

The shirt also has an unnaturally small collar, with a tiny hole in each wing (if that's the right term). The holes look like they're there for a reason, but I can't imagine what it might be.

Herman

July 17. I saw Heimlich again, tonight. He was coming out of the tube station, flowing with the crowd of exhausted, angry commuters. He took a copy of the *Metro* from the stand, and wedged it under his arm.

I say Heimlich, but there were none of the familiar Heimlichian elements – the terror, the pursuit, the Expressionist lighting. Which made me think that it could not be him, the real Heimlich. But when I looked again, I saw that he still resembled me, a little. And I realized that there could only be one explanation. This was not Heimlich, *my* dwarf doppelgänger, but *Heimlich's* dwarf doppelgänger. It must be the case that not only humans but also dwarves have dwarf doppelgängers.

And must I now name Heimlich's dwarf doppelgänger? Would he be Herman?

No, madness. I couldn't go on naming dwarf doppelgängers in an unending chain to the end of time. This dwarf had nothing to do with Heimlich. Any resemblance to Heimlich or to me was purely coincidental. I had no idea what his name was. It could have been anything.

And yet, deep down, I knew that he was Herman.

A Change of Key

July 18. Walking back from the bus stop this morning, I found that I was whistling the Elton John song 'Sacrifice'. People underestimate my whistling skills at their peril: it's one of the few things I'm really good at, and it's a shame there's little demand for it these days, outside the shepherding community.

Anyway, I became worried that people might take me for an Elton John fan, so I quickly recalibrated, and changed to whistling the lovely Sinead O'Connor cover version. Which is actually in a different key, E*b* as opposed to C (I think), so that's not as mad as it might sound.

At their peril. A stupid thing to say. Ignoring the DANGER! SHARKS! sign might put someone in peril, or neglecting to go to the GP about that large lump, but underestimating my whistling skills is unlikely to have serious, long-term consequences. I should moderate my language. And see the doctor about that lump.

The Real Thomas Cromwell

July 19. On the radio this morning I heard a passing reference to the last Abbot of Glastonbury, Richard Whiting, a bewildered seventy-eight-year-old, hanged, drawn and quartered in 1539. Reading Thomas Cromwell's own words acts as a useful corrective to Hilary Mantel's portrait of the sad-eyed humanist:

> Item. The Abbot, of Glaston to (be) tryed at Glaston and also executvd there with his complvcys.

So, the outcome of the trial was decided well before it took place. Cromwell had all the records destroyed, so no one knows what the charges were, or the evidence. Whiting was dragged naked across the fields with a couple of other monks, then castrated, disembowelled and cut up into chunks. His head was spiked over the gates of the empty abbey and his limbs carted off to various other locations, to encourage the people in their obedience.

Was He Really Sober?

July 20. The Faber Summer Party. Held in the lovely gardens behind the Faber offices in Bloomsbury. It was impossible to move without jostling someone famous, an Ishiguro, an Edna O'Brien, a Tom Stoppard. But I was too shy to talk to any of them. I briefly found refuge with a group I knew, but when I returned from a bar expedition they'd dispersed like insurgents into the local population. I figure-of-eighted through the party for a while, reluctant to be discovered at solitary rest. I took to making unnecessary visits to the snazzy Portaloos they'd erected. Saw a few old pals in there, though it wasn't the sort of place to linger.

I decided that for once I wouldn't be the last person to leave the party. On my way out a voice called to me.

'Not going to the pub?'

It was a rather beautiful literary scout I'd met at the same party last year. Literary scouts work for foreign publishers, seeking UK authors who might do well abroad. They're the kind of people you're supposed to suck up to, unless you're famous enough to be the one who is sucked. She had the lovely accent and slightly tragic air of a French Resistance fighter. She was never going to make it to the end of the war, but while she lived, she lived.

'I might see you in there,' I said.

The Crack of Doom

July 21. I was amazed it lasted this long. I'd splinted the old, broken drying rack. One of those up-ended concertina-like designs. Folded down quite neatly, but at the expense of robustness. Overburdened, it just gave in. And now the long search for a replacement begins. As drying racks count as 'technology', the task has fallen to me. With great power comes great responsibility. At the Council of Elrond I have been given the One Ring to bear. I shall carry it unto the Crack of Doom.

The Williad

July 22. Triggered by my experiences at the Faber party the other day, I've been working on an epic poem about all the children's book illustrators I've stood next to in the Gents'. This is part of the middle section of Book I (of XI)

I've moistened the urinal cake
Standing next to Quentin Blake,
And waved around my magic wand
Cheek by jowl with Michael Bond.
I've made the pissoire fag-butt drown
In unison with Tony Browne,
And smiled, as we shook dry our twigs,
At grumpy genius, Raymond Briggs.
I've pointed my albino carrot
In harness with that nice Nick Sharratt,
And even had the chance to piddle
Beside my hero, dear Chris Riddell,
Though tragically I never will
Relieve myself with Eric Hill,
Or spray my sloppy drunken shoes
Within the sight of Shirley Hughes.
And now I've found (it saddens me)
Is that when illustrators pee
They fail to do it artfully,
By painting on the porcelain,
A handsome prince or princess plain.
And so it does not pay to watch
Them piss away beer, wine and scotch.
But me, I carve sweet yellow prose
On newly fallen winter snows,
And pen amusing limericks
On grungy crumbling outhouse bricks.

And so I've proved, by means of wee,
The absolute sweet victory
Of word o'er image. QED.

Resting My Eyes

July 23. How good it feels to be under way on a new project, making stuff up that wouldn't otherwise exist in the world; and, even better, when you know that this time the book will become embarrassingly huge, enraging both friends and enemies with the vastness of the fame and riches it will bring: not just the occasional kind review in a newspaper, but national and international acclaim. The Booker, of course, and the Carnegie, but also that other vaguely Scandawegian prize that pays out hundreds of thousands – no, not the Nobel, though that, as well, obviously, the Astrid Thingy prize, that's the one, and as well as the cheque, you get a massive gilded trophy like the FA Cup, and I'll go on an open-top bus tour of West Hampstead and, er, Leeds, and the crowds will be a major headache for the police and local authorities, and handsome young women will hurl their undergarments at me, screaming like Maenads, but not the sort of Maenads who tore poor old Orpheus apart, but slightly nicer ones, and they'd settle for a bit of hanky-panky, not that I would. [A gentle touch on the shoulder] What? No, just resting my eyes. Snoring? Not me. Yes, I know it's a library… Isn't a fellow allowed to have a think with his eyes shut any more? Bloody 1984, fascist dictatorship, I didn't fight in the Falklands just to be woken up in the…

Going Postal

July 24. A satisfying morning working methodically in the library. Then, my mind still largely in my fictional universe, I went to post a letter. I didn't have a jacket with me today, so had my hands full of sundry things: wallet, phone, iPod, sandwiches, can of ginger beer, packet of crisps. As I approached the postbox in Judd Street, I re-emerged fully into this world, and had a sudden, startling realization that I was going to post my wallet, as well as, or instead of, my letter. I moved the wallet carefully to my mouth, where I carried it like a spaniel with a duck.

I was congratulating myself on this cunning manoeuvre as I posted the letter. Along with my sandwich.

I thought about trying to find someone to open it up for me, but lost the will to go on. Just wished I'd put an address and stamp on it, so it would be delivered and I could eat it tomorrow.

Leifheit

July 25. With enormous relief I can announce that our Leifheit 81514 Pegasus 180 Classic Coated Steel Drying Rack is on its way.

But that name – Leifheit 81514 Pegasus 180 Classic – it's trying quite hard, isn't it. Was there a Leifheit 81513 Pegasus 180 Classic? Or a plain Leifheit 81514 Pegasus 180, lacking the 'classic' moniker? I think I'd probably just have gone with the Leifheit Pegasus. I suppose it was a committee thing, and everyone wanted a different name, and some kind-hearted manager thought, 'Fuck it, we'll go with the whole damn lot.' I'm imaging a harried, overweight German, essentially decent, and ashamed of his father's role in the war making drying racks for the Waffen SS. He just wants an easy life, with time to drink beer and eat sausage and play with his grandchildren. I hope things go well for you, Otto Leifheit, I truly hope they do.

Breaking In Is the Easy Part

July 26. Things were going quite well: had a nice lunch with a writer friend, did a few hours' solid work in the British Library, bumped into another writer friend, and went for a quick drink. OK, not that quick… Returned to get my bike from the bike park in the library, only to find the whole place shut and locked down.

It then occurred to me that I could climb over the metal railing to retrieve the bike – my thought processes not entirely unaffected by the drink I'd taken.

They looked quite scalable from below.

Tottering twelve feet in the air I began to perceive the folly of the plan.

But it was now as grim to go back as to go on, so I leapt down, spraining everything that could be sprained from sole to scalp. But at least now I was in among the bikes. The fatal flaw in my plan now became evident: how was I to exit with the bicycle? I considered hurling the bike back over the fence, but it's newish, and not my usual heap of crap… So, reluctantly, and guessing it would entail some fawning, I had to wheel it round to the main entrance, and hail one of the security guards to facilitate my release.

A rather dour African gentleman, looking a lot like a less genial Robert Mugabe, gave me a serious talking to, then called his boss, who gave me a slightly less serious talking to. There was some discussion about calling the police, but I pointed out that trespass wasn't a crime. They countered by suggesting that, since 1994, it is. I retaliated in a friendly way by claiming that they were falsely imprisoning me. I think I might have pronounced this as 'flassly empoisoning me', which detracted somewhat from the force of my argument.

In the end they let me go, and we shook hands. I was late for dinner and Mrs McG gave me an earful, though not, alas, a mouthful.

Amid the Eunuchs

July 28. I was part of a panel discussion today, at a big conference, which was in itself a subset of one of those fantasy/science fiction conventions. There were several thousand people crammed into Earls Court, like the damned in a Bosch hellscape. Many of them were Wookies. A surprising number were Unsullied – the eunuch warriors from *Game of Thrones*. Alas, I'm not quite sure enough of my potency to confidently dress as a eunuch, even an invincible warrior eunuch.

The convention crowd was actually extraordinarily pleasant. These were the sort of utterly hapless people shunned by society: shapeless blobs, stooping beanpoles, the goofy, the nerdy, the lonely. But here they found each other, and love slopped and splashed around like pigs' blood in a badly run slaughterhouse. Enormous queues snaked outside booths where you could have, for £15, your photo taken with Stan Lee, or a perplexed old lady who used to be a pert-breasted member of a starship crew.

It was always especially sweet when strangers wearing the same costume collided – two Dr Whos, two Saurons, two Desmond Tutus... and they would embrace and laugh, even though they had never met before, and had only this connection. I really wanted to be one of them. But it seems that, even among the outsiders, I am an outsider.

I found this all immensely charming, and I was delighted that these people had somewhere to go, and something to give their lives meaning, amid their own kind. The human race is better for having them. Indeed, if I were God, I'd decree more of them, and fewer of me.

But then the debate came. Good people on the panel, including a couple of old bookworld friends. Everyone was agreeing. We were getting nowhere. Looking out at the audience, I deduced immediately what would enrage them. I supplied it. They were enraged. Of course I was counting on that, and the (quite literal) boos and hisses. But what mildly irritates me is when people claim to have been insulted. If someone goes up to you and says, 'Oi! you're ugly and stupid and you smell weird, and you've got shit shoes, and I bet you spend your evenings having sex with a stuffed orang-utan, because no human would have you,' then you might well have the right to say, 'I've never been so insulted in my life!'

But if you say to someone, 'Well, free country and all that, but instead of reading *Twilight* for the nineteenth time, you should read *War and Peace*,' then I'd suggest that you haven't really been insulted at all.

But maybe I'm lacking in empathy, as I'm essentially impossible to offend (although very easy to embarrass).

The Good Life

July 29. I think the best thing about my life at the moment is my window box of wild rocket. Those crinkly leaves don't hate me for saying at best mildly controversial things. Their minds are pleasantly open to ideas they might not entirely share. They are generous of spirit. And then I get to eat them.

Stella, Grins for a Living

July 30. I haven't earned enough money for a proper holiday this year, so we're staying again at my in-laws' farmhouse in Brittany. Before we left, Mrs McG's dad told us that the farmer next door recently went on a pyromaniacal rampage and then bought a one-way train ticket to the coast and committed suicide by walking into the sea. I've packed my Garrett Ace 250, hoping it will provide some amusement for the kids, and help take their minds off Brittany.

I'm in the bar on the ferry, watching the terrible cabaret. The children and Mrs McG have gone to skulk in the windowless cabin. A bald man plinks away at a Bontempi organ, while a young woman in a sequinned costume grins at the audience. As far as I can tell, that's it, just the grinning. She was probably the prettiest girl in her class at school. And now she grins for a living at a crowd of half-drunk lorry drivers and harassed parents.

Ah, no, I was wrong. I thought that was the whole act, but in fact a magician has now arrived late on stage. He has the look of a startled vampire, surprised in his lair by Van Helsing, the stake already one mallet-blow into his chest. The young woman is his assistant. His lateness meant she had to stand there for ten minutes, while the Bontempi man played 'Fly Me to the Moon', and 'I Lost My Heart in San Francisco'. Her smile never faltered. I'm a little in love. It's probably the Stella. And loneliness.

The magic is terrible.

One trick involves pouring liquid from one receptacle to another. Each time the amount of liquid appears to be very slightly different, in a way you wouldn't entirely expect. I'm feeling too much pain on behalf of the girl. Stella, I'm going to call her. But I also feel for the magician. This isn't what he wanted.

Time to find the back-end of the boat and gaze out into the starless night.

The Toy Crossbow

July 31. The house has a lot of character, if by character one means decrepitude and awkwardness and a tendency to shake a gnarled fist at the world. Open beams, crumbling stone walls, a weasel infestation in the attic. It's hard to avoid the sense that it has been the scene of atrocities, familiar, dynastic, sartorial. It's situated close to a hamlet called Dolo, the sort of place that may have bustled gaily before plague and war left it a refuge for bandits and wild dogs.

There are some sweet memories, though, human traces, such as the little toy crossbow I found, perched on the windowsill in the very rustic kitchen. I'd made it for my little boy, twelve years ago, from hazel wood and string and a brass picture hook. I tried it out, and it was still able to propel a sharpened pencil clean across the room. Back when the world was new, and Gabe was three, we used it for boar hunting in the woods, and spearfishing for shark in the stream at the bottom of the garden.

I like to think that when I'm dead, and everything else I own is lost and decayed, and the electronic trash of our age forgotten, some kid will be chasing his sister (or her brother) around the room with this toy crossbow.

'What's up, Dad?' Gabe said, finding me, holding the toy.

'It's this bloody house,' I said. 'The dust… my allergies.'

First Blood

August 2. Just taught my son how to shave. A rather emotional rite of passage, as it turned out. And now his legs are lovely and smooth again.

Just my little joke.

But his first shave is a French one, which I hope isn't significant.

The Find

August 3. We tried out the metal detector in the garden, in between the thunderstorms. I thought that there might be some Iron Age Celtic coins, or perhaps a small Viking hoard. The Garrett Ace 250 proved excellent at discovering bottle caps and aluminium ring-pulls amid the molehills. Then, just in front of the house, we picked up a very strong reading. The kids gouged at the wet ground with sticks until we'd excavated an impressive trench. But no hoard. We were about to give up when Gabe said, 'Dad, there's something…' And there was. And it was big. Big like the thighbone of an iguanodon.

We carried on. Eventually we unearthed it. Mrs McG came out to have a look.

It was the head of a sledgehammer.

I knew, of course, the sad narrative behind it. A sullen, silent peasant, hating his nag of a wife. A final enraged encounter. He goes for the hammer. Murder is done. Then, being an idiot, he buries the hammer instead of the wife.

I kept the story to myself.

Licking Anemones

August 4. The weather has improved, and we've found a beach that admits dogs. Unfortunately, Monty is a raving UKIP supporter, and keeps yapping at the suave poodles, straining to have at them, Agincourt-style. The shore is made of rock pools, and the nine-year-old me would have loved it. Even the fifty-year-old version can spend an hour, watching the guppies dart and the stealthy manoeuvrings of the hermit crabs. I even, at long last, got up the courage to touch an anemone. Not just the mucusy blob stage, but even when the arms are out and waving. The poison tips of the tentacles have little barbs, but they are not long enough to penetrate the skin. So all you feel is a slight sticking sensation, which is curiously addictive. I wondered what it would feel like on the tongue… but dipping your head into rock pools and licking anemones isn't really the sort of thing you can do on a nice bourgeois French beach.

But the McGowans at least are talking. Isolation and the absence of the internet can do that to you.

The Melancholy Roadkill

August 5. There's a new indoor water park thingy near where we're staying. I took the kids, hoping to wear them out so they wouldn't be bothersome during the evening's cider drinking. Marching out of the changing rooms (troublingly omni-sexual, by the way…) in my traditional baggy swimming shorts, I was told a firm 'Non!' by a swarthy Breton attendant. He pointed with unnecessary vehemence to a sign on the tiled wall, which indicated by means of pictograms that there was a 'no swimming shorts' rule.

I was instructed to go and buy some Speedo-type things at the reception. The poor girl there pointed me towards various trunks, most looking like the sort of thing used by David to hurl his stones at Goliath.

'Plus gros,' I kept saying. 'Plus, plus grande.'

Finally she disappeared into a back room and came out with a pair of XXXLs that still seemed pretty flimsy.

Anyway, I put them on in the changing rooms, trying to hide myself from the women and strange children wandering around in there, and then wobbled out, greatly amusing my offspring. I kept catching glimpses of myself in various reflective surfaces, and to my eyes I looked quite naked, as the trunks were enveloped entirely by fleshy overhangs and lardy extrusions. They were also, paradoxically, a little loose, and I kept having to pull them up, and tighten the shoelace arrangement around the waist.

Fortunately, the kids were soon distracted by the watery slides and tunnels and so forth, and I took a turn around the pool, doing my usual stately strokes – the reverse humber, the slaint, the breast-nurdle. Eventually my daughter came and insisted that I have a go on one of the slides, and I allowed myself to be dragged up the hundreds of steps to the top.

She gave me a friendly shove, overcoming my hesitation, and down I hurtled, blinded by the spray but not neglecting to scream like a schoolgirl. About halfway down I realized why the trunks were supposed to be tight. My brief-yet-saggy ones were shipping water, inflating, like some obscene balloon animal. I tried to rectify this, by squeezing the water out, but the gravitational forces generated by the slide were too great.

And then I realized that things were becoming critical. A hull-breach was imminent. My yelps became ever higher in pitch… By the time I reached the bottom, closely observed by some hundreds of fascinated Breton teenagers, puzzled toddlers and mirthful adults, my trunks had been radically relocated, and all of my reproductive equipment was entirely on the outside of the fabric, lying like melancholy roadkill or, no, like some mutant sea creature washed up on the Breton shore – part squid, part bleached sea anemone, part dead guppy, with a grey-brown fringe of weathered bladder-wrack.

Sensing the guards approaching, I hurried back to the polymorphously perverse changing room, and then out into the steady French drizzle, where I threw the stupid trunks out into the muddy lake waters; and, when a hand neglected to come forth and take them down into the depths, I hurled stones at them until a grizzled fisherman asked me to stop, as I was 'bouleverser les poissons'.

The Soft Clock

August 6. On the dramatic beach at Saint-Briac, watching Rosie and Gabe playing in the surf. They go further out, and I start to get nervous, pacing before them on the sand. You can see the current pushing them along, from left to right, without them perceiving it – they think they are staying still, relative to the beach. Almost as if the giant hand of a soft clock were sweeping round, carrying them with it. Impossible not to think of it all as a metaphor for time passing, with you gradually ageing without noticing it, pushed inexorably towards the rocks of death.

The other lesson of the sea is that your kids, splashing in the surf, can't hear you scream at them.

He Goes a Little Mad

August 7. I've found myself dismayed by the cloying animal and vegetative fecundity of this place, the damp heart of Brittany. The arthropodic and molluscine superabundance particularly distresses me. I'm beset by bloodsuckers. Mosquitoes swarm to me, like frantic spermatozoa around the drying fallopian's last ovum. And horseflies blindly hurl themselves at me, maddened by the call of my croissant-sweetened blood. They crash onto my blue-grey skin with an audible 'tock', like raindrops hitting the window. Great orange slugs appear each morning, turgid and ridged, like some obscene sex toy, or glumly deflated, like a used condom. Moles proliferate – the garden is merely narrow strips of dead grass in between the brown humps.

Occasionally you'll see a pink nose emerge, and the worm-gorged mole will fix its black eyes on you with a monstrous indifference.

By humankind the land is sparsely populated. Once in a while a hunchbacked peasant will come stumping across a field, muttering to himself. One foot is encased in a rubber boot, roughly sheared off at the ankle; the other is wrapped in bandages, a yellow seepage pooled and crusted at the toe. When he sees me, he utters some guttural ejaculation, and shakes his fist, although I cannot know if it is aimed at me or at God.

Since we lost the arrows for the bow, the children keep themselves busy with furious arguments. Gabe has found a severed pig's head to worship and Rosie is forever on the brink of an eruption. I've hidden the meat cleaver in the woodshed. Mrs McG has conceived an irrational hatred for a pair of white trousers I brought with me, but their story will have to await a later entry. However, the isolation is quite conducive to creative work. I've speculated about staying here alone, to write. But at night the black silence unnerves me, and I populate the emptiness with ghouls, stalking close to the house, red eyes at the shutters.

I suspect when the relief party reaches here, they'd find me crouching in the corner, my hands over my head, raving about the moles, the moles.

Lager

August 9. In France they have a brand of cheap lager, just called 'Lager'. It tastes agreeably of lager. I've accessorized it with a wine glass, on account of my embourgeoisification.

We go back tomorrow. I'll miss the lager called Lager.

I thought about bringing the little toy crossbow back with me, but it belongs here. I felt the old house complain, when I took it from its place by the window.

'Your allergies bad again, Dad?'

Return

August 10. I stood at the back of the ferry, alone, looking out into the greys and greens. And the longer I gazed, the more I thought I could discern cetacean forms out there, in the roiling, uneasy sea. The spray from the blow holes; the curving backs of rorqual and right, sperm and blue. And then dolphins and orcas breached, and porpoises, by kelp caressed. And then mermaids, sighing in the foam, their modesty protected by a brassiere of scallop shells. But then the door to the bar swung open, and a lorry driver came out for a smoke, and brought with him the noise of the bar and the cabaret. Bingo. They were calling bingo. No whales, no porpoises, no mermaids. And darker colours than grey.

Bad Faith

August 12. One of my hobbies is scratching, and I was wondering, this morning, if there's a spot on my body that I've never yet scratched, and how extraordinarily pleasant it must feel if I could find one, and then scratch it for the first time, like the explosion of sensual joy I experienced on eating that first ever curry, in Manchester, in 1983, when taste buds that had never before been fired up were suddenly bathed in kormic glory.

But then I realized that you can't just scratch something that isn't itchy; or I suppose you can, but it's what Sartre would call 'une égratignure de mauvaise foi'. So I suppose I'll just have to wait until an itch occurs in the new place naturally, and take it from there.

And Lavatory Cleaner

August 13. I've noticed that there often comes a point in the writing of a book when you suddenly stop getting it. You just don't see the point of the thing any more, can't work out what it is you were trying to say, or why. The words you've written seem totally alien to you, as though badly translated from a foreign language. And you lose your own style. Each word seems unconnected to those before and after. Like an inept relay team, each word drops the baton of meaning, stops, picks it up, stumbles on. And there are days when life seems like that. When you lose the internal music, your style of being. And then you think that perhaps going on a massive bender, a three-day orgy of self-destruction, might be the cure. Except you have to cook dinner for the kids. And buy toilet rolls. And lavatory cleaner.

The Universe Punishes Me

August 14. I found myself unexpectedly in Golders Green this morning. I worked for a couple of hours in the public library, which was full of a completely different sort of eccentric to the ones I'm used to in Swiss Cottage Library – crazy Jewish cousins rather than irascible Jamaican grandfathers. At lunch I bought a bagel, and cycled to Golders Hill to chew on it. I found a bench in front of the tennis courts. Two men were playing. They were comical to behold, even before the action commenced. They were both dressed in Lycra, and one was tiny and round, the other a beanpole, at least six and a half feet tall. When they started to play, I realized that something special was happening. I don't think I've ever seen a human perform an act with such ineptitude. It was almost heroic. If I were that bad at something, and it was optional, as tennis is supposed to be, I just wouldn't do it. I'd find another hobby.

For the most part tennis shots arrange themselves on the horizontal plane – backhands and forehands go roughly from side to side. (Of course there's serving, and the smash to spoil my analysis, but let's just put them aside, for now.) But these guys had only two shots – a sort of underarm scoop, which sent the ball sailing out over the back of the court, and a weak-wristed flap, which sent the ball into the bottom of the net. They failed to have a single rally of more than two strokes. But they performed all this with the deep seriousness of elite athletes, grunting with the effort, fists pumping exultingly when a point was won. It was all very enjoyable. And then one sent the ball looping over the fence, near me. I thought I should pay for my entertainment by fetching it for them. They seemed to take this as their due, rather gracelessly, the way pros do with the ball boys and girls at Wimbledon. Anyway, I retrieved the ball and underarmed it back over the fence.

Or I meant to. Used to the meatier mass of a cricket ball, I fluffed it, and sent the ball more or less straight up in the air. In fact, it landed a little way behind me. The beanpole sniggered. For some reason I found myself apologizing. I picked up the ball again, and this time chucked it back properly. Alas, a gust of wind came up, and the ball didn't quite make it over the fence. The little fat Oompa-Loompa tutted, impatiently. I thought about hurling their stupid ball away in the opposite direction, or lasciviously sliding it inside my trousers and rubbing it around my groin and crack and then returning it once more, but I just left it there in a patch of nettles, got on my bike and cycled off.

Thus the universe punishes me for indulging in a few moments of assumed superiority.

No One Could Make Me

August 15. Had a huge panic attack listening to the discussion of the Virginia Woolf ballet on Radio 4's *Front Row.* And then, with a sense of relief that came close to exultation, I realized that I didn't have to go and see it, and no one could make me.

Downward Dog

August 16. There's a large mirror just inside the main entrance of our apartment block, which you can see through the distorting glass of the door, and whenever I walk towards it from outside, keys in hand, and see the unfamiliar hunched, angry, hulking, scowling figure reflected back at me, I have a flash of apprehension, and assume it's a burglar or brigand of some kind, on his way out with the purloined loot, and I run through, in my mind, the various Ninja moves I plan to use to take him down: the crouching tiger, the flying monkey, the downward dog, etc., and then briefly worry that I might get these mixed up with some of the positions from the *Kama Sutra*, which could be awkward.

And then I realize it's just me, back with the shopping.

All this happens in about a quarter of a second, but I imagine each stage registers briefly on my face, like those time-lapse films of decaying mushrooms, and that would probably be worth recording.

It's Enormous

August 17. The author disrobes, ready for another night in which sleepless hours are interrupted by brief interludes of anxiety dreams. He uses his naked foot to pull the drawer containing his pyjamas out from beneath the bed. The action involves looming over the prone figure of his wife, intent on her book. A little annoyed, she looks up. Her eyes widen, registering first surprise, then a kind of horrified fascination. Her lips mouth the words 'Oh my God'. The author looks down at himself, and then up at his wife. He shrugs an apology.

'It's enormous,' she says, like a commentator on the Olympic long jump finals.

He looks down again, and knows that she's right. It hardly appears human. More like something out of a 1950s science fiction comic, or perhaps a nature documentary. And he feels alienated from this thing. It's not really part of him at all. More like an embarrassing uncle, or the sort of person you meet in Freshers' Week and spend the next three years trying to lose. He flicks it. It feels as solid and inert as a marrow.

'You have to go on a diet,' she says.

'I know. From tomorrow.'

Then he goes back into the kitchen and eats every biscuit in the house in preparation for the rigours to come.

Cob and Pen

August 18. Finding myself in Newcastle, I sat down by the Tyne and counted bridges. Bloody mad for bridges, the Geordies. And don't get me wrong – I love a good bridge, me, symbolizing, as they do, my need to get from one side of a thing to the other. But there seems to be at least one too many here, and they could have given it up, so some other place in bad need of a bridge or two – Bangladesh, maybe, or Peru – could have the benefit.

Still, though, it's a beautiful city. It has an interestingly layered topology, with the different levels and historical epochs connected by unexpected stairways and ginnels, like wormholes in Einsteinian space-time.

As I was sitting, feeling very alone, a pair of swans approached, a cob and a pen, flying in that heavy, methodical, rather dim-witted way. They looked as ill-suited to flight as some piece of domestic equipment – a vacuum cleaner or mop and bucket. The crowd on the riverbank fell silent to watch their progress. They flew under the span of one of the bridges, and over another, heading in towards town. And then they took a sharp left turn, almost as if there were a T-junction in the sky. And conversation broke out again, among those who were not alone, now that the swans were flying away from us.

But I carried on watching as the swans banked again, and slowly returned to the line of the river, but this time travelling in the opposite direction. It gave the whole thing a faintly absurd and homely aspect. The couple had just been out for a bit of a fly, and were now going back home.

'Is this far enough, dear?'

'Oh, I think so. Let's get back and put the kettle on. We don't want to miss *Strictly*...'

I Never Trod on a Dog

August 19. What I love most about sitting in the quiet coach on the train is the constant background threat of violence. You know that a single out-of-place noise could mean death by steely gaze, or Stanley knife.

But I also love getting quietly drunk on the train after a day spent shouting at children about crossbows, Balzac, Barthes, fights, and the softest thing with which to wipe your arse – the soft and downy neck of a goose, according to Rabelais. Even the glass of the window feels oddly comforting to the side of your head, slumped against it.

And I recall my favourite comment from the day's very enjoyable visit to Whitley Bay High School (imagine a lovely soft Geordie accent):

'Sir, I never trod on a dog, but I once stabbed a dolphin in the eye with me finger; then I bit the Chinese boy next to me.'

'Yes?' said the Count

August 20. Just dropped some books off at the Oxfam shop. Among them was Iris Murdoch's *Metaphysics as a Guide to Morals*, purchased at a remainder bookshop sometime in the early to mid-1990s, and resolutely unread since then. And I was struck by the futility of this whole process – the purchase, the moving with me to various London addresses, always neatly shelved, never read, and now dispatched to Oxfam.

While I was there I had a look through the stock, and saw in a not very striking coincidence a copy of Murdoch's *Nuns and Soldiers*. I've only read a couple of her novels, which I neither enjoyed nor hated. I had a quick look at this one, thinking it sounded quite racy. It began:

> Chapter 1
> 'Wittgenstein—'
> 'Yes?' said the Count.

And I was filled with an inchoate rage, and would have doused it in petrol, if I'd had any petrol, and set fire to it, if I'd had any matches, and stripped naked, and danced around the flames like a Red Indian, I mean Native Indian, I mean Red Native, well, never mind what I mean, I'd have been doing that. If I were insane.

The Mechanical Finger

August 21. Been invited in for a free NHS health check at the start of next week. The last time I had any kind of general check-up was at school, when we all had to stand in a line while an elderly man walked along, cupping our genitals in a gnarled hand for slightly longer than was necessary, while he asked us to cough. I expect things have moved on since then. They probably have a robot now to cup your testicles. Perhaps the same robot can be programmed to stick its mechanical finger up your bum to check for whatever they check for up there. But I am a bit worried about what they'll find, beyond the athlete's foot, mild to moderate cognitive impairment and hairy ears already diagnosed (by me). No doubt it'll be something embarrassing.

I'm Due Another Good Writhe

August 22. Shortly going off to be a Supportive Spouse, as Mrs McG is up for an award at the LSE – Teacher of the Year, or some such. I owe her this, as she's come along to a few of mine – including the first award I was ever up for – the Branford Boase – back in 2006. As well as my first award shortlisting, it was also my first heavy defeat. I consoled myself by getting so drunk on warm white wine that Mrs McG refused to sit in the same tube carriage as me on the way home. I have a memory of writhing around, my face crushed into the wooden slatted flooring tube trains used to have in those days. I couldn't one hundred per cent swear that I didn't befoul myself in some way. I expect Mrs McG will be more dignified, win or lose. Mind you, if they have free wine, perhaps I'm due another good writhe...

A Day Packed with Incident

August 23. If I'd known how traumatic that was going to be, I'd never have bothered even trying to post those letters.

First of all, one of our neighbours – a bald gentleman, from a few flats along – said, 'I see you've got your blue shoes on again.'

Now, those of you who have been taking an interest in my footwear will know that this is exactly what I've been anticipating. (I'd bought two pairs of near identical electric-blue Nike trainers, and was waiting for someone to say 'I see you've got your blue shoes on again,' so I could retort, 'Actually, no, this is the other pair, not the pair that you mean,' or some such.)

But now that the longed-for conversation had actually come about, I realized that, for all I knew, he *had* seen me in this particular pair of shoes before, and not the other ones. This momentarily took the wind out of my sails. By the time I realized that I could just bluff it, and pretend that these were my other shoes (and, in fact, they may well have been), the man had wheeled away, huffily.

You see, although friendly, he's had a long and troubled history of mental instability and is on anti-psychotics, so he probably took my silence for a rebuff of some kind, rather than the moment of puzzled contemplation that it actually was. I thought about chasing after him, and trying to explain. But, as you can imagine, it's not an easy thing to explain, about the shoes, I mean. So I thought I'd just give him one of my cans, next time we're on a bench together. But this was not the end of my troubles, not by a long chalk.

Right after that, I met Jim, the electrician from the estate. He pointed to my backpack and said, 'Going hiking?' I laughed, and replied that no, all that was in there was a couple of letters, but I couldn't trust myself to make it to the postbox without losing one or both. Then I opened the backpack to show him, I'm not sure why.

And of course the backpack was empty. This made me seem like the sort of mad person who carries round an empty bag, which he believes to be full of letters.

So I went back to get the letters I'd forgotten. While I was out I decided I'd buy a few things to put in the empty bag, as otherwise it would be vaguely pointless. I mean the wasted energy in carrying around the empty bag. So I popped into Waitrose.

As I was tying up Monty outside, an attractive lady came up. She had two Chihuahuas.

'Is he called Monty?' she said, excitedly. 'I heard you say Monty…'

'Yes,' I replied.

'Mine's called Monty, too,' she smiled.

'Oh, which one?' I said, looking at the two little dogs, while I tried to stop my Monty from killing them.

She looked mystified. Then I wondered if she might be a bit strange, and it hit me – she'd called both her dogs Monty.

'Are they both called Monty?' I said.

She looked even more baffled.

'No. He's not here.'

Then she pulled her dogs away down the street, checking back to make sure I wasn't following her.

When I got home I emptied the shopping out of my rucksack. The last things I took out were, of course, the two letters I'd gone out to post.

The Air Chief Marshall

August 24. I've long thought that other dog-owners judge not the dog, but the owner – for good and ill. Coming back from having walked with Mrs McG to her morning yoga class, Monty and I encountered a middle-aged couple, along with the sort of fluffy white dog that Monty (being a fluffy white dog) tends to get along with, rather than his usual passive aggressive snarling while backing away. So I let out a little line, and the two dogs engaged in some companionable bum sniffing.

I hadn't really noticed much about the human part of this interchange, but then the man said curtly and distinctly, 'No, Nanny, not with him! NOT. WITH. HIM.' He was rather short, very neatly dressed, in a vaguely un-English sort of way, as you'd imagine a late nineteenth-century German professor of linguistics to look. Both he and his wife wore those Reactolite lenses in their glasses. In fact, the impression was like a retired member of the Argentinian Junta, perhaps the Air Chief Marshall, in charge of the Department of Torture and Murder. I hardly ever take against people, but this couple emanated a distinct aura of evil. 'No, Nanny, not with him,' the retired torturer said again, and dragged the pooch down the road, in the direction of Nando's.

Why Is No One Talking About the Crisis of Overproduction and Tech Company Cash Hoards Pour Homme

August 25. I've discovered that you can buy lip-gloss in various 'classic' cocktail flavours – Negroni, Harvey Wallbanger, etc. If I were to bring out a range of lip-glosses, I'd try to get more complexity into the flavours – Vague Anxiety; Apprehension About Spitting When Talking; Do I Smell Funny? Are People

Staring at Me? Laughing at the Disadvantaged; Aren't Stamps Really Expensive These Days? I mentioned this to my friend Ian, and he suggested, Why Is No One Talking About the Crisis of Overproduction and Tech Company Cash Hoards Pour Homme, which I thought was nicely in the spirit of things, although more one for my line of aftershaves and body sprays.

Jumping the Gun

August 26. A letter came through the door yesterday saying someone's offer on a flat in our block has fallen through, and dangling an absurd amount of money before us – more than I can realistically hope to earn in the rest of my life. Pointless, of course, tied as we are to London for family reasons. So it's locked up, uselessly, like the large life insurance policy I recently discovered that Mrs McG has taken out on me.

When I challenged her about the insurance (though 'challenged' puts it a bit strongly – whatever I said came out more as a wheedle and a whine than a robust assertion of my point of view), Mrs McG said something about the fact that I was always complaining about how ill I felt, that I constantly said that I'd be dead soon, that the combination of drink and cycling would, in fact, quite likely be the death of me, and that she'd need some new outfits if she was back in the dating game.

The last was one of her jokes.

I didn't have an answer to any of it.

But mulling things over later on, it struck me that I'd seen her in some nice new clothes recently. A dress, with a shimmer to it like the sheen of petrol on a puddle; a skirt that flowed around her lower half like milk poured over ice in a tall glass.

Rosie, Sometimes

August 27. About eighteen months ago I was reading *Charlotte Sometimes* by Penelope Farmer to my daughter. It had been obvious for a while that she was more tolerating than loving the experience, and so, reluctantly, we stopped, and from then on she read by herself (not *Charlotte Sometimes*, which is, in truth, a rather difficult and awkward book, though certainly a fine one – but the usual things that thirteen-year-old girls like – *The Hunger Games*, *Twilight*, *The Brothers Karamazov*, etc. etc.).

Fifteen years of reading to my children had come to an end – and an end without a proper conclusion, as we never finished *Charlotte Sometimes*. I went through four of the five stages of grieving – Denial, Anger, Bargaining, Depression – without ever reaching the fifth: Acceptance.

And then tonight Rosie out of the blue suggested that we snuggle up and read.

Really hope it lasts long enough to get through *Charlotte*.

Anyway, it was one of my happiest parenting half hours.

Marinated in Anger

August 28. Was just wiping down the cooker with some Waitrose multi-surface cleaner, when I glanced at the label. The flavour (so to speak) appeared to be 'citrus and anger', which made me snort with laughter. It also chimed nicely with my recent riff about more imaginatively named lip-glosses (Spurned by the Office Photocopy Repair Man; Despair at the State of the Middle East, etc.). And anger might well help you really get to work on those hard-to-shift grease stains.

But then when I focused properly on the label I saw that it was 'citrus and ginger', which was a bit disappointing, although I guess it would make an excellent marinade for fish or chicken.

The Person from Porlock

August 29. Despite being a lover of Nature, I've grown to hate the London plane tree that grows smack in the middle of the pavement just over the road from here. It's right on my usual morning perambulatory route, and although I've never actually walked into it, at least twice a week I almost do, and the last-minute swerve or juddering stop interrupts my reveries and musings in an annoying way.

The tree is my person from Porlock (the insurance salesman who interrupted Coleridge's opium dream, and ruined *Kubla Khan*).

Or perhaps it's more like the opening of *Tristram Shandy*, Tristram's mother, in the midst of a bout of methodical love-making, asking her husband if he'd remembered to wind the clock, thereby quite putting Mr Shandy off his stroke, and leading to all kinds of future problems for Tristram, as this 'very unseasonable question… scattered and dispersed the animal spirits, whose business it was to have escorted and gone hand in hand with the Homunculus, and conducted him safe to the place destined for his reception'. One wonders, in parenthesis, if any other great novel begins not merely in the midst of the carnal act, but with an actual ejaculation, frothing its angry way into the female reproductive tract.

Back to my tree – which, like Mrs Shandy's ill-timed question, scatters and disperses my animal spirits, sucking the life-force from my spurting creativity. And I imagine the circumstances of the tree's conception. Two old lags and a gormless youth on the council planting team. The old stagers want to knock off early to get shit-faced at the Spleen and Gristle in Camden.

'You do this last one,' they say to the lad. 'Just don't plant it in the middle of the fucking pavement.'

The youth wanders off, lost in his own reveries. At a suitable spot he tries to recall what he's been told. Something about planting the sapling in the middle of the pavement...

Arsenic and Old Lace

August 30. Just been told off by an elderly lady for typing too loudly in the library. She put her hand gently on my shoulder and said, 'I can tell when you're writing well, because you bash away...'

Her look was part eccentric detective from the 1930s, part mad woman working in the charity shop. She gave off a faint whiff of Parma Violets. She was both charming and faintly sinister. Perhaps more refined lady poisoner than detective. Now tiptoeing with my fingers.

No, No One Pretty

August 31. Mrs McG surveyed my British Library outfit this morning: an unironed shirt, already darkened with sweat; khaki shorts mottled with stains, ancient and modern; odd socks (but, to be fair, both in vaguely similar shades of gravy); shoes seemingly assembled from severed sections of camel foreskin, randomly sewn together by a blind idiot.

'So,' she observed, not inaccurately, 'not meeting anyone pretty for lunch today.'

God Bless You, Plucky Norway

September 1. A pleasant authorial surprise awaited me on my return from an otherwise not especially satisfactory day at the British Library: a substantial (by my standards) royalty payment from Norway. It turns out I'm quite big in Scandawegia (by Scandawegian standards).

The windfall meant I could thicken the children's gruel with lard, while I feasted on Scandy delicacies – Ryvita and some kind of disgusting raw fish, apparently 'cured', although if it was cured, how come it was still dead, eh?

And Mrs McG is always softened, a little, by this sort of thing. Money, I mean. But not just money – the lustre, not of lucre, but success. It's because although for me failure is a kind of joke, a comedy prop, albeit a morbid one, like a skull or a shadow on the chest X-ray in the shape of a penis, for her it's a threatening, even a monstrous presence. She's treading water, and she sees, at the corner of her vision, a fin.

Not that she's ever failed at anything. She ran her own fashion business, and now she's nestled in the soft bosom of academia. But her friends are all top City lawyers or bankers or kept in obscene comfort by their successful partners. And when her friends, out of politeness, ask her what I'm up to, she has a mental image of me looking into the local charity shop windows, or mumbling curses as I walk the dog, or seeing visions of dwarves, and so she just has to lie.

'Oh, he's fine. All well. He's got a new one out next year.'

Anyway, God bless you, plucky Norway, land of Abba, volcanoes, Danish bacon, saunas, gloomy detectives, reindeers, trolls, sagas, Ikea and brown cheese.

Rabbit Pizza

September 2. Travelled to the University of East Anglia to deliver a talk. I'm staying in a glorified hall of residence on the campus, which is fine. But there are no other writers staying – a couple of old friends are also part of the festival, and I'd hoped to meet up for a beer.

There is, however, a group of sanitary-ware salespeople, here for a conference. I was initially mistaken for one of them, and thought about playing along, and joining them for the evening, but doubted I could convince them that I could tell my Armitage from my Shanks.

The lady on reception gave me a little map, and pointed out a joint where you can get 'either a pizza or an oriental, as the mood takes you'. I might go there.

When I became a writer I thought it'd be fun escaping for nights away like this, but I miss the kids fighting and Mrs McG's look of annoyance and frustration. And I don't really know what I'm going to say tomorrow, as I haven't got a clear idea of the audience.

And they have hundreds of giant rabbits here, all over the campus, and they stare at you, and don't move out of the way when you walk up to them. There's hunger in their eyes. You'd have thought word would have reached East Anglia's fox and weasel population that there's all the rabbit they could eat, stir fried or on a pizza.

Which has made me hungry. Time to go for my lonely pizza. Or my oriental. I hope she's in a consoling mood.

They Thought I Was Going to Be Benjamin Zephaniah

September 3. Five bloody thirty. Been awake since three. Should have brought my own special pillows. And then the deafening chorus of crows when I almost drifted off again. And the higher-pitched noise, like a finger run around a wine glass, that is the sound of the rabbits trying to communicate with me telepathically. Run naked among us, they say, and we will soothe you with our soft fur, nuzzle you with our gentle noses. Must resist, must resist.

Watching breakfast telly, which I never do at home. Rather unnerved by the woman presenter. I can't detect any relationship between her expressions – the vividly communicated joy, concern, anger – and the actual content of what's going on. It's as if it's all out of synch. Or maybe I am.

The lecture hall was vast; my audience, modest. A third of the way through my talk a row of elderly folk got up and left. I found out later that there had been a timetabling mix up, and they thought I was going to be Benjamin Zephaniah.

Pasta Troubles

September 4. I know it has the smack of a First World Problem, but it's still rather disheartening, not to say enraging, when your little pasta parcels come unsealed in the two-minute boiling process, giving forth their contents unto the water, resulting in some pointless, empty pasta, floating like dead jellyfish in a grainy porridge of pumpkin and pine nuts. Waitrose – you need to use a stronger pasta glue.

And a second culinary note: I plucked the last few enfeebled herbs from my window boxes – tiny basil leaves, the size of confetti; greyed rocket; a contorted radish, like the severed penis of an imp; some other things that may just have been weeds – and made a composite pesto. It was quite nice, in a grassy, rabbit-shitty sort of way.

But, overall, I'd have to declare my attempts to feed the family from a London windowsill as a failure. Next season I plan to monetize the space by intensively rearing badgers out there, and harvesting them for their hair, which is said to make the best shaving brushes.

Don't You Worry That Perhaps You've Wasted Your Life?

September 5. I always find it rather poignant going into Swiss Cottage Library these days. The building is still wonderful – a piece of 1960s modernism that really works, tastefully renovated and vajazzled in the early noughties.

And they had, miraculously – in storage, but still available – a copy of the 1965 biography of Montaigne I was after.

And yet… there are shelves full of books they're selling, almost giving away – some old rather touching non-fiction (*How to Dance the Highland Fling*, *The Ghana Yearbook, 1962*, *Cactuses for Beginners*, etc. etc.), but also some new, seemingly unread fiction. It seems wrong, but I know they have storage issues.

And the staff seem a bit subdued, beaten down by the cuts and the uncertainty. And then on this visit I was approached by a man handing out fliers for a talk he was about to do in one of the public rooms they rent out. He'd walked all over the world, around it, up and down it, breaking various records. And then written a book about it. He looked a bit bemused and befuddled, and was wearing the sort of train engineer's cap you occasionally find on the heads of benign lunatics.

'It's the real thing,' he said to me. 'Oh yes.'

I suppose he meant his talk, or the book, or his perambulations, rather than the hat.

I nearly went to the talk out of sympathy, but I feared I might, at some point, ask him, 'Don't you worry that perhaps you've wasted your life by aimlessly walking hither and thither, breaking records that don't really matter? Couldn't you have done something else, something more useful?'

But then he'd be within his rights to hurl the question back at me. Haven't I wasted my life? Thus forcing me to defend myself, when defending yourself is the one thing that's indefensible. And then I'd have gone off to the pub on my own, and got more depressed.

So it was probably a good thing that I had to come home to cook dinner for the kids.

A Death in Venice

September 6. The book I'm working on has a scene where two kids go fishing. It's set on the banks of the Bacon Pond – the small lake next to what used to be the Bacon Factory – a meat processing plant in my home town. The story was that the spoiled meat would be dumped in the pond, where it fed the pike until they reached symphonic proportions. We were told they'd eat you, if you swam in the water. I never succeeded in catching a single fish on my own few fishing trips as a boy. I'd bought a rod and a reel with my pocket money, but I didn't have a fishing friend who could show me how to set it up.

When I was twelve, I took my first girlfriend, Louise Craggs, fishing to the Bacon Pond. I got everything tangled up, and hurled the rod out over the waters. No hand came up to catch it, Excalibur like. I remember that my mum had made a packed lunch, and that it contained a Wagon Wheel. I liked Louise very much.

It was, of course, doomed. I had no idea what to do with girls, how to talk to them, how to kiss, even. We had a couple more dates – we went to see the Disney cartoon *The Rescuers*, at the Odeon on the Head Row in Leeds (now gone), and I put my arm around her shoulder. And then, the next week, we went to *The Spy Who Loved Me*. I knew she wanted me to kiss her at the bus stop afterwards, and I did, but it was a closed-mouth peck that really didn't deliver the goods.

And then there came the school skiing trip to Italy. I only wanted to go because she was going. My parents could barely afford it, and there was nothing left over for the right gear. My uncle Liam lent me a pair of motorcycle goggles. I had an enormous jumper knitted by my granny in Scotland. I skied in a pair of hugely flared Wrangler jeans, just as flares were going out of fashion. The sound of the denim flapping behind me as I hurtled out of control down the slopes haunts me still. I never got beyond the snowplough stage.

The upshot was that I was hopelessly uncool, as well as useless on the intimacy front, and so Louise really had no choice but to chuck me, employing for the purpose her friend, whose name I can't now remember. When I asked the friend why, she said that it was because I was boring. That was my original hurt, and it doesn't take much for the wound to open afresh, even four decades later. None of my close friends were on the trip, which added to my sense of isolation and despair.

On the way back to Leeds there was some problem with the flight, and we had an unexpected night in Venice. The glittering midwinter beauty of the place proved too much for me, and I stood on a bridge and declaimed to Louise that unless she went back out with me I'd jump in the canal. She didn't even answer, but simply walked away with her friends, leaving me to climb down from the wall.

A little later Louise started going out with a kid who was really good at table tennis. I heard years later that they were married, and ran a fish and chip shop on the outskirts of Leeds.

Slantwise

September 7. I've found that the best way of removing the grime from your hands after fixing a puncture is to wash your hair. I was lying in the bath thinking of other ways in which problems have been solved by coming in slantwise, from a new angle. The one that first came to mind was the way in which the hedge trimmer was originally invented purely as a means of ENRAGING SENSITIVE AUTHORS, and only later was its ability to neaten your topiary discovered. (When I got out of the bath, by the way, I found that my tyre had gone flat again, making this, officially, the worst day of my life.)

But now I've managed to half cheer myself up, by wondering who the first person was to think of holding out a digit, saying 'Pull my finger' and then farting. Something so specific must have had a single point of origin, a patient zero, so to speak, from which every other episode of finger-pulling flatulence has derived. Would quite like to write a treatise on this. Also, would like to track down the author of 'My Friend Billy Had a Ten-Foot Willy'.

In case you're not familiar with this masterpiece, which I heard in Yorkshire in about 1972, it goes, in full,

> My friend Billy had a ten-foot willy
> And he showed it to the lady next door.
> She thought it was a snake,
> And she hit it with a rake
> And now it's only four foot four.

I taught this to my kids, and there was a mild scandal when they introduced it to the junior school playground. Party invites dried up for a while. But if they don't get you for one thing, they'll get you for another.

Brent Cross Blues

September 8. Given my puncture-related downheartedness, I should probably never have gone shopping. But I was in the midst of an underpant crisis, so I cycled (puncture fixed with a second new inner tube) the weary way to the Brent Cross shopping centre, first through streets lined with the large but nondescript houses where the henchmen of the Oligarchs live, and then through the estates where teenagers get stabbed for carrying their school books in the wrong kind of satchel, and then over the Dantean North Circular Road.

Brent Cross was full of people looking happy to be there, which is in itself a sign of how low we've sunk as a species. Eventually, after a period of bewildered wandering, I found the sock and underpant section of M&S, and grabbed some items, more or less at random.

Then I saw some hysterically awful Y-fronts, of vast size, constructed from that perforated fabric – Aertex? Anaglypta? Something like that. I thought I'd get them as a kind of comedy thing, to amuse Mrs McG – you know, like Bridget Jones's giant pants. I imagined myself springing forth wearing them, doing a little dance, and we'd all fall about laughing, and then, perhaps… well worth the £8 (for two pairs). But in the rather long queue, I began to feel somewhat embarrassed by the giant pants, which seemed to be growing ever bigger even as I clung to them; and I also realized that I'd picked up some socks incorporating silver filaments, 'to control excessive foot odour', and I became convinced that the other queuers were looking at me strangely, seeing not the multi-award-winning novelist, acclaimed by critics and adored by both his readers, but a dishevelled man, almost like an ancient, scruffy schoolboy, a Tithonus shorn of poignancy, somehow cursed never to mature even as he becomes decrepit, with giant pants and smelly feet (which, weirdly, I don't have).

In a moment of irrationality, I conceived the idea that buying some handkerchiefs from the display near the tills would help ease the tension. I don't think I've ever bought handkerchiefs before, and these turned out to be 'antibacterial', which doubtless added to the overall impression that I was unclean and profoundly infected.

So I was feeling a bit panicky and paranoid, and then I turned around and saw three huge, blank-faced figures looming over me, looking like the baddies in that silent episode of *Buffy*, if you've ever seen it. Elongated featureless heads, as though modelled on Munch's *The Scream*. They were only manikins, of course, but I still emitted a guttural shout of terror, which I tried, unconvincingly, to convert into a cough.

I suppose I was looking a touch shabby and seedy, but it was still a bit much when a mother thrust her children behind her skirts, forming a human shield to protect them from me. Surely, now, I thought, the worst is over?

After that, I went, on a whim, to see if I could pick up something in the dying days of the Fenwick's sale. Everything looked terrible, except a blue Paul Smith jacket, reduced from £250 to £99. It had a faint sickly sheen to it, like a rainbow trout you really should have eaten a couple of days ago.

As I was checking it out in the mirror, an elderly West Indian gentleman of dignified bearing appeared next to me, wearing exactly the same jacket. He looked in the mirror, and our eyes met. After a few moments he shook his head, sadly.

'Not for us,' he said.

At the time I was a little taken aback, thinking he meant the jacket was too young and 'with it' for two old codgers like us, but looking back I think he was being more subtle, and his meaning was that the jacket was simultaneously too casual for him, and too formal for me. I also think he saw a bond between us, a link formed through our various sufferings and burdens. His life of prejudice and intolerance, my athlete's foot and problems changing my bicycle inner tube. Our ferocious and indomitable spouses…

I thought for a moment he was going to shake my hand, but instead he nodded and moved away towards the ties. I didn't buy anything.

Finally, I escaped from the moronic inferno of Brent Cross. Outside there was a fun fair, and the cries of despair and fear emanating from those trapped on the rides were most disconcerting. I thought, as I cycled along, of how such places were the haunt of old-fashioned perverts, bum fondlers, seat sniffers, etc. etc. And I wondered if there was scope for a *Call the Midwife* style comedy drama, set in the 1950s, about a flasher, a man who steals underwear off washing lines and a scout master, and the amusing capers they get up to. Martin Clunes could be in it.

I was pretty low by now, and then I saw something in the road ahead, and thought, oh God, no, not a dead dog. But then, when I got closer I saw it was only a bag. I thought about stopping and opening the bag, but then I was worried that it might contain a dead dog. And then speculated further that I might think it was a dead dog, but on closer inspection it would turn out to be another bag. And then I'd be trapped there forever in another of my infinite regresses, which was no good as I had to cook dinner for the kids. So I swerved round it and cycled home.

The comedy underpants didn't go down well. Mrs McG just told me to get rid of them. She said I should drive them out into the country, and set them out on the side of the road to fend for themselves. But I didn't have the heart. And, besides, I don't know how to drive. I tried offering them to the Oxfam shop, but they wouldn't take them. So I posted them through a random letterbox with a note, saying 'Please look after these underpants', in the hope that the house might belong to an old man, who could put them to some good use. I hope it doesn't turn out to be a house full of students, who'll abuse and mock them. Or bedsit types, who'll just leave them forever in the communal hall, slowly dying from lack of love. I might go back tomorrow and look through the letterbox.

In Which It Is Revealed that the Earl of Oxford Wrote 'My Friend Billy'

September 9. A British Library day today. My packed lunch consists of some mystery cheeses left over from a dinner party, and two slices of melon I found in the fridge. Obviously, fruit should play a role in a packed lunch, but I'm worried about the melon. If I saw someone randomly eating melon in the BL courtyard – as opposed to an apple or a banana – I'd find myself leaping to conclusions. I'd guess that they were the sort of person who spent their evenings alone in a bedsit, talking to their budgie. They'd be largely rational, but have odd notions and manias, believing in alien abduction, and that the Earl of Oxford wrote Shakespeare (as well as authoring the well-known rhyme beginning 'My friend Billy…').

I only brought the melon in as I felt sorry for it. But these acts of compassion have a way of biting you on the bum. Anyway, I'm putting off lunch for as long as possible.

Upwards of 45K

September 10. Writing in Swiss Cottage Library today, taking advantage of the fact there are no revising kids. But, in terms of distractions, there is a man being interviewed for a job over the telephone. His voice is very loud.

'I was on 50k at Mobil… No, nothing at the moment. Looking to get back in the game… Upwards of 45k…'

He looks like he should be in an Arthur Miller play. The armpit of his white poly-cotton shirt is dyed nicotine yellow. His world is falling apart. I hope he gets the job. He hasn't a chance.

Then another man spins round and hisses at me, 'Don't sit behind me!'

I don't really want to have an I'm-madder-than-you contest and I move to the area with the newspapers and periodicals. There are three people snoring, theatrically.

So I go to the library café and have a rather good cup of coffee and some madeira cake. I've just noticed that all the pensioners are wearing huge coats. Is summer truly over? Time is slipping away.

Quitting

September 11. Still trying to finish my book in the public library. I work in five-minute spurts, punctuated by longer bouts of wandering and mooching.

Vacantly perusing the library shelves, I came across the 'Hobbies' section. Large signs indicate that there are books dealing with NEEDLEWORK and KNITTING. There is also a sign that says QUITTING, and I thought, at last, a hobby for me. Finally, I can put my gift for giving up without a fight to some good use. But on closer examination it turns out to say QUILTING.

The Cyclopean Eye

September 12. In Sainsbury's today, with a shopping list that seemed deliberately composed to convey poignancy and loneliness – mouthwash, dogfood, toilet paper, athlete's foot powder, Haribo Starmix.

As I wandered along the toilet-roll aisle, a nine-pack caught my attention. There was something wrong with it. One of the rolls on the top layer had rotated through ninety degrees, so it stared out through the plastic packaging with a baleful, Cyclopean eye. I tried to ignore it, but it bored into me. So I attempted to manipulate it, massaging the misaligned roll back into the perpendicular.

And then I thought to myself how strange this must look, this kneading and caressing of the rolls. Like some quasi-sexual act. Or a particularly inept attempt at shoplifting. So I returned the misaligned one to the shelf, picked another pack, and hurried away.

But, in the queue, I remembered again that blank, hopeless eye, still staring out, and I went back for it, meaning to buy the mutant pack and fix it, at my leisure, when I got home. But when I reached the spot, that pack had gone. So I'll never get closure on this.

The Trees, the Wood

September 13. We hauled the children out for a walk in Golders Hill Park. It's a place rich with memories, most of them, unusually for me, happy, or not unhappy. When Gabe and Rosie were little I'd wheel them up to the playground there, and afterwards we'd have hot chocolate in the café, which for some reason was a hangout for a gang of campy old Jewish guys with a theatrical bent. And then we'd walk through the lovely woods, getting to know each distinct zone: the sandy section where a stand of Scots pines made it look as though half an acre of the Highlands had been transported into North London; the dense thickets of oak, where the gays lurked, looking for love; the open, airier ground, where grey-flanked beech trees loomed in slightly ominous silence; the silver birches, their metallic plating shining when young, but soon crumbling, and cracked, like the face paint on an empress dowager. And here the fallen tree, where some angry wasps took their resentment out on poor Rosie, stinging her through her long red-golden hair.

And even now, with Rosie thirteen and Gabe fifteen, we revert to childish ways, and muck about and joke and scramble over the logs, and kick piles of leaves in the air, and the kids still have hot chocolate, and those Italian wafer biscuits, light as a snowflake on the tongue, although the old Jews have thinned over the decade, and those that remain no longer know who we are.

Of course, I insist on turning it into a nature walk, pointing out interesting fungi (for which I usually invent obscene-sounding cod-Latin names) and birds' nests, and illustrating the difference between badger and fox excrement, or 'spraint' as we poo people call it ('With badger you get more of a taste of burnt almonds.' 'Awwwww, Daaaad!').

The kids and I dawdled on the way back, and Mrs McG raced home before us, having shunned the loos at the café.

And so she missed it.

It was Rosie who noticed him first.

'Dad,' she said, pulling at my arm. 'Is that…?'

I followed her gaze.

And there he was. Heimlich. Moving quickly on his crutches. He was on the other side of the road, and we watched as he ran past us, and then further up the street, his pace steady. But this time, rather than flight or even pursuit, his goal seemed different. He was wearing jogging pants and a headband. Looked like he was on a health kick.

'It's not what I was expecting,' said Gabe. 'But he does look a bit like you.'

'We should tell Mum!' said Rosie.

She's always been more sensitive to these things than Gabe. I mean the emotional currents. I think she knew the significance of Heimlich. Knew what the truth of him would mean. It would be like finding life on Mars – the squirming of a bacterium on the microscope slide would mean that all that money would not have been wasted.

Gabe was watching me as well, now. We were outside the front door of our block.

'You kids go in,' I said. 'I'll be there in a sec.'

'Come with us, Dad,' said Rosie.

'I'll be right up.'

And I sat on the wall, and looked down the street, at the diminishing form of Heimlich, becoming hazy now in the traffic fumes. And then I scraped whatever it was off my shoe (fox, I think, rather than badger), and went in.

Acknowledgements

My thanks, first of all, to my agent, Charlie Campbell, who salvaged this wreck from the rocks. And to Sam Carter, who saw beyond the broken keel and shattered masts and the raving, wild-eyed captain. And to the whole brilliant Oneworld team, who made her shipshape. And to Tamsin Shelton, who patched the final holes. And to Rosie and Gabe, pressganged into the crew.

Profound thanks, also, to the early readers, who offered either unconditional love or severe reprimands – both essential: Andy Stanton, Will Fiennes (thanks, Will, for the loan of those jackdaws), Nick Hornby, Alex Preston, Amanda Craig, Seema Merchant and Richard Beard loom large.

And it would be amiss if I didn't tip my cap to the dozens of Facebook friends who helped hone early versions of many of the sections in the book. I wrote most of it to try to make you laugh.

Finally, my love to Rebecca Campbell, the fearsome Mrs McG of these pages. She could have snuffed it out, but she nurtured the flame.